Something dark app_____ the
train but moving t_____nel
carved into the side _____.

Longarm, hunkered low atop the coach car, stared in
awe—could he get this lucky?—as the dark tunnel mouth
flew toward him and the day coach he lay prone upon, both
boots dangling down over the side. The peak of the arching
portal was only about four feet above the coach car roof.

Longarm looked at Rio Hayes and smiled.

Hayes had just gained his feet and grabbed another bowie
knife from somewhere on his scruffy person, and had turned
toward Longarm, a savage scowl that, coupled with his broken jaw hanging askew, made his entire face look horsey
and crooked and even more demented than usual.

Hayes hadn't seen the tunnel when Longarm had. But
now he saw that gaping, black portal rushing toward him
like a gigantic black bird from some hellish underworld
intending to scoop him up in its stygian wings.

Hayes had about one second to widen his eyes in awe and
dismay before the tunnel turned the world dark. About one
eye wink later, following a clipped scream, Longarm heard
a resounding, crunching thump!

Just like that, Rio Hayes was gone.

TABOR EVANS

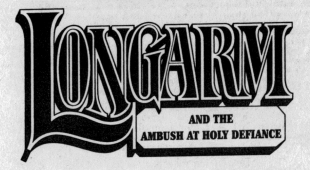

LONGARM

AND THE
AMBUSH AT HOLY DEFIANCE

JOVE BOOKS, NEW YORK

THE BERKLEY PUBLISHING GROUP
Published by the Penguin Group
Penguin Group (USA) Inc.
375 Hudson Street, New York, New York 10014, USA

Penguin Group (Canada), 90 Eglinton Avenue East, Suite 700, Toronto, Ontario M4P 2Y3, Canada
(a division of Pearson Penguin Canada Inc.) • Penguin Books Ltd., 80 Strand, London WC2R 0RL,
England • Penguin Group Ireland, 25 St. Stephen's Green, Dublin 2, Ireland (a division of Penguin
Books Ltd.) • Penguin Group (Australia), 707 Collins Street, Melbourne, Victoria 3008, Australia
(a division of Pearson Australia Group Pty. Ltd.) • Penguin Books India Pvt. Ltd., 11 Community
Centre, Panchsheel Park, New Delhi—110 017, India • Penguin Group (NZ), 67 Apollo Drive,
Rosedale, Auckland 0632, New Zealand (a division of Pearson New Zealand Ltd.) • Penguin Books
(South Africa) (Pty.) Ltd., Rosebank Office Park, 181 Jan Smuts Avenue, Parktown North 2191,
South Africa • Penguin China, B7 Jiaming Center, 27 East Third Ring Road North,
Chaoyang District, Beijing 100020, China

Penguin Books Ltd., Registered Offices: 80 Strand, London WC2R 0RL, England

This is a work of fiction. Names, characters, places, and incidents either are the product of the author's
imagination or are used fictitiously, and any resemblance to actual persons, living or dead, business
establishments, events, or locales is entirely coincidental.

LONGARM AND THE AMBUSH AT HOLY DEFIANCE

A Jove Book / published by arrangement with the author

PUBLISHING HISTORY
Jove edition / February 2013

Copyright © 2013 by Penguin Group (USA) Inc.
Cover illustration by Milo Sinovcic.

ISBN: 978-0-515-15353-8

JOVE®
Jove Books are published by The Berkley Publishing Group,
a division of Penguin Group (USA) Inc.,
375 Hudson Street, New York, New York 10014.
JOVE® is a registered trademark of Penguin Group (USA) Inc.
The "J" design is a trademark of Penguin Group (USA) Inc.

PRINTED IN THE UNITED STATES OF AMERICA

10 9 8 7 6 5 4 3 2 1

ALWAYS LEARNING   **PEARSON**

Chapter 1

The deputy U.S. marshal known to friend and foe as Longarm took a final drag from his three-for-a-nickel cheroot. He blew the smoke out his nose and then tossed the cigar away on the hot wind blowing past the stony escarpment he was perched on, in the San Juan Mountains of southern Colorado Territory.

He drew the flat brim of his flat-crowned, coffee-brown Stetson down low on his sun-leathered forehead and tightened his grip on the forestock of his Winchester '73.

Longarm stared down at the roofs of the train cars passing about fifteen feet below him. The train was moving only about ten, maybe twelve miles an hour as it climbed the steep slope from his left to his right. Still, one misstep, and a second later he'd be rolling off the train and into the deep, salmon-colored canyon yawning on the far side of the tracks.

"Billy, you don't pay me near enough," the big lawman in the tobacco tweed suit grumbled aloud, though not so loudly that the outlaws he knew to be aboard the train could hear him.

The Billy of topic, of course, was Longarm's boss, Chief Marshal Billy Vail of Denver's First District Court, who no doubt at this moment was safely ensconced behind his cluttered desk in the Federal Building on Denver's Colfax Avenue, not far from the Mint.

Billy's prissy male secretary was probably contentedly playing his typing machine in the outer office. The pretty, young, unattached girls of Denver were likely strolling along the cinder-paved streets around Union Station in their summer-weight frocks, breasts jostling enticingly against their stays and trusses, cheeks rouged from the pure, fresh, high-altitude air and sun.

"Well, let's unleash the wolves," Longarm said and stepped off the stony escarpment into thin air.

The roof of the second-to-last car in the combination widened beneath his boots, rising so quickly that he could clearly see several rusty rivets in the car's tin roof a second before his heels struck the roof with a heavy, tinny thump! Longarm threw his free arm and rifle out to each side for balance, spreading his boots a little more than shoulder-width apart.

He sucked a sharp, anxious breath.

Had the rough landing been heard inside the car?

He got his answer a second later, when a funnel-brimmed hat appeared just beyond the front of the car, on the car's right side, where the ladder must have been. As the hat rose higher, a face appeared beneath it—a broad, flat, tan face with blue eyes and a shaggy, red-blond mustache drooping down over the man's mouth. The man's right cheek had a deep, puckered scar, identifying him instantly as Oklahoma Charlie De Paul, who'd gotten the scar when a Lipan Apache had pierced it with an arrow back when Charlie had first started running guns along the Arizona-Mexico border.

When Charlie's eyes found Longarm, they snapped wide in mutual recognition. Longarm flung himself onto his butt and spun, raising his rifle at the same time that Oklahoma Charlie brought a pistol to bear.

"Fuck you, Longarm!"

The pistol flashed and roared, the slug screeching past

Longarm's left ear as the rangy lawman flinched and then yelled, "I take it that mean you don't intend on givin' yourself up, eh, Charlie!"

The outlaw opened his mouth to respond at the same time that he laid his pistol's sights on Longarm again, squinting down the barrel. Longarm lined up his own sights, squeezed the Winchester's trigger. As the stock kicked back against his right shoulder, he saw the top of Charlie's head turn red.

Charlie's revolver stabbed flames skyward. His hat blew away in the wind a half second before Charlie's head slipped abruptly down out of sight below the roof of the jostling train car. At the same time, a roar of panic erupted in the combination's three passenger cars, including the one beneath Longarm.

A woman screamed. A baby cried.

Beneath the din, Longarm heard someone he assumed was one of the outlaws yell, *"Son of a bitchin' law!"*

"On the roof!" another outlaw shouted.

Longarm gained his feet and moved toward the front of the car.

A pistol cracked twice in the car beneath him, causing another woman to scream and two ragged holes to appear in the tin roof about two feet behind Longarm. A hatted head appeared at the rear end of the car, and the black-bearded train robber flared his nostrils and brought up a Henry rifle, planting the brass maw on Longarm, who, planting his feet against the pitch and sway of the coach roof, fired his Winchester twice from his right hip.

The outlaw triggered his Henry into the stone cliff on the train's right side before falling back off the ladder and out of Longarm's field of vision.

More women were screaming now in the cars beneath Longarm. More tykes were bawling. Men were shouting. Someone, probably a sky pilot, was reciting scripture from his Bible in a loud but dull monotone that only slightly betrayed the precariousness of his situation.

As the pistol beneath Longarm cracked once, twice, three more times, Longarm ran toward the front of the car, hearing the bullets pop through the ceiling behind him. He saw movement on the vestibule between his car and the next one. He ran harder as he approached the gap and then launched himself into the air, landing on the roof of the next car and having to throw his rifle out to one side to regain his balance lest the train's violent swaying throw him into the canyon.

When he had a relatively firm purchase, he wheeled, cocked the Winchester, pressed the brass butt plate against his shoulder, and fired twice quickly. The two outlaws looking up at him from the vestibule, trying to plant their sights on him, were sent spinning and bouncing off the front, blood-splattered wall of the car Longarm had just left.

One desperado flew off the cliff side of the train and disappeared in a cloud of dust beside the rail bed. The other gave a terrified scream as he flew off into the canyon, the scream dwindling quickly as he plunged toward the canyon of the Looking Glass River far, far below.

More shouts and cries from inside the passenger cars. Boots thumped as the remaining outlaws ran around, probably trying to figure out how many lawmen they were dealing with.

Longarm knew he probably shouldn't have tried taking them all down alone, but he'd learned just a few hours before, from a former gang member, of the gang's intention to rob this narrow gauge spur line running between mining camps in the San Juans, and there'd been no time to throw a posse together. The Arkansas River Gang, as this bunch was called, was known for cold-blooded murder as well as rape and for kidnapping young women to sell as slaves in Arizona and Old Mexico.

For those reasons, he'd opted to risk his own hide as well as those of the innocent passengers who could get caught in the crossfire, and try to take them all down solo.

Hell, according to their former member, Scratch Gillis,

who'd gotten crossways with the gang when its leader shot Gillis's brother, H. C., when he found H. C. fucking Gillis's girl in a chicken coop, there were only eight members. Since Longarm had already killed four, that left only four more.

Hell, for a man like Longarm, those were bettin' odds.

Backing away from the end of the car, Longarm racked a fresh cartridge into his Winchester's breech. If more men ran out onto the vestibule, so much the better. He'd pick them off one at a time a relatively safe distance from the passengers.

Dropping to his knees, he continued to peer over the edge of the car and onto the blood-splattered wooden platform below. The rushing wind threatened to blow his hat off from behind. Vaguely, because he had more important things on his mind just now, he noted that the train's speed seemed to be increasing, which meant they were nearing the top of Horse Thief Pass.

A face appeared in the little dirty window in the rear door of the car behind Longarm. It was a round face with little cruel eyes and thin, sandy hair. The gang's leader, most likely—Rio Hayes. Longarm recognized him from the wanted dodgers that his ugly visage graced throughout the frontier.

When Hayes's eyes found Longarm, the lawman jerked back behind the roof's overhang. He heard the gang leader yell, *"On the roof, next car forward!"*

Longarm didn't want to shoot Hayes through the glass and risk a ricochet that might strike one of the passengers. Instead, he decided to buy himself some time and took off running forward along the roof of the car he was on, lunging to each side, setting his feet carefully so he wouldn't get thrown off. He was halfway to the car's other end when a pistol popped behind him. The bullet screamed past his right ear and plunked into a stovepipe poking up from the roof of the next car.

The pistol popped again.

Then again.

The shooter cursed angrily as the pistol belched once more, the third bullet kissing the right flap of Longarm's brown tweed frock coat. Longarm wheeled and fired two hasty shots at the shooter crouched atop the car's rear end. Then Longarm turned forward again and stepped off the edge of the roof.

As he dropped, he twisted around, aiming the Winchester out from his right hip. The man standing there—a beefy Mexican with bandoliers crisscrossed on his chest and holding a Winchester carbine slackly in both his big, brown hands—stared at the lawman in round-eyed, slack-jawed fascination.

The Mexican had a blond girl trapped beneath his right boot. She lay belly down, naked and squirming and sobbing against the Mexican's weight. The Mexican's pants were down around his knees. His dong jutted at half-mast from under the ragged tails of his red-and-black calico shirt.

Longarm triggered the Winchester once while he was still in the air and a second time just after he landed on the vestibule, near the naked girl's small, pink feet. Both shots blew dust from the Mexican's shirt, punching him back against the rear of the car behind him. He slumped there, gritting his teeth and gasping and trying to raise his carbine.

The girl was screaming and kicking. A quick glance told Longarm she couldn't have been much over thirteen years old. Longarm looked at the Mex, fury boiling up from deep in his belly, and smashed the rear stock of his rifle against the Mexican's face. The blow turned the man's nose sideways. The nose exploded like a ripe tomato blasted off a fence post.

Blood flew in all directions, painting the Mexican's big face. Several large, thick drops splashed onto the naked girl's smooth shoulders. Longarm stepped back, raised the rifle again.

"You got no manners at all, amigo," he said, the mildness in his voice belying the hot fury that had turned the tops of his ears red.

There was a thudding crack as the Winchester's butt plate met the Mexican's left temple resoundingly and sent the man hurling off the girl and over the side of the train. There was no longer a canyon to accept him, however. Trees and rocks had pushed up along both sides of the rails. The Mexican hit the ground, bounced, and rolled into the pines and boulders and was gone as the train rushed on.

The girl gained her knees, stared after the Mexican, and then half turned toward Longarm. He glimpsed a pair of perfect, peach-colored breasts with tender pink nipples. Her long, lustrous hair was the dark blond of ripe autumn wheat.

"That bastard stuck his filthy cock in me!" she cried, her face a mask of revulsion.

Vaguely noting from both her physical attributes as well as her command of farm talk that she was probably older than he'd at first thought, Longarm said, "You're all right now, miss. He's deader'n hell."

He edged a look through the glass of the coach door splattered with the Mex's blood. "Now it's time for the rest of his ilk to join him." He glanced at the girl once more where she knelt with her arms crossed on her breasts. "You stay here!"

He jerked the coach door open and bolted inside.

Chapter 2

There were about ten passengers in the car as Longarm ran inside, loudly cocking his Winchester and aiming straight out from his shoulder, staring down the barrel.

Most of the men were on their feet. A middle-aged woman screamed and clutched a towheaded boy to her bosom, pressing her back against the coach wall to Longarm's right, about midway down the car, squeezing her eyes closed.

Most of the men—stocky and rough-hewn, with drooping mustaches—appeared to be miners. There were a couple of women in frilly dresses revealing more flesh than customary and whom Longarm pegged as whores likely heading for the mining camps to ply their trade through the summer, now that all the passes were finally open after a hard high-country winter. On the left-side grouping of benches thinly upholstered in thin green canvas, a baby was crying in its mother's arms.

Longarm was looking for an outlaw, but the only person here apparently not a passenger was a black porter who sat on a bench on the car's left side, in a small open space in which a black, bullet-shaped stove hunched with a box heaped with firewood. The porter, a young man with obsidian-dark skin, stared at Longarm with as much wide-eyed fear as the others.

"I'm a U.S. marshal," the lawman announced, walking slowly down the middle aisle, sliding his rifle barrel from right to left and back again, ready to shoot the first man who poked a gun at him. "Any owlhoots here?"

Aside from the baby's crying and a woman sobbing, the small crowd was eerily quiet. Several of the standing men's eyes kept darting toward the rear of the jostling car. When Longarm was ten feet away from the rear door, a thick man in a round-brimmed, black felt hat scrambled up from the floor, holding a young woman in a skimpy, shiny red dress in front of him with one arm. He held a pearl-gripped, black steel Colt against the girl's head.

The girl was green-eyed and pretty in a hard way, and while she winced against the harshness of the man's stranglehold on her neck, she didn't appear overly frightened. She was one of those girls who'd seen it all, and this was just one more thing to see.

The outlaw dragged the girl to the car's rear door, shouting, "One more step, lawdog, and I'm gonna give this doxie an extra ear!"

"Drop it!"

"Uh-uh." The hard case grinned and shook his head. He had little pig eyes and a double chin, two holsters hanging low on his hips, one empty. "*You* drop it. You got three seconds, or I'm gonna blow her head off!"

Running footsteps sounded on the coach roof above Longarm's head. Two men were up there. They were shouting as they ran from the rear of the car toward the front.

Longarm's glance only flicked toward the hammered-tin ceiling before leveling on the hard case grinning before him and holding the cocked pistol to the whore's head. He wore a greasy, mocking smile.

Quickly, Longarm lined up his sights on the man's left temple. He knew it was a risky shot, and that the hard case would likely drop the hammer on the whore as he died, but it was a shot Longarm had to take to try to save the other passengers.

The hard case must have seen the flinty, flat cast in Longarm's brown eyes as he arranged the sights on the man's head, just above his right eye. The hard case's own eyes snapped wide in horror, and just as he dropped his lower jaw and opened his mouth to scream, Longarm squeezed the Winchester's trigger.

The rifle's blast echoed around the inside of the rumbling car like a Fourth of July rocket detonated inside an empty tin rain barrel. The hard case smashed his ruined head back against the door so hard he broke the window, painting the sharp-edged shards with his own blood and white bone and brain matter. At the same time, he triggered his pistol, and somehow the bullet sliced up in front of the girl's face to plunk harmlessly into the ceiling.

As the dying man released his hold on the girl's arm, she dropped straight down to the floor on her knees, looking more relieved than terrified, and cast her green-eyed gaze on Longarm. "Thanks," she said raspily, breathing hard and rubbing her neck.

The double-chinned hard case was slowly sagging to the floor, glass raining down from the door around him, his little pig eyes flat and lightless. His arms jerked as he died.

Longarm ejected his spent shell casing. As the cartridge clattered to the wooden floor and rolled, he wheeled toward the front of the coach, where two figures shone in the door's small window, one man looking inside. As the outlaw brought a pistol up, all the women in the car gasped in unison, and one of the miners said, "Good *Lord*!"

Longarm ran toward the front of the car. *"Everyone down!"*

They all cowered at the same time, and as the outlaw backed up, grinning, and aimed his pistol at the window to shoot into the car, Longarm stopped and fired three quick rounds—boom! boom! boom!—through the door. One bullet blew out the glass still splattered with the Mexican's blood, while the other two punched through the wood. All three must have ripped into the outlaw with the pistol, because he suddenly flew up and back, bouncing off the rear wall of the next car forward.

His pistol popped into the air above his head. Beneath the rumble of the train, which seemed to be picking up more and more speed and angling slightly downward now, the report sounded little louder than a twig snapping. The baby wailed louder, and the sobbing around Longarm grew more frantic as he ejected the last spent cartridge, levered a fresh one into the breech, and prepared to shoot the second shooter on the platform.

Foot thuds sounded atop the coach. Longarm lowered his Winchester. Apprehension caused the short hairs along the back of his neck to bristle. The man on the roof shouted, "You made a big mistake, lawdog!"

The train robber triggered two rounds through the roof—one hole after another appearing in the middle of the car, just behind Longarm. One bullet plowed into an empty bench while the other kissed the nap from the wool coat of one of the miners, causing the man to curse sharply as he grabbed that arm and lurched toward the side of the car. Heart thudding, knowing he might have a bloodbath involving innocent bystanders on his hands, Longarm fired three rounds into the ceiling, around where the shooter on the roof had fired.

Longarm ejected the last spent casings and stared at the ceiling, pricking his ears. The shooter laughed tauntingly, and fired three more rounds through the ceiling, these three bullets tearing harmlessly into the coach's floor or thumping into the wood box near the stove, thank God.

Longarm fired three more rounds desperately, gritting

his teeth and narrowing his eyes. He lunged to his left, and grabbed the brake chain. A sudden slowing of the train would likely knock the owlhoot off the coach.

He jerked hard on the chain four or five times. The train didn't slow an iota. He cursed.

"Tried that," one of the men near him shouted. "They musta rigged the brakes from the engine!"

Longarm triggered the Winchester into the ceiling two more times. His last shot was still echoing around the coach, and he could hear the shooter laughing, when he ran down the center aisle and out the bullet-riddled rear door. He turned sharply right, grabbed the ladder, and climbed, glancing once to his left and cursing.

The train had climbed to the top of the pass and was starting down.

If there'd been an engineer at the controls, he probably would have heard the gunfire and stopped the train. Since they were still moving, and gradually increasing speed on the backside of Horse Thief Pass, the engineer and tender must both be dead. The outlaws had probably shot them when they'd first boarded the train, so they themselves could control the combination, not wanting it stopped until they'd reached wherever they intended to get off and mount fresh horses waiting for them.

Longarm lunged up and over the top of the coach car just as the outlaw leader, Rio Hayes, fired one of the two pistols in his hands through the roof, about two feet from Hayes's left boot. Longarm brought up the Winchester quickly and squeezed the trigger.

The hammer pinged on an empty chamber.

He tossed the gun aside, and as it dropped onto the vestibule below, he palmed his Colt .44-40 but not before Rio Hayes gave a jeering whoop and triggered both his pistols at Longarm.

One hammered into the coach roof near Longarm's right knee. The other three sailed wide. The train was moving and pitching so violently now that the shooter couldn't draw an accurate bead.

Longarm raised the double-action Colt and fired. Hayes was laughing madly and dancing around, making it doubly impossible for Longarm to pink the son of a bitch.

Longarm straightened, walked forward, holding his left hand out for balance while he fired with his right. Hayes whooped and hollered and fired from a similar posture, his bullets flying past Longarm to thunk into the wood piled in the tender car beyond.

The wind whipped Longarm's hat from his head. Hayes had already lost his hat, and his thin, scraggly, greasy blond hair was blowing straight back behind his bald paint. He fired his pistols, squinting his eyes, grinning, his clothes flapping madly.

Longarm's sixth bullet nicked Hayes's left earlobe. The killer flinched. His smile instantly became a glare. Blood dripped from the ragged bottom of his earlobe and blew away in the wind.

Hayes moved toward Longarm taking heavy, lunging steps, continuing to fire until both his gun hammers clapped tinnily against the firing pins. The outlaw leader tossed both empty guns away with a savage snarl and slid a big bowie knife from a sheath strapped to his right thigh.

Longarm holstered his Colt and shoved his hand into his right vest pocket for the double-barreled derringer he kept there, attached by a gold-washed chain to a turnip-sized railroad watch residing in the opposite pocket. Hayes was on him before he could wrap his hand around the little popper. The lawman threw both his hands up, closing the left one around Hayes's right wrist, stopping the point of the razor-edged knife about a foot away from his throat.

He dug the fingers of his right hand into Hayes's neck, pressing his thumb hard against the man's prominent Adam's apple carpeted by a two- or three-day growth of prickly, sweat-greasy, dark-brown beard. Hayes snarled, gritting his chipped yellow teeth, eyes appearing about to pop out of his head.

Longarm was bigger and stronger. He pushed the outlaw's knife hand back and then released the man's throat only to slam his right fist twice and with all his power against the man's jaw, knocking it loose from its mooring.

"Unnghawww!" the broken-jawed Hayes screamed, falling back away from Longarm, dropping the bowie, and clutching his face with both hands.

Now Longarm had him. He lunged toward him to deliver the final blow and throw him from the train when the coach car dropped sharply forward, behind Longarm. The sudden descent caused Longarm to lose his footing. He fell hard against the coach roof on his back and rolled to the left, clawing at the roof for purchase, to keep from rolling off. As he did, dread rippled through him.

The sudden drop told him that the runaway train was heading down the perilously steep backside of Horse Thief Pass toward Horse Thief Gorge.

Moving as fast as they were without brakes, they'd never make it across the one-hundred-yard bridge across the gorge in one piece. The barreling train would shatter the bridge and end up—train, bridge, the innocent passengers, as well as Longarm—in blood-basted, iron-entangled debris at the bottom of Horse Thief Gorge.

Chapter 3

Longarm managed to fling one hand over the ridge of corrugated tin running along the center top of the coach car and use it to keep himself from being hurled off the speeding train and having his skull and every other bone broken amongst the rocks lining the trail.

Now, to get control of the train before it hit the bridge . . .

He heard someone moaning and groaning, and saw Rio Hayes lying facedown over the tin ridge. The man was trying to gain his feet.

Something dark appeared on Longarm's right, ahead of the train but moving toward Longarm fast. It was a tunnel carved into the side of the mountain.

Longarm, hunkered low atop the coach car, stared in awe—could he get this lucky?—as the dark tunnel mouth flew toward him and the day coach he lay prone upon, both boots dangling down over the side. The peak of the arching portal was only about four feet above the coach car roof.

Longarm looked at Rio Hayes and smiled.

Hayes had just gained his feet and grabbed another bowie knife from somewhere on his scruffy person, and had turned toward Longarm, a savage scowl that, coupled with his broken jaw hanging askew, made his entire face look horsey and crooked and even more demented than usual.

Hayes hadn't seen the tunnel when Longarm had. But now he saw that gaping, black portal rushing toward him like a gigantic black bird from some hellish underworld intending to swoop him up in its stygian wings.

Hayes had about one second to widen his eyes in awe and dismay before the tunnel turned the world dark. About one eye wink later, following a clipped scream, Longarm heard a resounding, crunching thump!

Just like that, Rio Hayes was gone.

Turned to jelly against the side of the tunnel, over the black, arching entrance. There was a clattering to Longarm's left, toward the train's rear. He heard it beneath the raucous din of the train echoing deafeningly off the tunnel's close, dark walls.

When the train caromed on out the tunnel's other side and into the blindingly bright daylight, Longarm saw what appeared a ragged, bloody bag of bones jouncing along a roof several cars back. It skidded off to the car's south side and slithered down over the roof and out of sight, leaving a wide smear of dark red blood behind it.

"Gone but not forgotten, Rio," Longarm muttered through a grunt, heaving himself to his feet, "you son of a bitch."

He stared forward, past the wood tender heaped with split pine and oak, to the black iron engine with its diamond-shaped stack spewing gray smoke that billowed in ghostly snakes behind. Beyond the smokestack, the rail bed was a thin swath of iron and rock leading arrow-straight through dark green walls of forest. It dropped perilously toward a distant, gray-blue fold in the dark ridges—a fold in which the broad, deep Horse Thief Gorge lay.

Longarm knew from having taken this line before that the grade soon got even steeper before bottoming out at the bridge over the gorge. Usually through here the engineer was clamping the brake shoes taut against all wheels, just creeping along, because he knew the bridge could only withstand a speed of less than twenty miles an hour. Any more than that, the force and pressure and vibration of the locomotive and trailing cars would rattle the whole thing apart.

As Longarm dropped quickly down the ladder to the vestibule, he judged they were traveling at least thirty miles an hour and were probably picking up an extra mile an hour with every few passing seconds. The wind rush over the train was enormous, blowing the lawman's close-cropped, dark brown hair flat against his skull.

"How come we're going so fast?" It was the girl the Mexican had been having his way with.

She was still naked and sitting with her back to the bloody front wall of the coach car, one arm crossed on her breasts. Having seen the other doxies inside the coach car, Longarm now realized this girl was likely with them. With her other hand, she was holding her blowing hair back from her face. She looked concerned but not horrified.

"That's what I'm gonna find out!" Longarm yelled above the screeching and clattering of the wheels over the rail seams and the incessant whooshing of the wind.

He climbed up into the tender car and crawled over the neatly stacked wood, wincing at the sharp edges of the wood digging into his bare hands and scraping his knees. Ahead, he saw the fireman and the engineer both slumped inside the locomotive. The fireman lay on the floor across from the firebox that heated the boiler. The engineer was half standing, as though he were suspended by something.

Longarm continued crawling, glancing at the engineer and then out beyond the train to the gorge that he could see opening now before him, the bridge stretching a thin, silver-brown line across it. It was a mile away but it was coming up fast. The lawman knew enough about trains to know that even this narrow-gauge affair needed at least a hundred yards to stop after the brakes were fully applied, maybe more than that considering how fast the combination was barreling down a steep pass.

Longarm dropped over the bulkhead and into the locomotive, stepped over the stout boots of the overall-clad fireman, blood gushing out the side of the man's head. He stepped over to the engineer, who had a similar hole as the fireman, in the same side of his head.

He saw now what had happened. The gang had shot the engineer and the brakemen before Hayes's men had leaped onto the train . . . probably from a perch similar to Longarm's.

They'd figured they could stop the train whenever they wanted by pulling the brake through chain from anywhere behind, in any of the cars. Only, they hadn't counted on the engineer falling over the dead-release lever that disengaged the through chain, rendering it impossible to brake the train from anywhere but in the locomotive itself.

Longarm pulled the engineer off the lever and let him drop to the floor. He turned the lever back to the right, saw the long, wood-handled brake, which looked much like the brake on a wagon, and hauled back on it. After a few seconds, he felt the locomotive tremble as the wood-and-metal brake jaws clamped over the iron wheels of all the cars.

Only, the forward momentum was too great for the brakes. They wouldn't hold. The lever leaped back upright, releasing the brake jaws and nearly tearing Longarm's shoulders from their sockets.

"Shit!" the lawman shouted into the wind, grabbing the handle with both hands and hauling back and down on it once more.

Again, he felt the engine tremble beneath his boots. It sort of hiccupped, but the handle jerked upward despite Longarm virtually hanging on it the way the engineer had been hanging over the dead-release.

"Need some help?" The feminine voice had sounded from behind.

Longarm glanced over his shoulder to see the girl he'd

left on the vestibule crawling over the wood stacked in the tender car. She'd thrown a thin, very low-cut, sleeveless pink dress on. The wind billowed it out in front, revealing her tender, sloping breasts, which jostled as she crawled, barefoot, across the wood.

Longarm continued to wrestle with the brake lever, encouraged by the hiccups he felt through the iron grate of the locomotive floor whenever he got the brake engaged, though he was having a devil of a time *keeping* it engaged. The girl climbed over the bulkhead, winced at the dead men lying around Longarm, and came over to where Longarm was clutching the lever with both hands and leaning far back toward the floor, grunting and sighing and cursing through gritted teeth.

Straight ahead, he saw the bridge and the canyon. It was sliding up on him fast as the train continued to barrel down the side of the pass, which was leveling out a little now though the train was still hammering along at forty or fifty miles an hour.

That was just too fast. He had to get the speed down to half that or they were all doomed.

The brakes screamed like a hundred terrified girls, but the jerking Longarm could feel meant they weren't continuously engaged.

"Let me help!" the girl shouted above the wind.

She climbed on top of Longarm, her back to him, the brake handle between them. She propped her bare feet up on the front bulkhead, and pressed her body back and down against the brake handle and Longarm.

He could feel her round rump against his crotch. Her hair blew around his face in the wind. It smelled faintly like sage and chokecherries. Her dress blew up in the wind, exposing the long, creamy length of her legs clear to her hips.

The brakes screamed more shrilly than before. The engine shuddered violently as the jaws clamped down hard over all the iron wheels.

Longarm looked through the golden cloud of the girl's blowing hair. The locomotive was nearly level with the bridge now, and it was still swooping toward them but not quite as quickly as before. To both sides, the trees were thinning out, exposing the clay-colored boulders of the ridge still angling down toward the gorge.

To the left of the rails, two gray coyotes watched the train from a stony ledge, ears raised curiously, one curveting as though it wanted to run but was too fascinated by the big iron, screeching contraption to hightail it just yet. Both brush wolves were wondering if the train would make it or pile up at the bottom of the gorge.

The locomotive jerked and shuddered. The brakes squealed so shrilly that Longarm thought his eardrums would pop. The girl screamed as she threw her head back against Longarm's chest, grinding the heels of her feet into the bulkhead and pressing her supple body down harder against Longarm and the brake handle.

Longarm closed his eyes. He was about tapped out, the power in his body draining. His tense muscles were turning to putty.

Gradually, the shuddering continued until Longarm looked to both sides and saw nothing but clear, blue Colorado sky stretching from horizon to horizon. They were over the bridge. And they were probably not moving over fifteen miles an hour. Maybe less than that. The train was still hiccupping and the brakes were still screeching, but, by damn, they'd done it!

They'd gotten the train slowed. The bridge should hold.

"We're over the middle of the canyon!" the girl cried.

Longarm kept his hands wrapped around the brake lever. He felt as though his knuckles were about to pop, his arms about to tear loose from their sockets. The girl's hair in his face was a tonic, however. So, too, was her rump grinding against his balls.

When he felt the engine grind to a final halt, he looked

to both sides. Red, rocky slopes rose around him, stippled with piñon pines and firs. He could smell the pine resin. It was like perfume. The locomotive panted like a dying dinosaur; the fire in its box hadn't been stoked since the outlaws had killed the fireman. Now that its momentum had been broken, and it was stopped, it wouldn't be going anywhere until it was fired up again.

"We made it," the girl said in a sexy, husky voice, rolling off of Longarm, setting her feet on the floor and looking around with girlish delight. "We made it, mister. You did it. You saved us all!"

As though on cue, a great, victorious whoop rose from the passengers behind the tender car.

Longarm gained his feet, straightened. The brake remained now in the locked position. He squeezed his hands together, wincing as the blood oozed back into them, as the damaged tendons and muscles barked their complaints.

He looked at the girl beaming up at him. "Couldn't have done it without you, miss," he said, panting.

"Call me Matilda."

He gave a weary half smile. "Call me Longarm."

She leaped up and wrapped her arms around his neck, pressing her breasts against his chest, her lips against his mouth.

"Longarm," she said, "when we get to Creede, you're gonna get the biggest thank you that any girl has ever given a man!"

Chapter 4

Two days later, riding north along a well-traveled stage road, Longarm reached into the pocket of his recently laundered tobacco-tweed frock coat, and pulled out the pink flimsy he'd received at the telegraph office in Creede. The missive had been sent in response to his request to have a few days off before heading back to the lawdog's grind in Denver.

REQUEST DENIED **STOP** AZ RANGERS AND U.S.
MARSHALS AMBUSHED IN ARIZONA **STOP** GET YOUR
ASS BACK HERE PRONTO END **STOP**

It was signed by Longarm's persnickety boss, Chief Marshal Billy Vail of Denver's First District Court.

Longarm frowned at the flimsy and then stuffed it back into his coat pocket. "Back to the grind," he muttered, and while he could have used a few more days to frolic with Miss Matilda Nightingale in Creede—he didn't know whether that was her real name but preferred to believe it was—the news of the deaths of his fellow lawmen graveled him.

He couldn't help wondering how many men had been killed and why and by whom, but he'd learn all that once he got back to Denver. That's where he was heading now, by way of Leadville, where he'd pick up the Old Leadville trail and take it up and over Mosquito Pass to the growing, mile-high city sprawled on the plain at the foot of the Front Range.

It was getting on toward night, however, so he'd spend the night in Leadville and then head east again first thing in the morning. He'd have taken the same narrow-gauge contraption he'd saved from the Arkansas River Gang six days before, but the locomotive's brakes were getting an overhaul at the Creede roundhouse and wouldn't be up and running until late next week at the earliest.

So Longarm had hired a stable boy to ride back along the tracks and fetch the blue roan gelding he'd left when he'd boarded the train. After he and the horse had had a badly needed night of rest, and his clothes had been laundered by a capable Chinaman, who also sold a rather tasty lager by the bucketful, now Longarm and the horse were pounding the trails for home.

He'd decided that despite the need to rush back to Denver, he had to stop overnight somewhere or kill both himself and his horse. Why not treat himself to a luxurious bed and a good meal in the stylish Grand Hotel built recently by Horace W. Tabor?

He felt lousy about the dead lawmen—he wondered who they were and if he'd known any of them—but he could only move so fast, and after taking down an entire gang of yellow-fanged devils and saving a train full of innocent folks including five pretty doxies, he deserved one night in a down-stuffed bed provided by the silver tycoon, Horace Tabor. Never mind that most of the country's newspapers had declared the man a hell-bent lecher, having divorced his wife and married one Elizabeth McCourt, deemed by the scandal-mongering newsmen and tabloid-reading public a home-wrecking charlatan.

It was said that old Horace had built the grandest hotel

on the western frontier, and named it appropriately, providing luxurious furnishings and tasty grub to weary travelers. Longarm had also heard from those who knew him personally that Tabor was a right generous jake to the families who patronized his mercantile, offering credit left and right, and that he was just as fair and honorable to those who worked for him breaking rock in his silver mine, the Matchless, outside Leadville.

Yes, the weary lawman was looking forward to warm, succulent grub and a good night's sleep. True to her word, the night before, the pretty, blond whore who called herself Matilda Nightingale had given Longarm about as much pleasure as one man could bear. But he hadn't gotten a whole lot of sleep.

Matilda had also made his daylong ride today a little uncomfortable, sucking, as she had, nearly all the skin off his cock. Well, not really. It was just raw enough to make sitting a McClellan saddle all day a tad uncomfortable.

Her wonderful mouth had sucked him long and hard, though, and despite the day's discomfort, he felt his balbriggans tent-poling a little at the memory of her soft and pliant mouth. Her warm, wet tongue had stroked him like a lollipop, causing him to grind his heels into the lumpy cornshuck mattress provided by the madam who ran the crude but functional Creede House of Love & Other Sundry Pleasures.

Oh, yeah—a soft bed was going to feel good. Especially after he'd been fogging the trail of the Arkansas River Gang for the past three weeks, every night spreading his bedroll out in the rough-and-rocky.

An hour later, he reined the roan up in front of the Grand Hotel in Leadville, the cobblestone street around him alive now with the crowd that would soon be filling all the saloons and stomping their feet and whistling their delight at the night's performance at the Tabor Opera House, just down the street from the hotel.

All types of westerners milled around Longarm—miners, drifters, gunmen, gamblers, Chinamen, blacks, soldiers, bib-bearded prospectors with the crazy eyes of men alone too long in the mountains, and, of course, the brightly dressed doxies showing off their wares from balconies.

The painted-faced girls resembled lovely birds of all colors of the rainbow, preening themselves for the ribald, rollicking crowd of half-drunk prospective clients whistling and yelling and applauding on the boardwalks below.

Some men threw scrip and specie at the girls, and then, when their chosen girl beckoned, ran through the parlor house's propped-open front doors. A few triggered pistols into the air. Young boys in knickers and watch caps ran around, selling sandwiches from tomato crates attached to small wagons or wheelbarrows, dogs barking and panting after them.

It wasn't yet seven o'clock, but the brick or wood-frame saloons were doing a brisk business, with burly, bearded men in overalls and hobnailed boots walking in and out of the batwings with frothy beer mugs clutched in their ham-sized red paws, conversing on the boardwalks in nearly every language Longarm had ever heard, and more.

The travel-worn federal lawman looped the roan's reins around one of the several wrought-iron hitch racks fronting the Grand Hotel, unable to take his eyes off the well-named structure though he'd seen it once before. Built of red brick and trimmed in crisply painted white wood, with a mansard roof rising from its second story, sort of like a king's crown, it resembled nothing so much as a lavish, triple-decker riverboat that plied the waters of the southern Mississippi.

"Incredible, isn't it?"

Longarm turned to the woman standing on the broad, stone paving, between the hitch racks and their dozen or so tied horses, and the building itself. She was staring up at the hotel, as well, but also casting sidelong glances at Longarm. The tall, handsomely weathered lawman stared at her, and for one of the very first times in his adult life, he was tongue-tied.

He'd rarely laid eyes on such a rare and sumptuous creature as the ravishing brunette before him. Long-legged and cool as a snowmelt stream, she was a goddess sent from heaven to bless mere mortals with her presence while both captivating and torturing men with her beauty.

She somehow had that air about her, too, with her thick, rich hair piled high and secured with a gold comb atop her patrician's head. Her eyes were hazel, set wide apart and accentuating the long, gallant line of her nose. Those polished hazel orbs matched the brocade and taffeta of her lavishly but tastefully appointed dress that was trimmed with cream silk sleeves, a cream silk collar, and an understated, gold, obviously expensive cameo brooch.

Her breasts were well concealed, as befitted a lady, but Longarm knew, as though he could see them through her dress and several layers of traditional under frillies, that they would be proud, firm, full, and perfectly shaped, with exquisitely jutting nipples.

One look at them, and a man would come in his trousers without her even laying a hand on him.

Quickly, realizing where his gaze had been, he jerked his eyes to her face. Too late. With a tolerant half smile, squinting those intoxicating hazel orbs and turning the beautifully clefted chin toward the hotel's front doors, she said, "Excuse me."

Holding her skirts above her fine ankles and teal, side-button shoes, she climbed the wooden steps to the hotel's broad oak doors.

"Ah, shit," Longarm said, the tips of his ears turning as warm as an overheated iron. "Fuckin' fool . . ."

He continued to scold himself while the girl's image continued to float around inside his brain, as though it had been emblazoned forever on his retinas. Girl? Young woman, rather, though he doubted that she was much over twenty. No, not more than a year past that, he decided, remembering how smooth her skin had been around her eyes and across her finely tapering cheeks, how its perfection, only slightly suntanned, seemed to soften the long, firm, yet delicate line of her jaw.

As he lifted his saddlebags off the roan's back and slid his Winchester from its sheath, setting the long gun on his right shoulder, he realized he had a semi hard-on. Grimacing, he brushed his hand across his crotch, adjusting his whipcord trousers so not to cripple himself.

He consciously wrestled the girl's image from his mind and, only partly succeeding, stiffly stepped onto the stone paving, climbed the hotel's entrance steps, and pushed through the heavy, giant, castle-like doors into the broad, high-ceilinged lobby.

There she was, ahead of him, apparently picking up her room key at the block-long, horseshoe-shaped front desk of gleaming cherry trimmed with silver and with ornate mahogany inlays. Over the lobby and between ornate balconies with rails of the same material as the front desk, hung a crystal chandelier the size of a Concord stagecoach.

Longarm only glanced at the lobby's fine appointments, having found the young brunette to be as breathtaking as anything that humans could ever construct. Just now the liveried, gray-haired lobby clerk handed her a small parchment envelope, which she opened, slipping out the note tucked inside. She bowed her lovely head to read the missive as she made her way to the wine-red carpeted staircase with its gleaming, polished rails.

The liveried oldster twisted a corner of his waxed handlebar mustache as he watched her go, dipping his chin just enough to tell Longarm that he was admiring the girl's ass. Longarm found himself admiring it, too, as he strode across the polished slate floor, saddlebags over one shoulder, Winchester hiked atop the other.

As the woman made her way up the stairs, slowly at first as she read the note, then more quickly when she'd read it, turning at the second-floor landing, Longarm set his gear on the desk and said, "Who in the roaring flames of the devil's hell is that?"

The oldster gave him a disapproving glance, jerking his black silk waistcoat down. "I do apologize, sir, but I'm not predisposed to give out information about the Grand's clientele."

"Well, excuse me all to hell." Longarm caught one last glimpse of the charming waif before she disappeared up the second leg of the stairs. "Don't suppose you'd be predisposed to renting a room to this tired old jake for a night, would you, friend?"

He hated uppity folks, especially those he knew to be little better heeled that he himself was.

The middle-aged desk clerk gave the tall, sun-weathered, dusty, rifle-wielding gent before him the critical up and down before saying with a haughty sigh and a slow, reproving blink behind steel-framed spectacles, "If you can pay in advance, such arrangements can be made, I suppose."

Longarm plunked the right amount of coins onto the desk, signed the register, gave the nasty old clerk instructions regarding the tending of his horse as well as his own person in the form of a hot bath delivered to his room, then pocketed his room key.

"Later, amigo," he said.

"Of course, sir."

"And don't be skimpy on the roan's oats," he said as he crossed to the stairs, not looking behind him. "I need him rarin' to ride first thing in the mañana."

As he made his way to his room, striding along the second floor's carpeted hall lit with gilded bracket lamps, he stopped suddenly, frowned, and glanced over his right shoulder. A door latch clicked, as though a door had been opened slightly, quietly, but not so quietly closed.

As if someone had been spying on him.

The girl?

Longarm's broad face with its late-day beard shadow acquired a wistful expression. "Hmmmm."

Chapter 5

Longarm lounged in the hot water that the young porter had filled his copper tub with, sitting back and smoking a three-for-a-nickel cheroot and sipping straight from the bottle of Maryland rye whiskey that the lad had also hauled to his room.

The lawman, grateful for the rare rye and to be able to sit right here in his nicely furnished digs without having to hammer the boardwalks looking for a tonsorial parlor or bathhouse, flipped the kid a three-dollar gold piece, and the kid—tall and gangly and looking like the sensitive black sheep of a mining family—left grinning.

When Longarm had scraped his jaws with his ivory-handled razor, he rinsed with a bucket of clean hot water the porter had also provided. Finding himself as hungry as a prisoner working the rock quarries, he scrambled out of the tub. He dressed in clean underwear from his saddlebags and then wrestled into the rest of his duds that he'd given a quick dusting with a horsehair brush. He'd cleaned his low-heeled cavalry stovepipes with a little spit and a gun rag.

He wrapped his gun and shell belt around his narrow hips, dropped his double-barreled, pearl-gripped derringer into the right pocket of his fawn vest, slid the old turnip

watch into the opposite pocket, donned his hat, and headed
down to the hotel's stylish dining room to sup.

Just after he'd ordered the roast beef with mashed potatoes and gravy with two hot buns and sides of fresh garden
greens and buttered carrots, his heart stopped. His chest
went tight, and his face swelled. It heated up like a pig carcass hanging in the full sunlight.

At least, he *thought* his ticker had seized up on him.
Maybe it only felt like that. He was dead certain his lower
jaw was sagging nearly clear down to his round table's crisp
white linen, twinkling silverware, and glistening crystal
water glass.

Vaguely, as he stared into the hazel eyes of the queen
he'd probably have met properly outside the hotel earlier if
she hadn't caught him staring at her tits, he considered summoning a sawbones but nixed the idea when he didn't pass
out but found himself looking at the top of the girl's beautiful brown head as she perused her menu.

She was sitting across the room from him. And she'd
been watching him. He knew she had. That's what had
almost killed him.

He'd been looking around the large room with its high,
pressed-tin ceiling painted off-white, and then he'd found
himself staring into those eyes that had been directed at
him. Sort of furtively directed at him, over the girl's menu.

Then she'd lowered those polished marbles quickly but
somehow casually to her menu, and he was now studying
the rich swirls of brown hair, his heart beating again. Not
really beating but fluttering.

The comb she wore in her hair was cherry colored. It
complimented her red, lace-edged dress perfectly, and it
also brought out the deep reds in her skin, including the red
of her wide, full mouth that had been so perfectly made by
God to wrap itself around a man's jutting cock, to suck him
and deliver him to bliss.

She hadn't been seated in the dining room when he'd

walked in five minutes earlier. He was quite certain she hadn't, because he'd looked around for her when the hostess had seated him at the corner table he'd requested, because he always requested corner tables, with his back to the wall. It was a safety precaution that he always took to prevent his ending up back-shot by one of the many men he'd offended over the years and finding himself facedown, dead, in a pile of potatoes and beef gravy.

The point being, he had a good view of the room, and he'd looked for her. But she hadn't been here. Till now. She must have just been seated, maybe when he'd been perusing his menu, and now she was here. Which meant that there was a very good chance that it had been her who'd been spying on him earlier, when he'd been hunting for his room, and that she'd followed him down here now.

Could she be stalking him?

The idea was no less intoxicating for being utterly preposterous. If he wasn't careful, he was going to ooze in his shorts like a love-struck schoolboy getting a peek through the half-moon in the privy door at his favorite girl with her frillies down around her ankles.

Longarm sank back in his chair, in the room's front corner. Time to get a hold of yourself, old son. You must have got your head overly battered aboard the train the other day. This girl was obviously a couple of social as well as economic rungs above your lowly, badge toter's station.

Why, she'd as soon tumble with a hydrophobic cur behind a trash pile as spread her legs for your big, leathery, unhealed person. Her daddy no doubt has part ownership in the hotel or the opera house, and she's here to take the holdings for a little ride.

She did seem to be dining alone, however.

Longarm noticed that the waiter had swept all of the extra place settings from her table. If the big lawman had any balls at all, he'd walk over and inquire if he could join her.

And get a glass of ice water thrown in his face for his trouble . . .

He dug into his shirt pocket for a cheroot, bit the end off, and fired a match on his cartridge belt. As he touched the flame to the cheroot's tip, he vaguely opined that the girl could be married and possibly meeting her husband later for after-dinner drinks. Any man married to such a queen as her was likely some mucky-muck with business doings in these expanding parts and was likely too busy to sup with his wife.

As he got the cigar going to his liking, Longarm squinted through his billowing blue smoke at the girl's table, trying to get a look at one of her delicate-boned hands still holding the menu in front of her. There did seem to be something shiny there, but from this distance he couldn't tell if it was a diamond ring or a wedding band.

Uh-oh. Shit. She'd just lifted her eyes to his, and she turned away before he could do same, giving her right nostril a very subtle but very real winkle of utter disdain. She even seemed to sigh in disgust.

Well, there was Longarm's answer. Now he could stop fantasizing like a schoolboy with his dick in his hands, and go back to being a man of pride and self-respect.

He was a professional, for chrissakes. He'd eat his meal, follow it up with a hunk of peach cobbler and fresh-whipped cream, smoke another cigar, sip a last shot of rye, and then tumble on into the old mattress sack. Just like he *should* do. He needed to be well rested for the last leg of his journey on down the long hills to Denver. The next day, he'd no doubt hear more about the bushwhacked lawmen, and get himself headed for Arizona to see about bringing the killers to justice.

His food came, and it was every bit as scrumptious as he'd dreamed it would be. He was so hungry, and the food was so good, that he looked up only a few times while he ate, using the warm, buttery buns as gravy sponges.

As far as he could tell, the girl, who was eating now herself—some kind of fish, he thought—gave him not a single glance. She kept her eyes on her food or on the book she had open beside her and whose pages she turned slowly as she ate, taking very delicate bites and following each bite with a delicate pat of her lips with her white linen napkin.

Occasionally, she became so immersed in her book, gazing down at the page before her, that nearly an entire minute would pass before she'd take another bite.

The gal obviously hadn't taken down a trainload of curly wolves the day before, and then ridden sixty miles over mountain and plain, Longarm thought with a restrained snort as he swabbed the last of the gravy and bits of roast beef from his plate with his last bun.

Finished with the main meal, he ordered the pie, coffee, and a shot of rye, then sat back in his chair, stifled a belch, and very purposefully restrained himself from ogling the girl anymore. He'd genuinely become ashamed of himself, downright embarrassed.

He was half done with his pie, which he savored with the coffee and the rye, which he'd poured into the hot, black coffee, when he suddenly looked up and found himself staring into those hazel orbs once again. From three feet away, this time. Her red dinner dress was lower cut than the one she'd worn earlier, and a small, gold cross was tucked into the top of her deep, lightly tanned, slightly freckled cleavage above the rich, full mounds of her breasts.

Her right hand was closed, and for a second he thought she was about to punch him with it. But then he heard a quiet clink and looked down to see a gold room key on the table before him, beneath her now-open hand. Stealthily, using two fingers, she slid the key across the table until it was partly concealed by his coffee cup and saucer.

"The number is on the key," she said, her voice low and sexily raspy. "Give me a half hour. Be clean."

She turned away, strode coolly out of the dining room

and into the lobby, heading for the stairs. Longarm sat staring at the broad, open doorway, hang-jawed.

Vaguely, he once again considered summoning a sawbones, because he thought for sure his heart really was about to seize up on him this time. Or that he'd gone insane and had dreamed up the unlikely encounter.

Maybe the dustup in the train had caused him to go all soft and squishy in his thinker box.

A half hour, huh?

He looked down at the half-eaten chunk of cobbler and slid it away. He was no longer hungry. All he could think about now was the girl.

Butterflies flitted in all directions in his stomach. When the waiter passed, he told him to take the pie away, and he ordered another double shot of rye and relit the cheroot he'd allowed to go out. When the double shot came and the waiter had cleared the table, he sat back, manufacturing a casual expression while he smoked and sipped the whiskey and listened to his heart drumming like a tom-tom.

The half hour passed as slowly as the last ice age.

He probably consulted the big grandfather clock at the far end of the softly buzzing dining room once every two minutes, until he watched the large hand click for the thirtieth time. No point in being early. She might expect him to go running up the stairs and down the hall, tripping all over himself, playing the fool, but that wasn't how you played a girl like her.

You took it slow. Acted casual. You acted like you were doing her as big a favor as she was doing you.

She obviously enjoyed playing it coy up to a certain point—the point of finally dropping a key on a gentlemen's public table, that was. But you had to break her of that false timidity. You had to tease the girl until she was fairly yipping and moaning like a feral bitch in heat and climbing on your cock.

Longarm paid his bill, stubbed out his cigar, donned his

hat, and made his way very slowly, very nonchalantly out the door and into the lobby. He smiled and nodded casually at passersby, pinching his hat brim to the ladies, half consciously aware all the while that the hotel was spinning slightly around him, as though he'd had far more to drink that he actually had, and that he couldn't feel his feet.

He held the key tightly in his left fist, glancing down at it twice as he sauntered up the stairs. The numeral 19 fairly shouted up at him, making his ears ring. In the second-floor hall, he stopped at the door and poked the key into the lock, fully aware of the metaphorical significance of the maneuver.

He turned the key and went inside.

The large bed straight across from him was made. It was also empty. A red Tiffany lamp guttered on the dresser to the right of the bed, but the girl was nowhere to be seen.

Suddenly, a warning tolled in the lawman's ears, and he slid his hand across his belly to the polished walnut grips of his Colt.

Ambush?

He'd just started to slide the revolver from its holster when a soft, sensual voice said behind him and to his right, "Fuck me now and fuck me hard, you randy dog."

Chapter 6

Leaving the iron in the leather, Longarm whipped his head around. His tongue grew as heavy as a beer schooner. His heart started hammering inside his head.

The girl sat on a fainting couch against the wall behind the door, a candle on a side table quivering over her dramatically, revealing that she wore nothing but a sheer black shift.

Her hair was down, spread messily across her bare shoulders, framing her face and smoky eyes. She still wore the gold cross; it dangled down to the top of her breasts, which the shift only partly covered.

Actually, it didn't really cover them, just laid a filmy shadow across them, showing them in all their heavy, opulent splendor. They were as perfectly shaped as he'd imagined—firm and pointing slightly outward, with large, dark brown areolas, nipples jutting against the cloth. Longarm idly speculated that she was covered in no more silk than he could tuck under his tongue and still be able to down a meal without choking.

She had one knee up and was leaning her left arm across it. Her other leg was curled beneath it. The position lifted the shift high up on her waist, revealing the auburn tuft of hair between her thighs as well as an alluring glimpse of fleshy pink.

She tilted her head to one side, smiled with one half of her mouth, and let her eyes flick down to his crotch. "You'd better get out of those trousers before you tear right through them."

Longarm looked down at the bulge in his pants. She was right. He could feel the pain now.

He quickly closed the door, cuffed his hat from his head, kicked out of his boots, and removed his gun and shell belt. He was out of the rest of his attire in less than a minute, letting it all fall where it may. As he tossed his longhandles away behind him, he saw her smoky gaze rake his rangy, broad-shouldered, battle-scarred body slowly.

Her eyes widened when they got to his crotch, his dong jutting high above his belly button—full and thick, the mushroom head looking as though it were about to explode.

"Oh, my God," she whispered, her breasts rising and falling heavily. Her voice seemed thick, even raspier than before. "You're hung like a fucking Russian plow horse."

Keeping her eyes on his thundering hard-on, she dropped both feet to the floor, rose, turned toward the couch, leaned forward, and swept the shift up around her waist, revealing her perfect ass and the auburn mound up under her butt cheeks. "Take me," she said, her voice quivering desperately, looking over her shoulder at his throbbing cock. "Bring it over here and fuck me with it."

Longarm didn't need to be told twice.

He followed his dick right over to her, reached around her waist with one arm, drew her toward him firmly, and then took his cock in his free hand and guided it up under her ass and through the moist, hot waiting doors of her pussy.

She jerked forward like a startled mare, throwing her head back. "Gawd!"

Longarm stopped halfway in, letting her womb expand gradually around him, and then pushed forward on the balls of his feet, shoving his manhood deeper . . . deeper . . .

deeper, until it would go no farther and she was leaning forward against the fainting couch, groaning from deep in her chest.

"Fuck me, damnit," she said through gritted teeth, spreading her legs a little wider for him, grinding her feet into the thick, black-and-red carpet. "Fuck me hard, you randy dog! I saw how you were looking at me. You were imagining doing this back out on the street, weren't you?"

Longarm was driving against her, pulling out, driving in, the otherworldly sensations ensconcing him like the world's more powerful opiate.

"Weren't you?" she demanded, glaring over her shoulder at him as he fucked her, causing her hair to slide back and forth across her shoulders.

"Yep."

"Do you like fucking strange girls you meet on the street?"

"Stranger the better."

"Oh, you're such a randy dog!"

"Uh-huh," he grunted, squeezing his eyes closed as he leaned forward, wrapped his arms around her, and grabbed her breasts in his hands. He kneaded them, rolled the nipples between his thumbs and index fingers.

They were as hard as small stones, jutting like sewing thimbles. The softness of the silk shift caressed the backs of his hands as he fondled her. Occasionally it would drop down in back to brush his belly, a pleasing sensation that complimented the more dramatic one going on inside the head of his cock, his belly, in his loins.

"Oh, God," the girl said raspily, sucking sharp breaths, releasing them sharply, sucking another one just as sharp. The back of the fainting couch tapped against the papered wall behind it as they moved together, in perfect rhythm now, Longarm squeezing her perfect, jouncing breasts while he rammed his hips against her ass, raising slapping sounds.

Occasionally, he'd straighten, hold her hips in his hands,

and really put the wood to her. The problem with this maneuver, however, was that it caused the back of the couch to bang more loudly against the wall.

"Keep going," she said. "Fuck me, damn you, you nasty dog. I saw . . . I saw . . . how you looked at me. I knew—oh, *fuck*!—I knew what you wanted to do to me!"

Longarm only grunted through clenched jaws.

"You uncouth brigand!"

"Uh-huh."

"Oh, fuck—your plow handle is going to bust me in two!"

"I'll stop if you want," he reluctantly offered while he continued to hammer away at her.

"Don't you fucking dare, you bastard!"

He'd known women who'd go on like she was. Talking mean and dirty seemed to be part of their pleasure, sort of cutting loose from the bonds that otherwise constrained them and kept them "proper." Personally, he liked to be quiet when he was hauling a girl's ashes, but to each his own. This girl had a body that could light a fire in God's own soul, and she sure as hell knew how to wield it. That's all he cared about.

In and out, in and out. Her hot juices engulfed him. He felt as though hot water were rising around his straining legs.

Suddenly, the warm folds of her pussy engulfed him, squeezing him gently, and she gave a guttural groan, tipping her head back, as though a bowie knife had been plunged into her belly button. She quivered almost violently, shoulders jerking, as she gained the crest of her passion. He rammed hard against her once more, held himself firmly against her ass, and cut loose, feeling his seed rocket into her.

He groaned loudly, throwing his head far back and tightening his jaws.

When she began to pant and waggle her ass against his hips, he continued to ram against her, bucking back and forth, no longer caring how much racket the sofa made as it banged against the wall. She screamed and cried and grunted, called him a dirty bastard and a few other things, and then screamed and cried and grunted again, until she seemed to sort of faint from exhaustion and passion, and dropped to the floor on her knees.

"Ohhh!" she said through a long, loud sigh, bowing her head and clawing at the couch the way a cat kneads a rug with it paws. "Oh, Jesus H. Christalmighty."

She rested her face against her hands and then slowly rolled over to face him, sitting on the floor with her back to the sofa, the corners of her fine mouth quirking a satisfied smile. "You do that rather well."

Longarm leaned toward her, feasting his eyes on her beauty, closed his mouth over hers. She wrapped her arms around his neck and returned his kiss hungrily. Pulling away, he said, "You're no slouch yourself, Miss . . ."

"No." She shook her head vehemently. "No names. You don't know me; I don't know you. You're a stud, and I'm a craven harlot. Understand?"

Married, Longarm thought. Mr. Mucky-Muck can't satisfy her. Understandable, given the obviously high grade of her demands. Why, she'd kill a man with any physical weakness whatever.

"Understand?" she demanded, splaying her hands across her ears and staring up at him, one of her eyes crossing beautifully. Her nipples were pebbling again.

"Lady, you're every man's dream."

He smiled and then lowered his head and kissed each nipple in turn, sucking as he kissed her until she rolled her head back against the couch and was groaning, arching her back, lifting her breasts toward his mouth, running her hands through his hair.

He lowered his head and ran his tongue down her fine, flat belly, swirled it around inside her belly button. Now she started convulsing, giving little spasming jerks and shivers.

"Oh, Christ, you're a devil!"

He continued to nibble and lick while gently kneading her proud breasts with his hands.

When his cock was fully engorged once more, he stood and reached for her.

"Oh, God, wait!" she said, and flung herself toward him on her knees. She grabbed his member in both her hands. "Oh, my God. You're a monster. A big, brawny monster with a cock like a plow handle."

Gazing at the organ of topic, she whispered, "You can really torment a woman with this thing, can't you? Make her think about you and want you even when you're no longer here."

She seemed to be talking to herself, so he kept his own mouth shut and let her run her tongue and fingers down the length of him. She sucked the head of his cock until he'd rocked back on his heels and groaned. Then she pulled her mouth off him and lowered her head to suck his balls while she continued to hold him in both hands, gently squeezing.

"Christ!" he said, when she'd brought him to the boiling point.

Almost savagely, he reached down and picked her up in his arms. She gave a half-startled, half-thrilled little gasp. He strode over to the bed, tossed her on top of it, and swung her legs around brusquely, positioning her for accepting him.

"Oh, you cur!" she cried, eyes flashing in delight.

He spread her legs with his arms and mounted her.

He stared down into those incredible hazel eyes that returned his lusty, smoky, erotic gaze. "Fuck me, you dirty dog!" she said, smiling devilishly, causing her eyes to cross, wrapping her arms and legs around him and giving a throaty laugh. "Fuck me like the rabid cur you are!"

He drew a breath, shoved his cock into her, listened to

her groan and yip softly, gently chewing on his shoulder and grinding her heels into his ass, and fucked her long and hard.

When he pulled out of her finally, a half hour later, he thought she was dead. She lay splayed out beneath him like a corpse.

Only, her lovely mouth was spread with a satisfied, half-delirious grin.

She drew a deep breath, causing her breasts to rise, the gold cross wedged sideways between them, and clung to him when he started to draw away from her. She lifted her head and kissed him passionately. She kissed his nose, nibbled it.

Keeping her fingers locked together behind his neck, she said, "Of any of them, I'd like to know who you are."

He started to open his mouth to speak, but she pressed a finger to his mustache-mantled lips.

"No. There's no point. No names. Sexier, this way. More mysterious. We're just a couple of animals who met one night to fuck like dogs in the Grand Hotel in Leadville. Nothing more, nothing less. If we ever meet again, we'll each walk on past, just two dirty dogs passing in the street. Understand?"

He smiled down at her. Yep, married.

"You're the boss, lady."

He kissed her again, swept his eyes over her again from her beautiful head to her long, delicate feet, marveling at her sumptuous, impeccable beauty.

And then he rose from the bed, took a whore's bath at her washstand while she watched him quietly, lying sideways and naked on the bed, head propped on the heel of her hand. Watching him, she slid a hand around on one of her breasts and slowly caressed one foot with the other.

Like a cat in a window.

He reached for a towel with which to dry himself and paused. Something on her dresser had caught his eye. Beneath a newspaper and an overturned book lay a small, gold-washed, ivory-gripped derringer. A popper very much like the one he carried in his own vest pocket.

He dried himself with the towel, pretending he hadn't seen the gun. A woman with her beauty and sexual precociousness likely couldn't be too careful. She probably never really knew whom she was inviting into her room.

Longarm dressed, donned his hat, tipped it at its usual rakish, cavalry-style angle over his left eye, and turned to her. She continued to lay there, naked and beautiful and catlike, her smoky eyes seeming to take in every inch of him.

"Been fun," he said.

She smiled, flung her hair back from her face, then rested her head on her hand again and rubbed her feet together luxuriously. "I'll be walking bull-legged for a week," she said in her sexy, raspy voice.

He walked over to her, bent down, placed one hand on her ass, and kissed her. She returned the kiss, and when he pulled away, she leaned toward him, wrinkling the skin above the bridge of her nose, wanting more.

He grinned down at her, winked. Her pretty face acquired a look of frustration, and then he pinched his hat brim to her, strode across the carpeted floor to the door, glanced back once more at her still lying there gazing at him with her lips slightly parted, and went out.

In the hall, he pulled the door closed behind him, sighed, and shook his head.

He felt the peace that comes after having his manly desires so thoroughly sated. After tonight, he likely wouldn't need a woman again for a week at the most. Wincing, he adjusted his crotch. Another like her inside of a month would likely cripple him for life.

Chuckling quietly, he dug a cheroot out of his shirt pocket and headed for the stairs. He needed some air and a fresh smoke. Then he'd head to bed and no doubt enjoy the best sleep of his life.

Chapter 7

Two days later and right on schedule, Longarm climbed the stone steps of Denver's Federal Building at eight A.M., nodding at his male acquaintances and pinching his hat brim to the office girls.

He climbed the stairs to the cavernous second floor and said howdy-do to a couple of attorneys he'd come to know over the years and who were going over some papers together on a wooden bench outside a federal courtroom. He followed his well-practiced route to the end of the hall that smelled of varnish and cigar smoke as well as the coal used to heat the sprawling building, and pulled open the stout wooden door whose frosted glass panel bore the name of his boss, Chief Marshal William H. Vail, First District Court of Colorado, and went in.

"How's it hangin', Henry?" he asked the prissy gent playing typewriter on the desk to his left, while he tossed his freshly steamed and brushed hat on the tree to his right.

Without looking up but continuing to pound the odd-looking contraption's keys with his long, slim, white fingers, Billy Vail's secretary said, "The chief marshal is expecting you, Marshal Long. Am I imagining things or are you on time for a change?"

Longarm stared down at Henry's dancing fingers, amazed as always that each finger seemed to know where each of the two dozen or so keys on the contraption was, and they never seemed to get entangled or miss a beat. And how did each key know where it was supposed to go on the travel voucher Henry was typing on? The world was changing mighty fast, Longarm thought, and he'd better figure out such things or get lost in the dust!

When the secretary's words finally made their way through his silent musings on the nature of progress and the fast fading of the old frontier, the big lawman glanced at the clock on the wall behind Henry, saw that the hour hand was on the eight and that the minute hand was pointing straight up at twelve.

"Well, look at that," Longarm said, as amazed as Henry was, planting one fist on a hip. "Henry, you'd better write this down in your work log. Custis Long was on time for a change. Put it on the page where you write down such things as why certain lawmen deserve a raise." He muttered grumpily and raked a thumb along the line of his freshly shaven jaw. "'Cause such tedious little insignificant happenings as his savin' a whole trainload of train passengers from being slaughtered by the Rio Hayes Gang or ending up at the bottom of Horse Thief Gorge don't seem worthy!"

He said that last loudly enough to catch Henry's attention. The young, dapper little gent's long fingers rose all at once from the keys, hovering over them, as the pale, bespectacled face lifted toward Longarm. Henry furled his slender, light brown brows over his pale blue eyes. "What's that, Marshal Long?"

Longarm smiled at having finally captured the seemingly always distracted little fellow's attention. "Did you hear about my most recent exploits?"

"Exploits?"

"Yeah, you know—about me takin' down the Arkansas River Gang. All by my damn lonesome. And then I noticed that train we was on was headed on the downhill side of Horse Thief Pass without brakes, and . . ."

He let his voice trail off. Henry stared up at him over the tops of his round spectacles, with the expression of a man who hadn't understood a word Longarm had said, as though the lawman had been speaking Sanskrit!

Longarm leaned forward, planting both hands on Henry's desk and lowering his voice for emphasis. "You just wait till you read my next report. Got Marcella over at the Black Cat scribblin' it all down for me even as I speak. When you read that, Mr. Henry, you're gonna be seein' old Custis Long in a little different ligh—"

The door flanking Henry's neat desk on the right opened suddenly, and Chief Marshal Billy Vail poked his round head out the door. It was ensconced in a roiling cloud of cigar smoke. "Get your ass in here, Longarm. You're late again, as usual!"

Billy pulled his head back inside his office and swung his door wide as he retreated to his desk. Longarm looked at the clock. The minute hand was now at a minute past the twelve.

"Goddamnit, Henry," he said, "now you went and made me late!"

As Longarm moved to the door, he heard the prissy secretary give a snort before the typing machine resumed its raucous clattering. Longarm stepped into Vail's office and closed the door behind him.

"I was just tellin' Henry about what a great job I did over the past few days. Wait till you see my report, Chief, you're gonna—"

"Yeah, well, Henry would appreciate it if you'd tell whatever doxie you have writing up your reports these days to go a little easier on the smelly water." Billy brushed a pudgy fist across his doughy nose. "Irritates the soft tissues in his nose."

Longarm scowled indignantly.

"Have a seat and see if you can shut your pie hole long enough to roll your eyeballs over this file," Billy Vail said as he sort of floated through the smoke cloud hovering over and around his giant desk, the surface of which Longarm doubted the chief marshal had seen since he'd first been promoted to his esteemed echelon of public service.

He plucked a manila file folder off one of the several stacks surrounding many small piles of papers hiding his blotter and slid it toward Longarm's side of his desk. "We'll be waitin' on your partner, due to arrive in ten minutes."

Longarm jerked the red Moroccan leather guest chair out of its corner near the door and angled it in front of his boss's desk. "Partner?"

"Detective from the Pinkerton agency."

"Ah, hell, Billy," Longarm said, sagging into the chair with a sour look. "You know I always work alone. And them Pinkertons are pains in the ass! They think they're real lawmen and all they do is get in the galldarned way!"

"Don't start pissin' in the Pinkerton well again, Custis. You know as well as I do that the James Gang would still be runnin' wild up and down the Midwest if it wasn't for Allan Pinkerton. It's an old and illustrious company."

"Maybe so, but their agents of late are either old men or snot-nosed shavers who haven't yet taken a piss standing up but think they know everything there is to know about bringin' owlhoots to bay. Uppity sons o' bitches. No, sir, Billy, you know I work best when I work alone."

"You're not workin' alone on this one. And that's an order. The Pinkertons think they have a stake in what happened to them lawmen down in Arizona, and they've sent an agent."

Billy leaned forward to read a name scribbled on a coffee-stained, ash-speckled notepad. "A . . . uh . . . Mr. Harvey Delacroix. That's with an 'o-i-x' at the end, and if I remember what little I ever knew about French, I believe it's pronounced 'oy.' "

The pudgy chief marshal, once a tough-nut lawbringer himself, sagged back in his chair and brushed cigar ashes from the bulbous paunch threatening to bust the buttons on the wash-worn white dress shirt he wore under a ratty brown wool vest. "As in 'Oy, oy, oy, Custis, you're gonna be part-nerin' up with this Pinkerton agent whether you like it or not!' "

Billy guffawed, delighted with himself. He stuck the stub of the fat stogie between his lips, blew more smoke into the already smoggy air over his desk, and laughed some more.

Longarm sighed in disgust. Sometimes, despite his knowing that Vail prized him above all the other deputies in his deputy U.S. marshal stable, he couldn't help thinking that Billy kept him around just to torture him. He certainly gave him the toughest assignments, and on this one the chief marshal was not only partnering him up with a wet-behind-the-ears Pinkerton agent who no doubt thought himself as skilled or better than Allan Pinkerton himself, but he was sending him to Arizona right smack-dab in the heat of summer.

And the summers in Arizona were second on the heat scale only to Hell itself.

"All right, enough of that," Billy said with a final snort, sitting up straighter in his chair and brushing his fist across his nose. "This is serious business. Five lawmen dead, fer chriss-fuckin'-sakes!"

"So I heard," Longarm said, glancing at the file he hadn't yet plucked off the chief marshal's desk. "Why don't you give me the lowdown on it, Billy. You know I don't read so well until after lunch. I'll peruse the whole thing on the train ride down to Las Cruces. Who was killed and where?"

"I didn't recognize the names of any of the dead," Billy said. "They're in the file. They were killed outside a little town along Defiance Wash. Town's called Holy Defiance on account of a stand the locals including a Catholic priest made several years ago against a bronco band of Coyotero

Apaches. Not much there now. Some old desert rat and his daughter. Anyway, the lawmen had banded together to go looking for a cache of gold that was stolen off a stagecoach three years ago but was never recovered.

"Everyone thought the gold was lost for good after a passel of border toughs robbed it and the toughs themselves were attacked by a small band of Apaches who'd jumped the reservation. Apparently, the bandits buried the loot when they'd forted themselves up in a nest of rocks in the Black Puma Mountains and then lit out under cover of darkness. They intended to return for it later, but they were all gunned down by a rival gang in Nogales a few weeks later.

"That there is all I know," Billy said. "There's a little more in the file there—names and dates and whatnot, the name of the ranch that the money's supposedly buried on. Some highfalutin rancher down there named Azrael, if I remember. Whip Azrael."

"How's this Pinkerton territory, Billy?"

"The Pinkertons had insured the gold shipment. It was headed for the bank in Tucson. Two Pinkerton guards were killed as well as two guards the bank especially hired—two fairly well-known gunmen at the time named Roy Dupree and 'Cougar' Charlie McCallum."

Billy puffed his cigar, staring pensively down at his desk. "Them two names I do remember, 'cause when I was ridin' for the Texas Rangers back in them days, them two were a couple of the most wanted curly wolves in all of Texas and half of Louisiana. Cold-blooded killers, both. Cougar Charlie cut down a good partner of mine back in Alpine, just north of the Chisos Mountains, after we'd run 'im down after a saloon robbery. Walked up to my partner, H. C. Boyle, in an alley and blew him in half with a double-barreled shotgun from point-blank range."

"Cougar Charlie and the other gunman . . . ?"

"Dupree."

"They're both dead?"

"Killed during the robbery."

Longarm was thinking over what he'd heard. In the meantime, he'd plucked a cheroot from his shirt pocket and bit the end off. Now he struck a match on the edge of Billy's desk, touched the flame to the stogie, and said between smoke puffs, "How did the Arizona Rangers and the two U.S. marshals get wind of all this and start thinkin' they had a handle on where the gold was buried?"

"I'm told that one of the rangers heard from a man named Three Wolves a few weeks ago. Three Wolves apparently had known a couple of the killers, including the leader of the gang that robbed the stage—Rafael Santana. Three Wolves and Santana played poker together one night in Nogales, the night before Santana and his bunch were killed.

"Three Wolves claimed that when Santana was about to lose his shirt to Three Wolves, Santana told him he knew where some gold was buried. When Three Wolves pressed the matter, Santana gave him some details about where exactly Santana's bunch had buried the gold. Three Wolves kept what Santana had told him under his hat, only half believing it was true, I reckon. But he never did go looking for the gold himself. Don't ask me why. Maybe you'll find out when you get down there.

"In the meantime, Three Wolves ran his own freighting service until about six weeks ago when he ran afoul of the rangers. Killed a man in a jealous rage, it seems. The rangers tracked him down and arrested him. Three Wolves exchanged the information about where the loot was buried for a promise of a possibly lighter sentence, and three rangers and two deputy marshals out of Prescott ended up deader'n last year's Christmas goose for their trouble."

Longarm scowled dubiously as he exhaled smoke through his nostrils. "Where's this Three Wolves feller now?"

Chief Marshal Vail nodded his approval at his prized deputy's instincts. Since Three Wolves apparently knew, or said he knew, where the loot had been buried, he might also know who killed the lawmen who'd ridden out to find it.

"He's being held at the Arizona Rangers post in Broken Jaw in the Arizona Territory, about fifty miles across the line from New Mexico. Holy Defiance is another fifty or so miles southwest of Broken Jaw, west of Tombstone and Bisbee."

"I'll stop in at Broken Jaw and have a little palaver with this gent before heading on down to Holy Defiance." Longarm rolled the cheroot around between his lips and bounced his fists off the arms of the red Moroccan leather chair. "When's my train leave, Billy? Don't reckon it's gonna get any cooler down Arizona way. Sooner I get this job started, the sooner it'll be over with."

Billy grinned devilishly. "You mean, when does your and your *partner's* train leave?" The chief marshal glanced at the banjo clock on the wall to his left. "In about one half hour."

"Ah, dangit, Billy."

Just then a knock sounded on the chief marshal's door.

"Must be him now," Billy said, raising his voice as he cast his gaze at the door. "Come in, Agent Delacroix!"

Longarm heard but did not see the door open behind him. He'd be looking at the Pinkerton agent's no doubt pimple-scarred face long enough on the journey down to Arizona.

He did, however, look at Billy and wrinkle his brows curiously when Billy's lower jaw dropped nearly down to his cluttered desk. Billy's eyes opened nearly as wide as his mouth, and a rosy flush colored his otherwise pasty cheeks.

"Uh . . ." Billy said around an apparent frog in his throat, rising slowly from his chair. "Uhm . . . Harvey . . . Dela . . . Delacroix?"

Longarm smelled a subtle, cherrylike fragrance at the same time he heard a raspy, vaguely female voice behind him say, "No, it's Haven. *Haven* Delacroix, Chief Marshal Vail. I've been sent here by the Pinkerton Agency, to join your deputy on the Arizona murder investigation. The one involving the stolen gold?"

Longarm jerked his head around. His heart turned a somersault in his chest.

The tall brunette whom Longarm had last seen lounging like a satisfied cat on her bed in the Grand Hotel in Leadville, naked as a jaybird, took two steps forward, extending her right hand toward Billy Vail. "I hope I'm not overly late. The stage from Leadville, where I was investigating a possible counterfeiting ring, got held up at a bridge failure around Conifer."

Billy shook the young woman's hand woodenly, staring at her as shiny-eyed as a love-struck schoolboy. Longarm stood slowly, feeling a grin like that of the cat that ate the canary flashing in his eyes and quirking his mouth corners.

"How do you do, Miss Delacroix?" Longarm said, taking his cigar in his left hand and extending the right one to the girl. "I'm just pleased as punch to make your acquaintance."

She turned to him. Her eyes widened in mute horror. She gave a silent gasp. As she stared up at him, likely trying to convince herself that her imagination was playing a nasty trick on her, her exquisite face turned as frosty white as new-fallen snow on Christmas morning.

Longarm tensed himself to catch her if she fell, because Miss Haven Delacroix looked like she was about to drop dead right there at his feet in Billy Vail's office.

Chapter 8

"Yes, sir . . . er, I mean, ma'am," Longarm said, chuckling. "I thought for sure you was about to drop dead right there in Bily Vail's office."

"Shut up, you clod."

She glowered at him from the seat facing him in the coach car of the Atchison, Topeka and Santa Fe flyer heading through the rolling buttes south of Denver, climbing slowly toward Monarch Pass.

"God, I've never been so humiliated in all my life," she said, hardening her delicate lower jaw and turning to stare out the window at the as-yet snow-tipped Front Range looming in the west. "What a sour bucketful of luck, that was." She turned to him again, smoke fairly curling from the corners of those beautiful, crystal-clear hazel eyes. "Finding you in Chief Marshal Vail's office, waiting for *me*! To travel to Arizona with *you*. My *partner*!"

She ground her jaws and groaned, turning her sharp gaze to the mountains once more.

"Well, hey," Longarm said, thoroughly enjoying himself, "at least we broke the ice back in Leadville." He chuckled.

She wasn't listening. Turning to him, the nubs of her

tapering cheeks flushed with horror, she said, "Do you think he knew? Do you think Chief Marshal Vail sensed that we'd met before?"

"You mean do I think he sensed that we rutted like a couple of horny old dogs two nights before our meeting in his office—two *professionals* about to be *partnered up* together on an *official assignment*?" He knew it was not to his credit that he so enjoyed how horrified she was having her nasty secrets known to those who knew her not only by name but were about to work with her. "Nah, I don't think so. He was too busy starin' at your tits. Besides, we weren't there long. Shit, we got out of the Federal Building just in time to meet the train."

"Please don't talk like that. You're a professional, for goodness sakes."

Longarm stared at her. Would he ever cease to be surprised by this girl?

Scowling his amazement, he said, "Just the other night you were callin' me . . ."

She silenced him with a cold, admonishing stare. Looking around to make sure none of the other passengers was listening, she leaned forward to say just loudly enough for him to hear above the low roar of the coach car, its iron wheels clacking over the rail seams, "Would you please stop bringing that up? How was I supposed to know you and I would be working together? Imagine my horror!"

"Ah, come on," Longarm said, digging a small, flat traveling flask from his coat pocket. "It ain't all that bad. You're obviously a hardworking agent. If you weren't, there ain't no way ole Allan would have you on his role."

"God, do you have to speak in that fashion?"

"Like what? Hell, I didn't even curse that time."

"In that lowly, country manner, is what I meant. You are a deputy United States marshal, Marshal Long. A professional lawman. You should speak like a man worthy of his station."

Longarm studied her, trying not to take offense. He knew
few other men who didn't speak like he did. Those who
didn't were overeducated twerps or bankers. One and the
same. You could throw attorneys on the same pile. She must
have been spawned by one of those, so he'd have to give her
a little leeway. Besides, it was hard to take umbrage with
one so sexy and downright, soul-searingly beautiful, even
if she was fully aware of her assets.

"As I was sayin'," Longarm said, trying to keep his impatience out of his voice, "you're obviously a hardworking
agent. Just like hardworking men, includin' myself, you like
to let your hair down once in a while. Nothin' wrong with it."

She drew a frustrated breath and returned her gaze to the
soot-stained window.

Longarm flicked the top off the travel flask and held it
out to her. "Here, have a snort o' rye. Take the knot out of
your panties."

She scowled at him. "I don't drink when I'm on the job."

"You ain't on the job. You're on a train. Have a sip. Take
the edge off."

"No, thank you. Don't you think we should perhaps discuss the case we're on?"

Longarm took two swallows from the travel flask,
exhaled a long, satisfied breath, shoved the cork back in the
flask's mouth, and returned it to his coat pocket. "Let's do
that, though we have a ways to go before we roll into New
Mexico. We could see if this combination's pullin' a saloon
car, have us a couple of snorts back there and play a round
of Red Dog."

"I neither drink nor gamble when I'm on the job."

"Which reminds me—why'd they send you out on this
one?" Longarm leaned back in his seat and hiked a boot on
his knee. "I assume the Pinkerton ladies mostly work undercover, don't they? I don't see much need for 'assuming a
role' here, as Pinkerton calls it."

"True, that's why Mr. Pinkerton originally began hiring

female agents, but I do much more than assume roles, Marshal Long. I'm a detective, and I'm very good at it. As good as any of the men I know *inside* or *outside* of the service. Besides, I just happened to be the most indisposed agent closest to Denver at the time of the killings. That's probably why they gave me the assignment."

"I see no reason why you shouldn't go ahead and call me Longarm, since we know each other better than most folks ever get around to." He grinned.

She drew a deep breath and blinked her eyes, coolly tolerant. "Look, you mastodon. You must forget what happened back in Leadville. It certain will not be repeated. Not in the near future, not ever. We are two professionals working together, and that is all we are. So I will appreciate it if you'd respect me for the professional that I am and treat me accordingly. In exchange, I will do the same for you."

Longarm plucked the flask out of his coat pocket again, giving a weary sigh. "Oh, all right. I reckon I'll try to see it your way. There are five lawmen dead, after all." As he popped the cork on the flask, he glanced at the well-filled corset of her traveling dress made of some shiny, spruce-green material. "But you'll forgive me if it takes a while for me to forget two nights ago. That there was a tussle and a half!"

He tipped his head back, let the soothing rye wash down his throat, into his belly and deeper, into the regions where he'd been fighting a hard-on ever since he'd seen her again in Billy Vail's office, of all places.

Haven's cheeks reddened. She fought off the flush, however, and entwined her hands in her lap, beside the feathered green picture hat resting beside her supple left thigh. The manila folder containing the report rested against her opposite leg.

"Now, then, since our relationship has been clarified, let's get down to brass tacks, shall we? I read a copy of the ranger's report on my journey from Leadville, but it's pretty thin, not to mention nearly illiterate. In your meeting with Marshal Vail, did he mention anything about the rangers having any suspicions as to who might have shot their men and the deputy marshals?"

"Billy didn't say. But if it's not in the report there, I reckon it's a subject we'll have to cover when we get to the ranger post in Broken Jaw. I know a few of the boys down there. They're likely hell-bent on finding the men who shot their pards, and they'll most likely want to be the ones who serve up the gun justice good and hot, but they'll be as helpful as they can be."

"If they had been able to serve up this gun justice, as you call it, they probably would have by now. Which means they must be pretty much in the dark about who killed those men."

"Most likely." Longarm sat back in his seat, tipped his hat brim down over his eyes. The rye had worked its magic on him. "Well, if you'll forgive me, I reckon it's time for a nap. We got a long pull ahead. Figured we'd ride horses from Belen. The train south of there is notoriously slow and the Southern Pacific west through Broken Jaw ain't quite finished yet."

He squinted one eye at her beneath his hat. "You can ride a horse, can't you?"

"Of course I can ride. Just as well as you, Marshal Long."

"Well, proof of that will be in the puddin'," he said, chuckling ironically. "But I do apologize. This is the first time I've been paired up with a woman. I mean, *professionally*, of course."

"Of course." Haven rolled her eyes in disgust.

"Since I have my hoof in my mouth, anyway, I might as well go ahead and ask you if you have proper riding attire. That dress . . . while it does fit you dang nice . . . would be a little uncomfortable—"

"You worry about your own proper attire, Deputy," she said crisply, "and I'll worry about mine."

"All right, all right." Longarm pulled his hat down lower

on his forehead. The improbability of their situation continued to amaze him, and he realized he was grinning again
when he heard her say, "I realize this is all very amusing to
you, Deputy Long, but I really must insist that you put the
other night behind you. I know I have."

He opened his left eye and was about to respond that he
was dearly trying to do just that but held his tongue when
he saw a group of men in dusty leather trail gear studying
him and Agent Delacroix from their seats a few rows up
from Longarm and on the left side of the aisle. Most of their
attention was on the girl, of course, and they weren't so
much studying Haven as ogling her.

Speaking just loudly enough to be heard above the train's
irregular roar, he said, "Watch yourself."

She'd immersed herself in the file but looked up at him
curiously. He lifted his chin to indicate her admirers. She
turned her head to follow his gaze, then turned back to him
and gazed down once more at the open folder in her lap.

"Don't worry, I'm capable of taking care of myself."

"Yeah, I seen that little popper you had in Leadville."

"That 'little popper,' as you call it, is quite the efficient
weapon. I've turned many an hombre toe-down with it."

Longarm arched a surprised brow at the girl. " 'Many an
hombre toe-down'?" He snorted a laugh and closed his eyes,
knowing that if any of the girl's oglers approached he'd
likely smell him before he heard him.

"What's so funny about *that*, pray tell?"

"I do believe you've read too many yarns by Deadeye
Dick, Miss Delacroix."

"I thought you were going to take a nap, Marshal Long,"
she said in a strained, admonishing tone, suggesting that
she'd long come to the end of her leash regarding one Custis
P. Long.

Longarm opened his right eye halfway, looked at the
girl's admirers once more through sun-bleached lashes.
They occupied two seats, beneath a billowing cloud of

cigarette and cigar smoke. There were five of them, and from what Longarm could see of them, they appeared well armed with both long guns, short guns, and knives.

A Mexican with a sweeping mustache grinned at the girl with his sombrero tipped back of his broad, sun-blistered forehead. Catching Longarm's scrutinizing eyes on him, he blinked his own eye mockingly at the lawman and then spread his lips with a lascivious grin.

Longarm shook his head. He knew there'd be trouble. You couldn't go anywhere in the West with a beautiful young woman, especially one as beautiful as Agent Delacroix, without there being trouble. He was surprised old Pinkerton allowed her to travel alone, doubly surprised that she'd been traveling alone and was still alive, not having been raped and shot and thrown in a deep ravine.

She may have been damn beautiful, but he'd had his fun with her in Leadville. And the novelty of the situation had worn itself out.

When it was all said and done, he worked better alone. Hell, he'd have preferred a male partner to one he was going to have to play bodyguard and nursemaid to . . .

He gave a fateful sigh and closed his right eye, allowing himself to tumble slowly into a light doze, one in which he could hear all the sounds around him but one that still offered a modicum of refreshment.

He had no idea how long he'd catnapped before the train shuddered suddenly, and the girl screamed shrilly.

Chapter 9

Longarm wasn't fully awake before he realized his revolver was in his hand and he was sitting straight up, extending the gun out in front of him, swinging it from left to right, looking for a target. His heart was not hammering but warning bells were tolling in his head.

The girl sat straight across from him, a horrified look on her face. Only, the look of horror, he quickly realized, was because he was aiming his cocked Colt in her general direction.

Not because she was being accosted by the five brigands, because the five brigands were still seated where they'd been seated before. Three of the five, in fact, appeared to be sleeping while the other two were leaning forward, probably playing cards on their knees though Longarm couldn't see below their seat backs.

The train continued shuddering, rocking Longarm back in his seat, nudging the girl slightly forward in hers. Longarm looked outside past the tattered clouds of coal smoke sweeping past the windows. They were on a brown, sage-stippled plain, and they were slowing—likely for the little settlement of the appropriately named Jerkwater. Longarm had traveled this way more times than he could count, and they'd always stopped in Jerkwater to take on water after climbing and descending Monarch Pass.

Longarm depressed the Colt's hammer, raised the barrel, instantly feeling the heat of chagrin rise in his cheeks. Then he heard what he must have heard in his sleep—the train whistle announcing their arrival in Jerkwater.

The girl continued to stare at him, maybe wondering what grade of crazy man she'd found herself being accompanied to Arizona with, but she didn't say anything. Longarm returned his pistol to its holster and snapped the keeper thong home across the hammer.

When the train had come to a final, shuddering stop, all the passengers, of which there were only around a dozen, detrained to take advantage of Jerkwater's amenities. There was only a small café run by a gnarled Mexican lady, a saloon run by a fat Swede, and a feed store that doubled as a dry goods and post office, last time Longarm was through here. The buildings were all lined up along the tracks, their primary function to patronize the trains and the few area ranchers.

Since the five men who'd been appraising Haven's wares had also gotten off, and Longarm could see them now stretching and sauntering over in the direction of the saloon, he decided to get up and see what the Swede was serving for sandwiches. And a beer on a hot, dusty dry day of travel might be a welcome bit of nourishment, as well . . .

He told Haven his intentions.

"I'll stay here," she said. "I can't sleep while the train is moving, so maybe I'll indulge in a doze while it's stopped."

"Sandwich?" he offered. "A beer? The Swede don't keep it cold, but he makes a right malty ale."

"No, thank you," she said with her customary, strained tolerance as she sat back in her seat and crossed her long, fine legs under her dress.

Longarm indulged in a quick look, for it was hard not to look and keep on looking at a beauty as radiant as she, despite how much trouble she'd likely turn out to be. He pinched his hat brim to her, turned into the aisle, and left the coach car via its rear vestibule.

He stopped to stretch on the halved-log platform.

To his left, the engineers were maneuvering the wood-and-canvas spout into place, swinging it over the locomotive from the water tank that stood on stilts near a scraggly cottonwood that was currently being thrashed by a mean wind. The four crude board buildings that comprised Jerkwater lay straight out from the train, across a wide freight road. The wind was blowing dirt and sand and tumbleweeds every which way, and it was causing shingle chains to dance and squawk beneath porch awnings.

As Longarm headed on past the little, privy-sized shack that served as a depot here in Jerkwater toward the saloon, Longarm saw that most of the passengers appeared to be heading into the Mexican lady's café sitting just left of the Swede's saloon. She was deservedly reputed for her burritos, but she didn't serve beer or allow it on her premises, so Longarm continued on up the saloon's porch steps and through the batwings that the wind was flapping raucously.

"Swede, does the wind ever not blow here?" Longarm asked the big, blond-haired, blond-mustached gent slicing what appeared a deer or possibly an antelope quarter on the cottonwood planks that served as his bar. The lawman batted his hat against his whipcord trousers, causing dust to billow.

"Every night around midnight it settles down for about five minutes." The Swede grinned his rosy-cheeked grin as he regarded the big lawman, who always asked the same question as he walked through the Swede's doors, to the Swede's customary reply. "You on the hunt for curly wolves again, Custis?"

"What the hell else would I be doing out here on this blister on the devil's ass?" Longarm grinned. He always said that, too. The Swede didn't take offense; he was only here because his wife's father willed him the store and he'd had his fill of the big city Denver had become since the War Between the States.

It might be windy and ugly out here, but he was making a living, by God, and it was better than the stench and crowds farther north.

"Thought maybe you rode out here for my beer, got tired of that swill they serve up on Larimer Street."

"Serve it up, Swede." Longarm gazed at the meat the man had been slicing onto a big tin plate. "Any of that for sandwiches?"

"You betcha," the Swede said. "Shot that antelope buck last night just before dark. Good dark meat—dark as a Norwegian's soul!"

The Swede guffawed.

Longarm looked around. There were only two men in the place. He thought he recognized the two—a half-breed and an Anglo—from the group that had been paying such tribute to Agent Delacroix earlier. Vaguely, he supposed the others had gone over to the Mexican lady's café.

The Swede drew him a beer, scraped off the cream foam with a flat stick, and set the frothy schooner on the cottonwood planks before going to work on Longarm's sandwich. The lawman leaned against the planks and sipped the beer slowly. It was room temperature, but the Swede had a special way of making it—thick and malty, with just enough of an alcohol kick—to make it a welcome treat that tempered the tedium of the long, slow ride into New Mexico south of the formidable Raton Pass.

"Damn, that's good," he said. "You know, Swede, you should bottle that and . . ." He let his voice trail off and turned to gaze through the window left of the fluttering batwings.

He could see the train stretched out along the far side of the freight road, veiled by windblown grit and the occasional tumbling tumbleweed. He thought he'd heard something beneath the squawking of the shingle chains. The wind peeled a shake from the little depot building's roof and whipped it southward.

Deciding he'd only been hearing the wind, Longarm turned back to his beer. A half-formed thought pricked the short hairs beneath his shirt collar, and he turned to the two men from the train. They sat near the batwings, playing cards, but they were grinning at each other from beneath their hat brims.

The Anglo gave Longarm a furtive glance before dropping his eyes to his cards and whistling with feigned casualness. Longarm's pulse quickened. He turned full around to the two cardplayers.

"Where's your friends?" he asked.

"Huh?" replied the half-breed. He looked more Indian than white though he was dressed in a long, tan duster, black Stetson, and black batwing chaps. "What friends, brother?"

"Don't 'brother' me," Longarm muttered as he pushed away from the bar and started for the doors.

He was six feet from the batwings when the Anglo bounded up from his chair facing the table and the wall, wheeled, and threw himself violently into Longarm, slamming the lawman against the saloon's south wall. Longarm managed to stay on his feet and get turned to face his attacker, but then the short, solidly built gent punched him twice in the face.

Fortunately, Longarm had a big, thick face that was accustomed to such abuse. It took a lot of it to affect him overmuch.

He shook off the blow and then head-butted the stocky Anglo, who sagged back on his heels, dazed, before Longarm grabbed him by the collar of his denim jacket and hammered him twice against the wall, hard. The reverberating blows caused dust to sift from between the wall's whipsawed pine planks.

The stocky gent groaned and dropped straight down the

wall to his knees before leaning forward against the wall as though in prayer.

Longarm turned toward the room in time to see the flash of the wan sunlight off steel. He jerked his head to the right, and the big bowie knife that the half-breed had thrown embedded itself in the wall behind Longarm with a dull thud. The half-breed stood crouched about six feet from Longarm, in front of the jostling batwings, his boots spread in the fighter's stance.

He had another big knife in his right hand, and he flipped it dexterously between his thumb and index finger.

The savagely upturned tip glinted in the sunlight.

"We just give them a few minutes in the train—okay, brother?" the half-breed said, his malicious grin revealing chipped, yellow teeth between weathered pink lips. "Just a few minutes with your girl. Then it's my turn." He grabbed his crotch with his free hand. "Don't worry, I'll leave some for you, but you might have to sew her back together before you can fuck her again!"

The half-breed laughed, squinting his large, evil black eyes.

He flipped his bowie knife in the air, tauntingly, and just as he caught its handle, there was an enormous cracking boom that sounded like a barrel of dynamite exploding inside a one-hole privy. Longarm was staring at the half-breed's menacing face one second. The next half-second there was nothing but the man's shoulders and the ragged hole where his hat had been, the head itself with its remaining evil leer and long, black hair flying out over the batwings in a hail of buckshot.

The man's black hat left the head to tumble against the batwings and fall to the floor.

The man's headless body staggered bizarrely back against a chair, his hand still wielding the knife until both his arms fell and the headless corpse dropped back against the chair, knocking the chair to one side and then falling to the floor and rolling up beneath the table.

Longarm looked to his right. The big Swede grinned down the double-barreled shotgun he still held to his shoulder, aiming over the top of the bar. Slowly, he lowered the smoking weapon.

"There ya go, Custis. Compliments of the house. He was a good bit Norwegian. I'll bet you anything!"

"Thanks, Swede."

Longarm gave the headless corpse a dubious glance where it lay quivering beneath the table and then, as he ran through the batwings, he looked at the half-breed's head lying out in the street in front of the porch, at the end of a long blood trail.

The half-breed still had the same leer on his face as in the seconds before he'd lost his cap. Longarm leaped the grisly object that looked like a coffee can that had been used too long for target practice, and broke into a sprint toward the train, angling toward the coach car in which he'd left the girl.

A scream sounded beneath the wind's keening.

Longarm stopped suddenly about twenty feet in front of the train, left of the little wind-battered depot building.

A man flew out the rear door of the coach car. The round-faced Mexican with the drooping mustache bounced off the front of the next car back and then tumbled down the vestibule steps to the rail bed. He lay groaning and writhing and clutching both hands to his bloody crotch from which a knife handle protruded.

There was a loud boom, almost as loud as the thunder of the Swede's barn blaster.

Another scream.

A clattering rose inside the coach car, and then another man—this one the Anglo with the squash-yellow hair—flew out the coach's rear door backward and slammed against

the front of the next car back. He hit the car so hard that
Longarm heard the car's door crack in its frame, its window
glass breaking.

The man with the squash-yellow hair bounced off the
door, dropped to the vestibule, and tumbled down the steps
to pile up beside his amigo still writhing on the ground
beside the rail bed. Longarm looked again at the knife protruding from the Mexican's bloody crotch.

Slow footsteps sounded in the coach car. Haven Delacroix stepped through the door and onto the blood-splattered
vestibule. As she turned toward the dead or dying men lying
beside the rail bed, she held two smoking revolvers in her
hands, down low by her comely legs clad in the silvery-green
traveling frock.

The pistols were LeMats—five-shot revolvers with a
stubby, dark-mawed shotgun barrel situated beneath the
main .45-caliber one. Both guns were silver-chased and fancily scrolled. Longarm could see the pearl grips showing
between the girl's fingers wrapped tightly around the
handles.

Agent Delacroix stood staring down at the dead or dying,
her dark brown hair blowing around her lovely head in the
wind. Her lips were pressed tight together, her eyes narrowed in disgust.

"Teach you to trifle with defenseless women," she said
in a cold, hard, razor-edged voice.

She dropped the LeMats into soft, leather holsters belted
to her slender waist and which she must have donned after
Longarm had left the day coach, because she hadn't been
wearing the guns before. She must have anticipated a move
by the cutthroats.

She tugged her shirtwaist down and looked at Longarm.
"I could go for that sandwich now. Fetch it for me, will you,
Deputy Long? This wind wreaks havoc on a girl's hair."

She turned back through the coach car's open door.

Longarm stood staring, dumbfounded, at the space she'd

vacated. Footsteps rose behind him, and he turned woodenly to see the stage passengers approaching from the direction of the Mexican lady's café, both men and women holding their hats on their heads and looking wary.

The spindly, gray-haired depot agent stood staring hang-jawed through the open door of his little shack. The two engineers and the fireman were walking slowly, cautiously toward Longarm from the direction of the engine, staring down at the dead man and the slow-dying Mexican rolling from side to side and clutching at the knife in his crotch.

He was sobbing now and begging for mercy as he died.

Longarm looked up at the coach car again, his rugged face creased with amazement. He scratched the back of his head. "Well, I'll be damned."

Chapter 10

The dead man wore only a ratty Stetson with a braided rawhide band and a bullet hole in its crown.

He was about halfway from being dead to being a skeleton. Bits of sun-cured skin clung to the pale bones where the birds hadn't yet finished pecking it away. Long, thin, grizzled strands of hair dangled from the cadaver's eyeless skull to its spindly shoulders.

Where the man's clothes had gone was anyone's guess. Longarm was sure he hadn't died up there on the boulder towering beside the narrow, jagged entrance to a canyon deep in an unnamed jog of rocky bluffs and sloping mesas, somewhere north of Broken Jaw in the northeast Arizona Territory. The dead man had been placed atop the rock as though he'd climbed up there to look out across the sloping desert hills to the south and gone to sleep and expired.

"What on earth?" Haven said, sitting a rented steeldust gelding to Longarm's right. "Someone's idea of a joke, isn't it?"

"Sort of a joke," Longarm said. "Mostly, a warnin' to posses, lawmen, anyone with their hats set on scoutin' that chasm." His own mount was a strawberry roan with a cream-speckled hindquarters that he'd rented in Belen, New

Mexico, when he and Haven had ended their train journey. The sure-footed mount cropped gama grass growing up around the rocks strewn out in front of the canyon mouth.

"Outlaw hideout?"

"Most likely. One of their amigos likely took a bullet some months back, and they decided to put his carcass to good use. An old tradition in these parts."

Longarm glanced once more at the grisly totem. He reined his horse away from the canyon and touched heels to its flanks. "Well, we got other matters to tend to, but I'll keep that old boy in mind. His friends might prove to have some federal paper on their heads. Every other rascal in these parts does."

"How many times you been through here, Marshal?"

She put her horse up beside him, her steeldust keeping pace with his roan. In Belen, she'd exchanged her fancily stitched traveling dress for more practical trail gear, and while the men's shirt, slacks, and suspenders worn beneath a long, tan duster and the light brown Stetson made her resemble a typical thirty-a-month-and-found cowpuncher from a distance, from close up she was as beautiful as ever. Maybe prettier, even more alluring, for the form-fitting albeit rough riding gear revealed more of the swells and curves than the dress had.

Her full breasts, which Longarm couldn't help remember fondling, rolling the nipples between his thumbs and index fingers, pushed out from behind her striped shirt, straining the buttons, jiggling enticingly as she rode.

"Too many times to count, I reckon."

"I haven't traveled this far south." She was looking around, taking in the high-desert landscape with a fascination that made her otherwise cool eyes glow. "Most of my work has been done in cities."

"What kind of work has that been, Miss Delacroix?" Longarm still had trouble addressing the girl so formally. He couldn't remember ever having tumbled with a woman, especially with such abandon, and her still not letting him call her by her first name. That was a first, but then, Agent Delacroix was many firsts for Longarm.

Including the first woman he'd ever seen so expertly dispatch three would-be rapists like those she had dispatched back in Jerkwater.

She swung her head toward him, her hair flying about her shoulders. "You mean, where did I learn how to shoot so well—isn't that what you meant, Marshal Long?"

After the bodies were hauled off and the train had resumed its journey southward, they hadn't discussed the killings in Jerkwater. Longarm had thought it her place to broach the subject. Obviously, Miss Haven Delacroix was a girl of many mysteries, and he doubted she'd tell him a damn thing about anything until she was good and ready, and she may or might not be ever be ready.

"Well, now that you mention it . . ."

"My father was a rich man from back East. He owned a lot of weapons. He had no sons to teach how to use them, so he taught me. We hunted in the Allegheny Mountains and throughout Appalachia. Deer, bear, turkeys, ducks, geese . . ."

"Killin' men's a special kind of shootin', Miss Delacroix."

"Is it, Marshal Long?" Haven looked at him askance. "Oh, but when we're talking about men, we're not including those three back in Jerkwater, are we?"

Longarm looked back at her, finding himself growing more and more curious about her. What he saw in her hazel eyes now was a peculiar, unsettling edge. He'd seen it before, when they were fucking like dogs back in her hotel room in Leadville. He'd chalked that up to raw desire. But here it was again after she'd killed three men, having stabbed a stiletto into the balls of one.

Men who'd had it coming in spades, certainly. But she'd killed them just the same. And she was cooler about it than most men would have been.

Yes, there was much that was mysterious about Miss Haven Delacroix. And while she'd proven that she could defend herself against three half-drunk cowhands, she was just too forthright and too damn pretty to be partnered up with on a murder investigation on the mostly untamed frontier, where a good many men would as soon shoot a man, especially a *lawman*, as let him pass in the street.

The same held true for Pinkerton detectives.

A pretty girl was a lightning rod for trouble, and Miss Delacroix's being a Pinkerton made her stand all the taller against a stormy sky. Likely sooner rather than later, she was going to get herself and probably Longarm, too, in more trouble than either of them knew what to do with.

They rode throughout the afternoon, stopping now and then to rest their horses and drink from springs or muddy streams coursing down from the White Mountains in the northwest. Longarm followed an old wild-horse trail he'd taken through the area before, knowing it was the shortest route between Belen and Broken Jaw though the traveling was often rough. Wild horses knew the best routes between springs, however, so while they had to travel up and around some stony bluffs and steep mesas, water holes were relatively plentiful though a couple were already dry this late in the southwestern summer.

Late in the afternoon, they rode down a crease between slanting mesa walls. The trough was shaded by the west-angling sun, the hot air tanged with cedar. When Longarm rode around a thumb of rock jutting out from the mesa wall on his right, he reined up quickly, reaching a hand across his belly toward the Colt .44-40 holstered on his left hip.

Three men were at the springs he'd been heading for. Two were mounted. One holding a canteen, with a second flask draped over his shoulder, was kneeling near a small trough down which the water trickled as it issued from a crack in the rocks. They'd all heard the clomping of Longarm's and the girl's horses, and they all had their hands on

the butts of their own pistols and were gazing cautiously
toward the newcomers.

Agent Delacroix rode up beside Longarm and, seeing the
men by the spring, jerked back sharply on her own horse's
reins. She looked from Longarm to the strangers and back
again. Longarm said nothing but kept his expression mild.

The two mounted men by the spring eyed the lawman
and the girl suspiciously. The one with the canteens rose
slowly, shoving a cork into the lip of the canteen he held in
his left hand, smiling and nodding. "Afternoon."

"Afternoon," Longarm said.

"We was just ridin' on," said the man with the canteens,
flicking his dung-brown eyes from Longarm to the girl and
keeping them on Haven for about two beats too long.

"Good water." He held up the canteen he'd just corked.
"Help yourselves, friends."

He pinched his hat brim to the girl and then turned and
mounted a dun while the other two regarded Longarm and
Agent Delacroix with cold, calculating expressions. All
three were sun-browned and bearded Anglos in long, filthy
dusters. They had the wild-eyed look of desperadoes, and
the number of weapons they wore did nothing to temper the
impression.

When they rode off, Longarm removed his hand from
the walnut grips of his Colt. He watched the three ride on
down the cactus-bristling hills to the south and into a shaded
draw. They grew small beneath the vaulting, slightly darkening sky in which not a single cloud floated.

When they'd disappeared from view, Longarm swung
down from the roan's back. "We'll fill with water here, ride
on a few more miles, and camp."

Feeling owly, he slipped the roan's bit from its mouth so
it could drink freely, and then unbuckled the saddle cinch
so it could move around and get some air. He removed his
two canteens from his saddle horn. He could feel the girl
watching him pensively as he walked over to the spring.

"What's eating you?" she said.

"Nothin'." He didn't want to talk about it. She was here now, and he had to shoot with the loads he'd been given.

Kneeling beside the spring and plucking the cork from one of the canteens, he lowered the flask to the pencil-thin stream trickling out of the rocks.

"You think I'm trouble," she said.

Longarm gave a caustic snort.

"Well, I'm here now, and you're just going to have to get used to it. Mr. Pinkerton has assigned me to represent the interests of Wells Fargo in this matter, and that's exactly what I intend to do. If at all possible, I intend to see that the stolen gold is returned to its rightful owners."

Longarm said nothing. There was no point arguing with the girl. Arguing with females of any stripe only got a man a headache. A bad one.

Standing over him, looking down at him with her fists on her hips, a canteen hanging from each shoulder, she tapped her right boot impatiently. "Oh, I see."

Longarm glanced up at her. "See what?"

"I was just fine to have around as long as I could amuse you with my embarrassment. I was even finer to have around the other night in Leadville, wasn't I?"

Longarm corked his filled canteen. "I'll say you were!"

"But out here where I have a serious job to do, I'm trouble. Is that it?"

Despite knowing he was wasting his breath, Longarm glared up at her through one narrowed eye. "Yeah, that is it, Agent Delacroix. Women don't belong out here. Especially ones as pretty as you. A lawman has enough trouble out here with the additional trouble of a pretty girl!"

"Is that really what has your longhandles in a bunch?" she asked.

Longarm didn't say anything as he finished filling his second canteen.

"Or maybe it's because you're having such a hard time

keeping your eyes off of my shirt?" Her smile had as little
humor as an icicle hanging from a Dakota porch roof in
February. "Maybe you're not so afraid of the trouble I might
attract from other men, but of the distraction I am to *you*.
That's why you suddenly think I shouldn't be here, isn't it?
Because you can't keep your eyes off of me, or stop thinking about the other night!"

Longarm felt his face heating up. His hands shook as he
corked the second canteen and rose, trying hard to keep
both his chagrin and his anger on a short leash. "Yeah," he
said, honestly, "maybe that is it!"

He stared down at her. She had him so damn worked up
that he was having trouble finding the right words with
which to defend himself.

Hell, truth be told, now that she'd laid out her view of it,
he was having trouble understanding what it was he himself
thought about the whole matter. His own embarrassment
over her having read him so clearly, however, made him
even angrier than her presence did.

She gave him a mock smoky look, half smiling as she
turned her head to one side, drew her shoulders back, pushing her breasts out, and dropped her eyes to the buckle on
his cartridge belt. Her gaze was brashly jeering. "Would you
feel differently if I promised to sleep with you tonight?" Her
lips broadened her smile, and she shook her head slowly.
"And I don't mean *sleep*."

Longarm felt an instant, involuntary pull in his crotch.
It was followed by a sharp burn of anger. At what, he wasn't
sure. He only knew that his knees felt far weaker than they'd
ever felt when he was facing a whole passel of long-coulee
riders, and his ears were fairly scalding the sides of his head.
He wheeled and stomped over to his horse, hanging the
canteen lanyards over his saddle horn.

"Fill your goddamn canteens," he said through gritted
teeth. "Then we'll water the horses and hightail it before

those three come back to get what they were thinking about getting when they saw you ride out from behind that rock."

Digging a cheroot out of his shirt pocket with an angry-shaky hand, he added, "I don't think they were just thinkin' about *sleepin'* with you, either, Agent Delacroix. They're no doubt swinging back around us right now, chucklin' about how they're gonna skin them nice tight denims down your purty legs and hoist your knees up around your ears!"

That didn't seem to faze her a bit. She uncorked her canteen. "I can take care of myself very well, Marshal Long. You saw how well back in Jerkwater."

"You got damn lucky back in Jerkwater, lady. If I hadn't been there, all *five* of 'em would have been on you, and I doubt even Annie Oakley could have kept her legs together against those odds."

Hazel eyes fired javelins of hatred at him. "If you think I need your protection, Marshal Long, you're badly mistaken."

"Hah!"

Agent Delacroix's pretty face turned as red as a rose. "Next time, you just sit still and leave it all up to me. Hell, you might even learn something about how to handle yourself out here!"

She wheeled from him angrily, adjusting the Lemats holstered on her hips, and dropped to one knee beside the spring to fill her canteens. As she filled the first one, she narrowed her eyes over her shoulder at him. "You know what I think has you madder than an old wet hen, Marshal?"

Longarm fired a lucifer to life on his cartridge belt. "I know you're gonna tell me."

"You feel challenged after having witnessed how capable I am. A strong woman out here in this *man's land* threatens you."

Longarm removed his cheroot from his mouth and

pointed at the girl, dipping his chin and narrowing his eyes once more. "I ain't threatened by no woman, Agent Delacroix. Never have been, never will be."

"Oh, you're threatened, all right," she said, her self-assured smile vexing him further. "I threaten your manhood because I can take care of myself and because the only thing you know to do with a woman like me is to fuck me. But you'll never, ever do that again as long as I live!"

Longarm ground his molars as he glared at her from beneath his down-canted hat brim and blew smoke out his nostrils. Now, she genuinely had his goat, and they both knew it, and the only words he could find with which to respond were: "Wouldn't want to!"

He wheeled and stomped off into the brush. Seething and chewing his cigar, he took a piss. She had some goddamn nerve, telling him that *he* was threatened by *her* when they both knew it was the other way around.

Didn't they?

Angry and confused, he pissed in a complete circle around a square rock and then stomped back over to the springs. Both horses had wandered over to the water and were drinking while she stood beside the steeldust, adjusting a stirrup on the other side of the mount from Longarm. He sat on a rock in the relative shade of a large boulder and energetically smoked his cigar.

He didn't look at the woman.

Anger burned in him.

He wished like hell he'd never met her even the first time in Leadville. Never met her at all. What particularly burned him, he realized as he smoked, was that he couldn't keep those devilish little images from their night together in the Grand Hotel from creeping into his brain and causing his balbriggans to pinch.

Had she been right? Was his real problem with her the fact that he couldn't get the sexy memories out of his craw? That he wanted—*needed*—her again?

Well, if it *was* true, and he had to admit that that might be a *small* part of it, she sure as hell wasn't going to find out about it. From now on, he wasn't going to see her nor treat her any differently than he would a man trailing along with him. If she got herself in trouble for wagging those pretty tits in men's faces, she could get herself out of it.

He took the last puff from his cigar, toed the butt out in the dirt, and stomped over to his horse.

"All right, goddamnit," he said through a growl, pulling the mount's head up from a patch of grass growing along the spring. "Time to get a move on."

"That's just fine with me," said Agent Delacroix, slipping the steeldust's bit through its teeth. She flashed her wrathful eyes at him. "The sooner we get this assignment over, the better."

"Ain't that a coincidence," he said, chuckling as he swung up into the leather. "That's just how *I* feel about it!"

"Oh, and another thing."

Longarm looked at her.

"I didn't have half as much fun the other night as I was letting on."

Longarm laughed. "The hell you didn't!"

He booted the roan on down the southern hills in the direction of Broken Jaw, laughing.

Chapter 11

"Well, look what the cat dragged in! If it ain't ole Custis P. Long his own mean an' nasty self!" said Arizona Ranger Roscoe Sanders the next afternoon as Longarm and Agent Delacroix rode up to the squalid-looking ranger outpost in the desert town of Broken Jaw.

"You keepin' out of trouble, Roscoe?" Longarm asked the ranger kicked back in a hide-bottom chair on the outpost's front porch that was missing as many floorboards as it boasted.

Ranger Sanders was a small, compact, middle-aged gent with a horsey face trimmed with a long, Mexican-style mustache and one wandering eye. He wore a shabby wool vest over a grimy, cream shirt with blue pinstripes, a tarnished silver watch chain dangling from his vest pocket. His baggy wool trousers were patched in several places, their cuffs stuffed down inside his ancient stovepipe boots that were as worn as Apache moccasins.

Apparently, Sanders hadn't heard Longarm's question. He was squinting his good eye at Agent Delacroix riding up beside Longarm and facing the crumbling adobe shack that served as a ranger post, and he was slowly sitting up straighter in his chair. He poked his battered, old sombrero up off his pale forehead and widened his good eye.

"Say, now . . . what you got there?"

Longarm glanced at his partner and turned his mouth corners down in disgust. "This here is Miss Haven Delacroix, Pinkerton Agent. She's taggin' along on account of the Pinkerton's representing Wells Fargo in the matter of the stolen gold."

He and Haven hadn't exchanged more than three words since they'd left the springs, though they'd spent one night camped together afterward, in a crease in the hills a few miles south of it. Fortunately, the girl's latest three admirers hadn't shown up on their back trail, but Longarm wasn't convinced they still wouldn't. His lawman's sixth sense told him they were being shadowed.

"Pinkerton agent, eh?" said Sanders, rising slowly, his stiff knees popping audibly, good eye riveted on the willowy, heart-twistingly beautiful brunette who had Longarm by the balls and knew it though Longarm was doing his best to convince her she didn't.

A woman with that kind of power was a dangerous thing.

"Say, now, they're comin' in purtier packages these days, ain't they? The last one I seen was uglier'n last year's sin. Couldn't hold his liquor, neither."

"I can assure you I can hold my liquor," Agent Delacroix told the ranger, giving a haughty little smile directed at Sanders but meant for Longarm as she added, "Though I, unlike some, prefer not to drink when I'm working."

"You're makin' me thirsty," Longarm said with a grunt, flaring his nostrils at her and trying not to even glance at the two generous lumps in her shirt.

"How could you be thirsty?" she said without looking at him. "You've been sneaking sips from that flask of yours since early this morning."

"Sneaking sips!" Longarm said with an annoyed chuckle.

"I don't sneak nothin', and I had two drinks all day to cut the trail dust and make the company I been keepin' somewhat *tolerable*."

"Say, now . . ." said Roscoe Sanders, rolling his good eye between the two newcomers, deep lines cutting across his pale forehead and spoking his eye corners as he sized up the pair. He looked like he was watching two half-feral cats meet in an alley and was determining when the fur would fly.

With an air of impatience, Agent Delacroix said, "Getting down to business, Ranger Sanders, we understand that you're incarcerating one Frank Three Wolves here, who may or may not have some information leading to the cache of stolen gold as well as to the killer or killers of the three rangers and two deputy United States marshals." She offered a smile, which Longarm grudgingly had to admit was radiant. "Could we visit with this man, please?"

Sanders swallowed nervously as he stared at the woman, the deep, leathery tan of his craggy cheeks darkening with a schoolboy blush. "Well, sure, sure, ya can." He grinned, showing tobacco-crusted teeth.

When he said nothing more but just stood staring at the woman and probably imagining doing much more, Longarm swung down from the roan's back and said testily, "I take it he's inside?"

Sanders raked his eyes from the girl reluctantly, frowning as though trying to understand what he'd just heard, then said, "Oh, no! He ain't in the jailhouse. I got him over to Slim's drawin' drinks, as the boys from the Prickly Pear Ranch are in town, and Slim's been laid up since the doc cut his appendix out."

Longarm and Haven followed the ranger's gaze to a saloon on the other side of the street and about half a block to the east, the direction from which they'd come. A crude, hand-painted board sign over the brush-roofed gallery announced simply: SLIM'S. There was a good dozen or so ranch ponies standing at the two hitch racks fronting the place, their latigos drooping. A black-and-white collie dog lay on its side in the shade atop the gallery, sound asleep.

Haven scowled skeptically at Roscoe Sanders. "You have a prisoner working at a saloon? A man who might know the whereabouts of stolen gold as well as whom might have killed *five lawmen*?"

"Ah, heck, Miss . . . uh, what was the name again?"

"Delacroix."

"Ah, heck, Miss Delacroix, Big Frank ain't goin' nowhere. He's got nowhere to go and even if he tried, he wouldn't make it as far as the livery barn." Sanders snorted a laugh, brushed his fist across his nose, and walked down off the building's sagging porch.

"Follow me—I'll introduce you to Big Frank." Sanders swung back around and thoughtfully fingered his chin. "You don't mind goin' into a saloon, do ya, Miss Delacroix? Slim's place . . . well . . . there might be some business upstairs, if you get my drift?"

"I wouldn't doubt it a bit if Slim's place doubles as a sporting parlor, Rangers Sanders," Haven said, reining her horse away from the ranger post. "I wasn't born yesterday, and my investigations have more than a few times required me to enter drinking establishments possibly even more raggedy-heeled than that of Mr. Slim."

Sanders glanced at Longarm, who merely shrugged.

Sanders brushed his fist across his nose again, fidgeting, obviously uneasy, and then spat to one side as he swung around and tramped on down the street, angling toward Slim's, the mule ears of his boots flapping this way and that with his badly bowlegged stride. Longarm and Agent Delacroix followed the man, put their horses up to the less crowded of the two hitch racks, swung down, and looped their reins over the cottonwood crosstie polished to a smooth, silver shine.

Longarm had heard a loud commotion from inside the saloon when he'd passed on his and Haven's way through town a few minutes before. He heard it again now—a raucous din like only cowpunchers fresh off the ranch after payday could make.

Ranger Sanders stopped in front of the batwings, hooked a thumb at the doors. "Kinda rowdy in there. Maybe you'd like to wait out here, Miss Delacroix, while me and Custis talk to Big Frank."

Longarm looked at her just now walking up the gallery steps and crouching down to pat the shaggy, dusty dog still lying there as though he'd run hard all day. He didn't lift his head but merely flapped his tail against the gallery floor in acknowledgment of the woman's ministrations.

"Boys will be boys. They don't bother me at all." She gave the dog one more pat, winked at Sanders, nearly causing the ranger's knees to buckle, and then brushed past Longarm and pushed through the batwings.

The dog lifted his head suddenly, watching her go and giving a forlorn moan.

"Forget it, feller," Longarm muttered to the dog. "That woman walking away is the best thing that ever happened to you. Let her keep on walkin'!"

He followed her and Sanders into the saloon. Most of the sweaty, dusty punchers seemed to be grouped around a table at the back of the room, holding up wads of greenbacks and yelling out bets. A big, long-haired man with Indian features—probably a half-breed—and wearing a white apron shuffled amongst them, delivering frothy beer mugs from a round tray. As he turned from the group at the back of the room and started toward the bar, he tripped on something and would have fallen if he hadn't caught himself against a table.

Just then his molasses-dark eyes found Sanders, and he snapped out angrily, "Goddamnit, Roscoe, how'm I supposed to work when I keep trippin' over this goddamn ball an' chain?"

Just then, Longarm noticed two things about the big,

hawk-nosed half-breed with close-set, angry eyes. He had only one arm—the right one. And around one of his ankles was a stout iron shackle to which a six-foot length of chain trailed away to an iron ball hooked behind a chair leg.

Longarm had no sooner finished sizing up the half-breed than he saw what the cowboys were betting on at the back of the room. Apparently one of them was fucking a dark-haired girl bent forward across the table in front of him, the whore's skirt pushed up around her waist, the cowboy's denims and longhandles shoved down around his ankles.

He was crouched low over the whore, who was propped on her elbows on the table, leisurely resting her chin against the heel of her right hand as the waddie hammered away behind her. The whore was laughing and yelling encouragement in Spanish-accented English.

She was a big, comely girl, and her full, brown breasts raked their heavy nipples across the table beneath her.

The men around the hip-thrusting waddie were calling out times, betting on how long it would take him to finish, some cheering him on while others yelled for him to slow down and take his time.

One of the gamblers had him at twelve minutes while another—an older, short, wiry gent with pewter hair—had him at twenty. The little, older gent stood atop a chair near the whore's head, yelling and stomping one boot as though to the beat of a mariachi band, his spurs ringing like rusty chimes.

Longarm looked at Haven, who stood to his left, staring toward the back of the room. "Are they doing what I think they're doing?"

"Maybe you'd better wait outside."

"Men are disgusting." Haven drew a deep breath and turned to Sanders. "Mr. Three Wolves, please, Ranger?"

Sanders beckoned to the big half-breed, who had just returned his tray to the bar and was glaring at the old ranger. The half-breed had apparently noticed Haven, because his

eyes were riveted on the beautiful Pinkerton as he went over
and picked up the iron ball and carried it down the bar to
where the newcomers stood clomped at the end near the
batwings.

"What do we have here?" he said.

Sanders said, "Can you take a break, Frank? These folks
wanna talk to you."

"Who are they?" Three Wolves had only glanced at Longarm, his gaze remaining on Haven.

"Law."

"Really?" Big Frank's dark eyes flashed surprise as they
roamed up and down the woman's busty frame clad in tight
denims, long duster, and dusty stockman's boots. "They sure
don't *look* like law!"

"Why don't we have a drink?" Sanders said.

"I don't drink while I'm working," Haven said
reproachfully.

"Don't you ever get tired of the same old song?" Longarm looked at the half-breed. "I'll have a beer and a shot
of rye."

Haven flared her nostrils with disdain.

Longarm, Agent Delacroix, and Roscoe Sanders took
seats at a table near the front of the saloon, a good distance
away from the festivities, which were continuing, Longarm
couldn't help noticing though the hip-thrusting waddie
looked about ready to blow his load at any second. His face
was red and swollen and he was shouting, "Ah, shit! Ah,
shit—I ain't gonna last!" while the whore said, "Two more
minutes, Elwyn, and you will make Carmella one rich
puta!"

She cackled wildly.

A couple of the waddies clapped. The little, pewter-
haired cowboy on the chair was bellowing encouragement
in a heavy Scandinavian accent. Apparently, a couple of the
bettors had lost out and were slumping into chairs to ease
their loss with beer and whiskey.

Three Wolves came from the bar carrying his iron ball as well as his beer, not an easy maneuver for a one-armed man. He'd already delivered beers and whiskey shots to Longarm and Sanders, and a glass of water to Agent Delacroix. He looked worn-out and angry but Haven's appearance had gained his attention and tempered his owly mood. Like every other man who encountered her, he couldn't take his eyes off her.

Haven looked at the iron ball as the half-breed dropped it onto the floor, and scowled at Sanders. She said, "Making a one-armed man serve drinks while chained to an iron ball. Is this your doing, Ranger Sanders?"

"That was my flash of brilliance, yes, sir. I mean, *ma'am.*" Sanders chuckled. "I figure Slim needed a barman, and Frank here wasn't doin' nothin' but eatin' and shittin'— pardon my language, miss—over at the jailhouse while we was waiting for you two to show up. So why not put him to work slingin' drinks? The ball ain't nothin' personal, but Captain Leyton—that's Captain *Jack* Leyton," he told Longarm, "said to make sure he don't escape. Don't see how even ole fleet-footed Big Frank here could escape with an iron ball chained to his ankle!"

Sanders laughed.

"Oh, don't go feelin' sorry for ole Frank, Miss Delacroix. Frank's strong as an ox and mean as a hydrophobic wildcat. He got himself in this here sichyation when he cut the head off a poor little, unsuspectin' greaser he found diddlin' his girl in their shack out by Diamondback Canyon. Stuck the head on a post in front of his place, as a warning to others who might get the same idea, and fed the rest of the little Mex to his hogs."

Sanders pointed at the big half-breed, who sat glowering at him murderously, and laughed.

Chapter 12

The half-breed looked as though he were about to dive across the table at Ranger Sanders, so Longarm said, "All right, all right—enough about Big Frank here and the Mex, fer now." He fired a match to life on the marred tabletop and touched it to the cheroot sticking out of his mouth.

Haven said, "We're here about the stolen gold, Mr. Three Wolves. And the dead lawmen."

"I was locked up," Big Frank Three Wolves said, his dark eyes flaring out of his big, broad, pockmarked face at Haven and then at Longarm. "I didn't kill no one!"

"No, but you know who did, don't ya?" Longarm smiled knowingly at the man through the smoke wafting about his head.

Haven sat staring at Three Wolves, one fine, pale hand wrapped around her water glass, one brow arched with interest.

Longarm waved the match out and tossed it on the floor. He continued: "I got a feelin' you sent them down there, right into an ambush. Didn't you?"

Three Wolves shook his head, the nostrils of his big nose flaring. "You got it wrong, mister."

"Then tell me how it really went."

"I killed the Mex, all right. Caught him with Estella. Everyone knows how I feel about her. I get back from a freight run to Tucson early, and I find Cruz an' Estella . . . in my cabin, goin' at it like a coupla wildcats." He looked at Agent Delacroix as though for sympathy.

She jerked with a start as a shrill cry rose from the back of the room. The whore laughed. A roar went up, and the old, pewter-haired cowboy whistled and clapped his hands, leaping down from his chair and running over to congratulate Elwyn, who stumbled back away from the whore, his dick drooping between his bare thighs.

He looked as though he'd run a long ways over rough ground.

Longarm glanced at Haven. At the same time, she cast her hazel gaze at him, and it was like she'd touched those sweet lips to his balls. A shudder rippled through him. Flushing as though she'd just read his mind, she dropped her eyes quickly to her water glass around which she'd wrapped both her hands, gripping it tightly, as the revelry continued from the back of the room.

The whore sat on the table she'd been fucked on, drew her low-cut, fancily stitched dress up over her dark, swaying bosoms, and swept her curly hair from her face with the backs of her hands.

A man was calling for a beer for Elwyn. Sanders told him to get his own damn beer, that Big Frank was busy, and then Longarm glanced once more at Haven's hands, suppressing certain memories from a few nights ago, and turned back to Three Wolves.

"All right, you killed the Mex in a jealous rage. For consideration of a lighter sentence, you sent the rangers and the marshals down looking for stolen gold you heard about years ago from Rafael Santana. Have I got the dog by the tail?"

"That's right," Three Wolves said, nodding.

"Don't wash," Longarm told him. "If there really was gold to be found down there, why didn't you go after it a long time ago?"

"Oh, I thought about it," Three Wolves said, nodding. "But it wouldn't be so easy—a big half-breed Apache with one arm. Besides, Santana said he buried the gold on old Whip Azrael's range. White rancher with a whole lot of men on his roll, some of 'em cold-steel artists. I bought the freighting company with money I earned swampin' saloons and livery barns up on the Rim. Always thought I might go down and scratch around for that gold, but I also knew that gold could lead to a whole lot of trouble. I've had trouble all my life, lawman. Some big, some not so big."

"Got him a wicked half-breed Apache temper," Sanders said, sitting back in his chair, holding his beer in one horny, red fist and gazing amusedly at the half-breed. He looked at Longarm. "Why do you think he sent them lawmen into an ambush, Custis? Not that I don't agree with you, but how would he know they'd take his bait and go down and look for the gold? Hell, that gold was lost three years ago. No tellin' who woulda dug it up."

Longarm kept his eyes on the half-breed, trying to read the man, which he thought he was doing fairly well. He'd had plenty of experience reading the eyes of questionable men. "Where's the gold?"

"I gave the map I drew, based on what Santana told me, to the dead rangers."

Agent Delacroix said, "How do you know Santana told you the truth?"

"I didn't. Till them lawmen took the map down there and ended up with a bad case of lead poisonin'."

"Doesn't necessarily mean they were near the gold. Anyone might have thought they had a reason for killing the lawmen." Haven looked at Longarm coolly, her professionalism edging aside her disdain for her badge-toting partner.

Sanders said, "Where Big Frank here sent them boys

wasn't far from where the stage got hit all them years ago. There's got to be somethin' to Big Frank's story, I think."

Longarm looked at the old ranger. "Where's Jack Leyton? I thought he was the captain in charge around here."

"He is. He rode down south toward Holy Defiance, lookin' fer the gold around where the other rangers and the deputy marshals got ambushed. Figured he might kick up somethin' before you got here, Longarm. Him and Lieutenant Sullivan." Old Sanders hiked a shoulder and smiled at Haven as he nudged his shoulders back, obviously proud of himself. "I'm in charge till he and Sullivan get back."

She arched a mock-impressed brow at him.

Longarm said, "Ranger Matt Sullivan?"

"That's right. They both rode down there."

"How long have they been gone?" Agent Delacroix asked Sanders.

"Nigh on two weeks. Left here a week after we got word from Azrael's men about the killin's. Double D men found 'em, and the Azraels sent a man up here to report it."

"Two weeks, eh?" Longarm rubbed his cheek and glanced at Haven, who gave him a skeptical look. Could Jack Leyton and Matt Sullivan have ended up as dead as the other lawmen?

Longarm glanced at Big Frank Three Wolves. "You think the gold is really where Santana told you it was?"

Three Wolves shrugged. "All I know is I didn't send them into an ambush. I thought if they found the gold—good. On account o' that and being as it was just a dirty little Mex I killed, I'd prob'ly get a light sentence. I know I'm gonna end up in Yuma, but I been there before and I'd just as soon not stay long enough to get to know all the rattlesnakes in the hole by name."

Longarm took a deep drag off his cheroot and looked at the coal, running all the information he'd learned about this case through his head. "You can go back to work, Big Frank."

The half-breed studied Longarm skeptically. He'd drank

half his beer and now he polished off the rest in one long draught, scrubbed his mouth with the back of his hand, and rose.

He walked over and picked up the ball to which his chain was attached, glanced once more with brash male interest at Haven, and then hauled his ball back behind the bar and hazed away the pewter-haired cowboy who'd been drawing beers and splashing whiskey into shot glasses for his partners.

Ranger Sanders polished off his own beer and looked from Haven to Longarm. "Was Big Frank any help to you folks?"

"Not really." Haven shook her head, glanced at Longarm as though for corroboration, and sipped her water.

Sanders said, "Well, I reckon I had my beer and my whiskey, and now I reckon I'm gonna drift on back to the ranger office fer a nap. You two gonna be in town long?"

Longarm tossed back his whiskey shot. "We'll be pullin' out first thing in the mornin'. I'd like you to draw me a map to where we're goin', Roscoe."

"I'll help any way I can, Longarm. You know that."

"The Arizona House still standin'?"

Sanders nodded. "Best hotel in town. Right where it's always been." He grinned at Haven, raking his randy old eyes across the girl's well-filled shirt. "You might be able to get you a nice, hot bath, Miss Delacroix, purty yourself up."

"Whatever for?" she asked with an ironic cast to her hazel-eyed gaze.

Sanders glanced from the girl to Longarm and back again, a strained smile creasing his face. Looking as though he'd just walked into a rattlesnake nest, he rose stiffly, pinched his hat brim to them both, and sauntered in his bandy-legged fashion through the batwings and out into the brassy, unforgiving Arizona sunshine.

Haven rose. "I believe I will go have that bath. Where's this best hotel in town?"

"Back behind the ranger office." Longarm grinned at her. "You need any help, you just ask polite-like. Just remember, though—it's strictly *professional*."

"No, thank you," she said crisply. "But I suppose we should meet later and compare notes on the case."

"As long as it's only the case we're comparin' notes on." Longarm finished his beer and belched.

Ignoring him, she strode away through the batwings. He refused to turn his head to get a good, long look at her ass.

A man had his pride.

Chapter 13

When Longarm finished his beer and lowered his glass he found himself staring at two billowy, tan breasts sloping down into an incredibly low-cut, lacy cream dress. The frock was so low-cut that one nipple was poking out. The *puta*'s necklace dangled against the table where Agent Delacroix had been sitting a few minutes ago.

The whore's broad, red-painted lips spread a smile, and her dark eyes sparkled as she said, "How 'bout it, cowboy? You want me make you happy?"

Longarm looked at her breasts again, and smiled. "I'd like to get happy with you, senorita, but I'm all wiped out. Long, hard pull in the saddle." He thought she'd be tired after her recent workout at the back of the room.

"How 'bout a long, hard pull between my legs, cowboy?" The whore, who looked to be in her mid-twenties but was probably younger, glanced at the ceiling. "Come on, you can handle it."

She slid her eyes to one side, indicating the drunken cowboys behind her, some of whom were now playing cards while two others were dancing to an imagined band. "These boys are all played out, won't be game again until tonight. I get bored in the afternoons. Might as well make some money. And a big hombre like you could use his ashes hauled, uh?"

She smiled again, broadly. She pulled her dress down until both breasts spilled out onto the table. They were large and well shaped if losing their firmness, and the girl was probably damn good at her work. Longarm just didn't have any interest. He certainly had some time to kill. But no interest.

"No, thanks, senorita. You're purty as punch, but I'm plum tuckered. Here." He flipped her a gold dollar. "Buy yourself a new dress on old Longarm."

She palmed the coin and straightened, shaping a surprised smile. "*Gracias*, amigo!" She jerked her chin at the batwings. "The one who was in here earlier—she's yours, huh?" She smiled insinuatingly. "*Muchacha muy hermosa!*"

Longarm felt the old tug in his groin again, remembering. "Her? Ah, hell, she ain't nothin' so damn special!"

With that, he stood, tugged his hat brim low, and sauntered on out through the batwings. The black-and-white dog lay at the bottom of the gallery steps, chewing the fur off a dead jackrabbit. As Longarm descended the steps, the dog looked at him and dropped a proprietary paw over its supper.

"Looks good, dog," the lawman said, untying his reins from the hitch rack. "But I believe I'd prefer mine cooked. Enjoy yourself!"

With that, he swung up into the saddle and rode over to the livery barn that sat about fifty yards east of Slim's and on the other side of the street. As he approached the barn, he saw Haven exit the place by a rear side door and stroll back past the rear paddock, making her way through the brush toward the Arizona House behind the rangers' jail, her tan duster swirling around her long, denim-clad legs.

Longarm left the roan with the old, bib-bearded ex–desert rat, Hostetler, who ran the place, and then slung his saddlebags over his right shoulder, took his sheathed Winchester in his other hand, and headed farther east along the shadowy main drag of Broken Jaw. He'd seen a bathhouse on his way into town, and he decided to while away the last hour before supper in a tepid path and scrape the two-day growth of beard from his jaws.

He stopped suddenly as he angled toward the street's south side, frowning wonderingly. Why in hell was he thinking of a bath? That wasn't usually a big concern for him. Even less of a concern was the length of his beard stubble.

Agent Delacroix?

Was he so plum taken with the girl that he was allowing himself to be led around by some semiconscious impulse to look good for her?

Nah.

He just had some time to kill, that's all. And why smell yourself when you didn't have to? Besides, he had a feeling it was going to be a long time before he'd see another bathhouse again . . .

The appropriately named Chinaman's Bathhouse, owned by a Chinamen who dressed like a Mexican peasant but also wore the traditional coolie hat with a braided rawhide chin thong, sat about midway down the main drag. The house was constructed of vertical cottonwood planks and cream-colored canvas that snapped and flapped in the hot breeze.

Fronting the place was a fire over which several iron kettles were suspended. The Chinaman and a Chinese woman, similarly dressed, were tending the fire and boiling clothes as Longarm approached. There were two clotheslines strung lengthwise along the side of the tent shack, and a young Chinese boy was hanging wet wash from a handcart on one of the lines.

Longarm walked under the flapping front awning and asked if he could have a bath.

"Teef poo?" the Chinaman asked grinning and bowing.

Longarm scowled, puzzled. *"Teef poo?"*

"Si, si," said the Chinamen, apparently getting his Span-

ish and English confused. He pointed at his own front teeth with a finger. "Teef poo?"

He nodded at a sign hanging beside the one announcing the price for a bath. The second sign offered TOOF PULL for a mere dime. Another little sideline that the Chinaman had going, apparently. For the convenience of the customer with a grievous tooth, there was a wicker chair situated in the shade beside the tent, opposite the side on which the wash was hung. Pliers and a bottle of whiskey sat on a tree stump beside the chair.

"No teef poo," Longarm said, shaking his head and smiling tightly. "Just bath, please, amigo. Not too hot, not too cold." It was too hot for a hot bath; he wanted the water just warm enough to cut through the trail dust.

The Chinamen extended an arm to the bathhouse, and Longarm ducked through a flap and into one of the place's two rooms equipped with a stylish copper tub sitting on a slatted wooden floor. There was a long wooden bench and a row of pegs for hanging clothes on. The canvas was so old and thin in places that he could see through it to the outside street.

It was warm and musty in here, smelling like boiled burlap, and Longarm quickly shucked out of his clothes and tossed them by the front flap. A few minutes later he was soaking in lukewarm water, and the Chinese couple was washing his clothes outside, for an extra four bits. He figured that with the air being as dry and as hot as it was even this late in the day— around five—the duds would be ready to go by six.

That had no more to do with the girl than the bath did, he reminded himself. It just made good horse sense. Why clad a clean body in soiled duds?

With his own horse brush and an egg-shaped cake of lye soap, he scrubbed himself from scalp to toe, singing, "O, Susanna, o, don't you cry for me! I come from Alabama with a banjo on my knee!"

Finished soaping and scrubbing, he whistled for the Chinaman to come in and pour another bucket of lukewarm water over his head, to rinse off the soap. When he sat back in the tub, the Chinaman offered him a fresh cigar for a nickel. The price was a little steep given that Longarm could buy three for that much at a little drugstore just down from the Federal Building in Denver. But the Chinese family was in business to make money like everyone else, and it wasn't a bad-quality cigar.

Grinning and bowing and speaking rapidly in his undecipherable tongue, the bathhouse proprietor cut the end off the cigar, stuck it between the lawman's lips, and lit it with a long stove match, bowing like a waiter in a fancy restaurant. He stayed long enough to make sure that the cigar was to his customer's liking, and then, giving one last, resolute head bob, he shuffled back out the tent flap to his fire.

Longarm sat back in the tub. While he'd been washing and getting rinsed off by the Chinaman, he'd heard voices outside—the Chinese woman's and someone else's. Now he saw through the threadbare stretch of canvas forming a wall between his tub room and the one to his left, someone moving around. He had to lean forward a bit in his tub to see through a particularly thin part of the canvas. Normally, not being the sort who peeked on other bathers, he'd keep his eyes to himself.

However, in the back of his male brain he was remembering that one of the voices he'd heard outside a minute ago had sounded vaguely feminine. He'd thought he'd heard a soft, familiar, female laugh. Now as he stared through the threadbare patch of canvas, he felt the cool tip of an unseen tongue rise up out of the floor of his tub and gently touch his ball sac.

He winced from the pleasant shock.

The silhouette he could see beyond the canvas wall was clad in a long duster, which she was just now removing, along with her hat, and hanging on a wall peg. The Chinese family's fire was on Agent Delacroix's side of the tent, and its light through the wall beyond her silhouetted her in alluring mystery, all the more so when she stood in profile to Longarm, threw her long hair back, drew her shoulders back, and thrust her breasts forward, stretching.

Longarm's cheeks warmed with shame, staring through the tent like a devilish child watching through a parsonage window as the preacher's pretty wife skinned out of her Sunday duds, but he couldn't help himself.

His heartbeat quickened. His rod began to stiffen under the soapy water when Haven—what was she doing here; he'd thought she was going to bathe at the hotel?—raised her hands to her chest and began unbuttoning her shirt.

Longarm licked his lips. He was on the verge of clearing his throat and announcing himself. That's what an honorable man would do. Instead, he found himself sucking his lower lip and watching intently as the girl peeled out of her shirt and then her camisole and bent forward to lay the garments over the bench on the room's far side, beyond the tub.

She'd sat on the bench to remove her boots when the Chinese woman said something in badly broken English.

"Come in!" Haven called.

The Chinese woman entered, carrying two buckets by their handles. She filled the tub, prattled off some broken English mixed with Spanish, then shuffled back out the tent's front flap and secured the flap behind her.

By the time she'd left, Haven, who'd been continuing to undress, was down to her panties.

Leaning toward Longarm, her full, firm breasts slanting away from her chest, and silhouetted by the amber firelight and fading sunlight behind her, she daintily slid the panties down her legs, stepped out of them, raising each long, slender leg in turn. She dropped the panties on the bench and then leaned far forward, her back to Longarm, to pick up her gun belt and holstered LeMats, which had slid off the bench and onto the floor.

Longarm sucked a sharp breath as he stared at what appeared a gopher looking out from between her legs, up high near her comely, round ass. His cock lifted its purple head above the surface of the soapy water between his legs, and nodded like an old man waking from a short nap.

He stifled a groan.

She turned toward him, and he sat back quickly, water splashing against the sides of his tub. His heartbeat quickened further. Had she seen him? He was in deep shit now if she found out he was over here.

He leaned forward, felt a slight wave of relief. Facing him, she was pinning her hair up on her head, chin lowered. He could have sworn she was looking right at him, but she must not have been or by now she'd have filled her fists with her LeMats. Her breasts were pulled up slightly, bulging back against her chest, spilling slightly over the sides, both nipples aimed right at him.

His mouth turned to dust as she stepped into the tub, sat down in the water and gently splashed it over her shoulders and rubbed it into her breasts, caressing each orb in turn. His cock became fully erect as he watched her stand and soap herself—not quickly, just to get it over with, as he'd done . . . but slowly, enjoying the sensation of the soap and her soft brush on her fine, smooth skin.

He watched her breasts jostle as she turned this way and that, lifted each leg to wash it, and then reached behind to run her hand gently up between her butt cheeks. She closed one hand over her breast as she massaged the soap slowly, tenderly into the hair between her legs.

She groaned softly, sighed luxuriously.

Longarm drew a slow, deep, calming breath.

She sank back down in the tub and then called to the Chinese woman to come rinse her off. When the Chinese woman had come and gone, Longarm's heart thudded. He saw Haven resting with her head back against the back of her tub, as though dozing. Knowing that he couldn't leave here until his clothes were dry, and that she was bound to find out sooner or later that he was over here, he began splashing loudly and sing, "O, Susanna, o, don't you cry—!"

Her loud gasp cut him off.

"Marshal *Long*?" she said.

Longarm feigned a surprised grunt. "Holy moly—is that you over there, Agent Delacroix?"

Chapter 14

Longarm did not risk looking through the thin stretch of canvas, but he could vaguely see Haven Delacroix's murky silhouette as she sat in the tub with her arms crossed on her breasts, hands on her shoulders.

"Have you been over there all this time?" she demanded.

He chuckled. "I reckon I could ask the same of you. I just now woke up from a little nap. Like to doze in the tub, don't ya know. What're you doin' over *there*? I thought you was going to take a bath at the *hotel*!"

"Can you see me?"

"Why, no. Can you see *me*?"

Pause. He could see that she was staring toward him but that was about all he could see.

"I can only see a vague shadow."

"That's about all I can see, too."

"Thank God," she said.

"Thank him for me, too, will ya?" Longarm chuckled. "No wonder what you'd do, if you saw me naked again. Why, you'd probably tear right through this here canvas wall, and—!"

"Oh, please hush, will you? God, what a tiresome man you are! I just want to take a long, quiet bath. I was going to have one at the hotel but they had no wood split for a fire and the hired boy apparently got bit by a rattlesnake two days ago. His leg is swollen up, and I quote, 'thick as a cottonwood stump!' "

"Ouch!"

"You can say that again."

"Well, okay—*ouch*!"

She sighed. In the corner of his eye, he saw her lean back in her tub and lower her hands from her breasts. He leaned back in his own tub and looked down. His cock stood up like a brake handle, angling up over his belly button. He felt like giving it a knock against the side of the tub, to discourage it, but there was no denying the male organ when a woman like Haven was within twenty feet.

And naked.

Agent Delacroix said, "Since we're both here, and I intend to lock myself in my room for the night with a good book, let's go over what we know about the case, shall we?"

Longarm tried again to suppress his desire for the girl, to think and act like a professional. Why in hell did he have to be cursed with such a beautiful partner? Especially one whose wares and talents he'd been treated to once, just enough to make him ache for more.

"Shoot," he said with a sigh.

"You're the one with the most experience—you tell me what you know so far."

"Hell, that's easy," he said, rolling his cigar from one side of his mouth to the other. "I know that five lawmen ended up dead down here and that they *might* have been killed because they'd gotten close to a cache of gold that was stolen three years ago."

"But we don't really know why they were killed, correct?" she said.

Longarm nodded and rolled his cigar to the other corner of his mouth. "They could have been killed for any number of reasons. They might have run into cattle rustlers

or border bandits who thought the lawmen were shadowin'
them. Or they might simply have been killed because of the
badges pinned to their vests. I've had guns aimed my direction for no better reason than that one there."

"Right, it's actually quite silly to think the killings had
anything to do with the gold, isn't it?"

"Silly?" Longarm plucked the cigar from his mouth, and
studied the coal that had gone out while he'd been ogling
his partner. "Well, I wouldn't call it silly. Damned unlikely,
though. Truth be told, I got a feelin' we're never going to
learn who killed them fellas. The killer's trail is likely cold
as a grave digger's ass—uh, pardon my French."

"I believe I've grown inured to your French, Marshal."

He wanted to mention something about the French les-
sons she'd given to him back in Leadville, but congratulated
himself for resisting the notion and keeping his mind on
business. "If the gold's still where Santana's boys buried it,
though, there might be a chance we'll find it when we ride
down there and scout around."

"If it's still there."

"Check."

"And if Big Frank's information is reliable."

"Check again."

Haven asked, "Do you believe Three Wolves's story
about why he never went looking for the cache himself?"

"Yeah, I reckon I do. Not sure why, but I can usually tell
when a man is lyin'. I didn't see that look in Big Frank's
eyes when he was explainin' his side of it. He does only have
one arm, remember. And if he got anyone to help him, he'd
have had to tell 'em where the gold was buried and risk a
double cross in the form of a knife in his back. Big Frank's
seen enough trouble, just wanted to run his freight business
in peace."

"Until he discovered his woman's dalliance . . ."

"Yeah, there's that."

"I feel sorry for Big Frank." Haven's voice was thin and

wistful. "Being a one-armed half-breed cannot be an easy way to go through life."

"Yeah, and one with a nasty temper."

"There is that."

Longarm drew on his cigar and was reminded that it had gone out. He climbed out of the tub and walked over to the bench where'd he'd placed the contents of his pockets. He found his box of lucifers, struck one to life on the bench, and touched the flame to the stogie as he stepped back into the tub.

There was a shrill gasp.

"You filthy dog!" the girl fairly shrieked.

Standing in the tub, Longarm turned to see her milky silhouette leaning far forward in her own bath, gazing toward him . . . through the thin patch of canvas.

"You were watching me, weren't you?"

Longarm opened and closed his mouth, but the words were all tangled up in his tonsils.

"Sleeping, like hell!" she said, rising up out of her tub. "Well, here, take a good look, you depraved son of a bitch!"

She walked over to the thin patch in the canvas, to Long-arm's right, three feet away from him. She turned this way and that, catlike, bending each knee in turn, hefting her breasts in her hands, caressing them alluringly, glaring at him, curling her upper lip back with a feral, feline anger.

"Like what you see? Would you like to have your hands on these?" She dropped her eyes to his cock, which had dwindled during their business conversation but which was now beginning to swell again, lift its thick head once more from between his thighs.

"Does that make your big plow handle stand up and take notice? Oh, it does, doesn't it!"

She paused for just a second as she stared down at his cock, and he thought he saw her hesitate. A slight shudder rippled through her. She snapped her angry, flashing eyes back to his through the sheer spot in the canvas.

"You're a beast!" she railed once more, her voice thicker this time. Covering her breasts with her elbows, she turned, stomped over to where her clothes hung from pegs, and began to dress.

Outside the tent, the Chinese couple was prattling away in their mixed tongue, obviously alarmed by the verbal skirmish that had erupted inside their place of business. "It's all right," Haven called angrily as she dressed, glaring at him through the thin patch in the canvas wall. "Don't worry, good people—I'm very well armed and can take extremely good care of myself!"

Longarm bit down hard on his cigar and was about to stomp over to his bench and begin dressing, forgetting that his clothes were being laundered, his embarrassment about his current physical condition tempered somewhat by his knowing that Agent Delacroix was every bit as randy as he was.

Or at least nearly as randy. She was just too pigheaded to admit it. He'd have bet that her silky snatch was as hot as a freshly brewed pot of coffee at that moment.

Since there was nothing else on the bench save his hat, his saddlebags, and his Winchester, he grabbed the hat and clamped it down hard on his head, half-scowling and half-grinning over his shoulder at Haven, whose shadow he could see dressing against the fire on the other side of her.

Just then, the flap to his tub room opened, and the Chinese man entered, holding his clothes in a neatly folded pile in his hands. He was flushed and nervous, and his wife, who stood little higher than Longarm's breastbone, entered behind him holding a double-barreled shotgun that must have weighed as much as she did.

She scowled at Longarm and prattled away angrily, but when her eyes dropped to his dong, which was at half-mast now, she fell silent.

The man shuffled over to the bench, bowing anxiously and not meeting Longarm's gaze, and set the pile of clothes on the bench. He swung around quickly, like a chicken running from a dog, and started back to the flap, where his wife stood, holding the shotgun down in front of her and staring wide-eyed at Longarm's manhood. Her husband prattled at her and turned her toward the door, and she shuffled out in front of him, turning her head to get one more look at the well-hung man behind her.

Then they were gone.

Longarm took his clothes in his lap and sat down on the bench. Haven's shadow was still moving around on the other side of the canvas wall. Suddenly, he felt more confounded than amused.

"Oh, for pete's sakes, don't you think this is rather silly? Don't see no reason why we couldn't meet up again. What's it gonna hurt? We're both professionals. We can have fun and still do our jobs."

She was shrugging into her duster. Turning, she grabbed her hat off the peg and carefully set it on her head with both hands, carefully adjusting its angle. She said nothing but was being overly fussy about the hat.

"You got what I want, and I got what you want," Longarm said. "Why not admit it? We had fun once."

She lowered her hands from her hat and stood staring at him through the canvas wall. He could see her chest rising and falling slowly, heavily as she breathed.

As she thought it over.

She was as confounded as he was . . .

"No," she said resolutely. Then louder as though convincing, reprimanding herself. "Not ever again."

With that she turned and strode out of the tent.

"You got nothin' to be embarrassed about!" Longarm called after her. Then he stuck the cigar back in his mouth and said mostly to himself, because the girl was gone, "Hell, we all got wants. It's only natural!"

Chapter 15

Fully dressed and with his rifle riding one shoulder, his saddlebags slung over the other, Longarm slipped through the tent flap and out into the refreshingly cool air of the late afternoon, early evening.

The Chinese couple was still tending their laundry. They must wash clothes for nearly the entire town of Broken Jaw.

The Chinaman was removing dry clothes from one of the lines, folding them neatly, and placing them in a hand-cart. The woman paused in her stirring a pot of boiling clothes with a long paddle, giving Longarm a speculative, vaguely amorous look, a lock of black hair sliding back and forth above her right eye in the breeze.

Longarm flipped the woman a three-dollar gold piece.

"Sorry for the trouble." He pinched his hat brim to her and then walked on down the street in the direction of the hotel.

The street was busier than it had been earlier. There were two saloons in town, and cow ponies stood droopy-headed before the hitch racks of each. Horseback riders in the traditionally colorful, billowy neckerchiefs and dusty, weathered sombreros of the Arizona cowpuncher rode back and forth along the street, meeting each other and calling out or pinching their hat brims, laughing with the relief of the end of another long workday in the blazing Sonoran sun.

They'd have a few drinks, maybe a woman, and buck the tiger or play a few rounds of cards, likely losing every penny they'd made that day, before mounting their ponies again and riding back out to their respective bunkhouses.

A breeze rose, swirling the dust and bits of straw at Longarm's feet. It jostled a few of the tumbleweeds that had blown into town earlier that day. The breeze would die soon, as soon as the sun had sunk behind the Rincon Mountains in the west, and then the stars would come out to flash like near beacons.

Already the colors of the sunset were showing over the brown western peaks and ridges.

Longarm stopped at the ranger post to get directions to where Big Frank Three Wolves had claimed the cache of stolen gold was buried. With a pencil provided by Ranger Roscoe Sanders, he marked on the map that Big Frank Three Wolves had drawn for him where the dead rangers and U. S. marshals had been found, as well, near a creek about a hundred yards from the general area in which the gold was said to be buried though no one had discovered its exact location and retrieved it.

At least, no one the ranger or Big Frank knew about. A lot could happen in three years.

The stolen gold was supposedly on land that was part of the Double D Ranch of Whip Azrael, the headquarters of which was farther on down the streambed known as Defiance Wash, which could have been renamed Dead Man Creek, for it was the same creek around which the dead lawmen had been discovered. Defiance Wash ran through the little ghost town of Holy Defiance as well as the Azrael Double D Ranch eight miles to the west of the town, tucked inside a valley of the Black Puma Mountains.

Longarm pocketed the map that Three Wolves had scribbled on simple lined notepaper from memory, a copy of

which the now-dead lawman had used to find their way
twenty-five miles south to what had become the end of their
trail in more ways than one. Leaving Sanders playing check-
ers with Three Wolves through the big half-breed's cell door,
empty supper plates on Captain Jack Leyton's small, cluttered desk, Longarm headed out for a meal of his own.

Later, he went on over and paid for a room at the Arizona
House, a two-story adobe-brick affair framed in weathered
pine no doubt hauled down from the White Mountains when
Broken Jaw had still been burgeoning. The hotel sat on the
north end of town, nothing but sage and greasewood rolling
up toward high, salmon-colored mountains to the north.

A few years ago, this country had been terrorized by the
Coyotero and Lipan Apaches, and Longarm remembered stepping carefully, with a hand on his pistol's grips, waiting for an
attack at any moment. Because that's how they'd come—hard
and fast, anytime, anywhere, the savages wanting nothing
more than to rid their territory of the white invader.

It had been a bloody time across several decades, many
ranches raided, stagecoaches run down and burned, men
tortured, women raped and murdered. Secretly, Longarm
sympathized with the Apache plight, but he was glad that
the bulk of those depredations seemed to be over. Now and
then, bronco Apaches led by some war chief who couldn't
bring himself to be heeled by some Indian gent and the cavalry, would bust off their reservation and go on a wild, killing tear, but those "red cyclones," as he'd heard some settlers
call them, were happening less and less frequently in these
slightly more civilized times, thank God.

The most formidable war chief of them all, Geronimo of
the Chiricahua Apache, had finally surrendered only the
year before and had been taken with his family to Fort Per-
kins in Pensacola, Florida. Just as Longarm sympathized
with the Apache plight—no one wanted to be driven away
from their homes and plucked from the only way of life they
knew; the cavalry was trying to make them farmers, of all

things!—he admired the tough, crafty old leader, Geronimo, who, though sorely outnumbered and ill-equipped, had given General Crook and General Miles fits for many long, hard years.

When Longarm had signed his name in the guest register manned by a stocky German with a tangled bib beard, he headed on up the narrow stairs to his second-floor room. It was nearly dark now, and a couple of candles in wall-bracketed sconces offered a flickering, shadowy light.

When he was a third of the way down the hall, a door latch click behind him. He turned quickly, ready to snap the rifle down off his shoulder and ratchet the hammer back.

"Oh," Haven's voice said, an eye showing through the three-inch crack between her door and the frame. "I was . . ."

Longarm turned half around and arched a brow. "Feels like old times. Need somethin', Agent Delacroix."

Something seemed funny about her. She blinked, opened the door a little wider, poked her head out. She turned to look down the hall toward the stairs.

Thickly, she said, "I was just . . . needing some water. I thought you might be Mr. Berger." She glanced at Longarm coolly, and then stepped out of her room with a stone jug in her hand and strode off down the hall to the stairs. She was walking fine but the thickness of her voice and the shine in her eyes was odd.

Was she drunk? Assuaging her desires?

She stopped at the top of the stairs and called down to the German at the desk, her voice echoing hollowly. The man said something back to her and then Longarm heard the man's boots thumping on the steps.

Sure enough, Longarm thought—she was in her room, getting drunk alone, needing more branch water to mix with whatever tanglefoot she was imbibing in. He only vaguely realized he was staring back at her incredulously when she turned to him from the balcony rail and said in a typically peeved tone, "Everything is fine, Marshal. Good night!"

Longarm nodded, still puzzled. "Good night, Agent Delacroix. You need anything tonight, I'll be just down the hall." He winked at her. "Room four, just beyond yours."

She didn't say anything but merely handed the jug to the stocky German, who'd climbed the stairs to retrieve it.

Inside his room, he himself had his own few libations, but just a few. He wanted to get an early start tomorrow, to beat the heat, and he needed to be on his toes. If any sign remained at the spot where the lawmen had been murdered, he had to find it. That was likely his and Agent Delacroix's only hope of running the culprit or culprits to ground.

Having shucked down to his longhandles, he corked his bottle, stuffed it into a saddlebag pouch, and hung the saddlebags on a peg by the door. He wrapped his shell belt around a post at the head of his lumpy bed, which sagged in the middle, beneath a motley patch quilt that bore a Christmas design though it was not yet the Fourth of July, and then shucked the Colt from its holster.

He spun the cylinder, liking the familiar click of the well-oiled and fully loaded revolver. Returning the gun to its sheath, he blew out his bedside lamp and stared at the door for a while, trying to get his comely partner out of his head.

His lovely partner was drinking alone to quell her own heated cravings . . .

Longarm's cock still ached the heavy, dull ache of lust—not a comfortable sensation. He was not accustomed to not having his desires satisfied, and oh, what he wouldn't give to have Haven Delacroix's sweet mouth wrapped around his cock again tonight, satisfying that desire the way she had a few nights ago in the Colorado mountains.

Maybe he should have gone ahead and taken a tumble with the *puta* over at Slim's.

Well, he was here now, and he needed a good night's rest, so he'd turn his mind to the case at hand until he drifted off to sleep. And that's what he'd nearly done, his face in the pillow, opening his mouth to begin snoring, when he snapped his eyes suddenly wide in response to something his half-asleep lawman's senses had picked up in the building around him.

The click of a door latch?

Hinges squawked quietly. A door just down the hall was being drawn open slowly. Which direction?

In Haven's direction.

Longarm rolled eagerly onto his back and then sat up, like a boy listening for Santa Claus.

His dong immediately began aching again, though it was a pleasantly expectant sensation this time, like the thrill he always felt when he knew he was going to soon be "visiting" his old pal, the moneyed, young, and beautiful Miss Cynthia Larimer. He and the scrumptious daughter of General Larimer, Denver's founding father, rarely visited, however.

What they did do more than anything was fuck in nearly every position humanly possible and a couple of poses that required the often bittersweet strain of several obscure tendons, muscles, and joints.

Thinking about Cynthia now and an imminent visit from Haven Delacroix, who obviously hadn't been able to get him out of her craw, caused Longarm's heartbeat to quicken and his hands to slicken. Already, he felt his manhood pushing against the wash-worn fabric of his longhandles.

He breathed through his mouth so that he could hear better beyond his door. There was that click again. Had she gone back into her room?

No. A floorboard squawked. It was followed by another squawk slightly louder than the first.

Longarm fairly licked his chops. She was heading this way!

He heard the girl's soft tread in the hall, but he stayed where he was. He wasn't going to go running to greet her and make a fool of himself, by God. Let her knock and ask to be let in.

The soft footfalls grew louder until he saw a shadow

move under the door. He grinned as he stared at the shadow, waiting. The shadow remained in one place directly beneath the door. Longarm frowned.

Go on and knock, galldarnnit . . .

Suddenly, the shadow moved back to the right. It disappeared. He could hear Haven's footsteps again, but they grew quieter now as she retreated.

"Shit!" he muttered, flopping back down against his pillow.

He stared at the ceiling. Should he go after her? If he did, she might only give him the sharp chin again, frustrating him even more. Nah, he'd better stay right here and get rested for the trail tomorrow.

His cock was heavy, however. It yearned for the girl's soft lips and wet tongue, the expanding and contracting of her throat against its swollen head.

He chewed his cheeks as he stared at the ceiling in frustration. In the hall, a floorboard squawked.

Longarm jerked his head up, eyes wide in renewed anticipation. Again, a shadow appeared beneath his door. He stared at it. He lifted his gaze to the dark door panel.

"Come on," he whispered. "Knock. Go ahead. You know you want to."

The shadow wavered as though Haven herself was wavering, about to tramp on back to her own room again.

"Ah, for chrissakes!"

Longarm threw his covers back and rose from the bed. He was halfway to the door, making his way through the darkness, when a loud roar caused him to leap a foot in the air with a start. It also caused his door to blow open and swing within two inches of his nose before it slammed against the wall.

Or what was left of the door after two loads of double-ought buck had blown two watermelon-sized holes in it.

Chapter 16

One of the two figures standing in the hall outside Longarm's ruined door laughed raucously as he stepped aside for the man behind him to move forward and lift his own sawed-off double-barreled barn blaster.

By this time, Longarm was airborne, diving across his bed that the double-ought buck had shredded and dusted with slivers from the door. He slammed belly down on the bed, closed his right hand over the grips of his .44, and pulled the revolver from its holster as he rolled to the right, over the edge of the bed.

As he hit the floor on his butt, there was a bright, orange flash against the silhouette of the big man in his doorway. The expansive thundering report filled the room, causing the floor to leap beneath Longarm's ass.

The full load of buckshot flipped Longarm's pillow up high against the headboard, instantly turning it into a billowing cloud of feathers stitched with shredded ticking. The man with the shotgun swung the savage popper's barrels sideways, tracking Longarm and shouting, *"Die, you son of a bitch! Die!"*

Longarm dropped his head down below the edge of the bed but triggered his pistol over the top, aimed at the door.

He fired twice, one shot on top of the other. The Colt's second belch, sounding little louder than a knuckle pop after the shotgun's skull-shattering reverberation, was drowned by the ambusher's detonation of the coach gun's second barrel.

The man must have dropped the barrel just enough as he fired that the swarm of screaming pellets did not blow Longarm's Colt and fist off the end of his arm, but blasted into the end of the bed, causing a rain of corn leaves similar to that of the continuing drift of feathers. It also heaved the mattress across the frame and into Longarm's chest, knocking him back against the wall beneath the room's sole window.

From here, he watched the shooter stumble back into the hall as the man who'd been so unkind to the lawman's door swung his own empty shotgun behind his back, where it hung from a lanyard, and reached for one of the pistols on his hips.

Longarm rested his gun wrist against the top of the shredded bed once more, lined up his sights on the man's chest, and fired. The bushwhacker groaned and stumbled backward, twisting around and ramming his right shoulder against the hall's opposite wall, knocking a tintype off its nail.

The gunman had unleathered one of his pistols, and as he gave a great bellowing yell of pain and rage, he lifted the weapon.

Longarm fired two more times. One bullet punched through the man's chest while the second turned his left ear to jelly and painted the wall behind him with it. His head smacked the wall violently, with a thudding crack.

He screamed shrilly, dropped his own gun, and crumpled up on top of his partner, who lay parallel to the base of the wall, jerking as he stared glassily at Longarm, blinking rapidly, blood oozing from a corner of his mouth and pooling on the floor beneath his head.

An angry female scream sounded down the hall.

A man's scream followed it. A pistol popped.

Longarm scrambled to his feet and ran to the door in time to see a man run out of Agent Delacroix's room, a knife in his right hand. He was the hombre whom Longarm remembered filling his canteens at the spring that Longarm and Haven had ridden up on two day's ago. The now-dead men had been mounted on horses behind him.

The pistol popped again in the room behind the man as he glanced at Longarm and gave a snarling scream. He bounced off the hall wall opposite Haven's room as another bullet plunked into the pine boards beside him. He flung the knife toward Longarm, who ducked. The knife embedded itself into the doorframe behind the crouching lawman.

The attacker wheeled and took off running toward the stairs.

"Demon!" Agent Delacroix screamed.

She fired three more shots from inside her room, and the bullets blasted through the wall, spraying wood slivers behind the fleeing attacker. The man ran hard, elbows and knees pumping, casting horrified looks behind him as yet another slug blasted through the hall wall behind him and into the wall opposite.

Longarm extended his own revolver straight out from his shoulder, and shouted, *"Hold it, asshole!"*

At the top of the stairs, the man stopped, slapped his belly holster, and brought up a horn-gripped hogleg. Longarm's triggered slug puffed dust from the man's brown leather vest up near his left shoulder. He screamed again as he bounced off the rail post, dropped his pistol, and tumbled down the stairs and out of Longarm's sight, behind the hall's left wall.

Longarm ran to Haven's room. She was just climbing up from the floor, wearing a pink robe and holding a hand to her right cheek that matched the color of her robe. She held one of her LeMats in her right fist. Smoke curled from both barrels.

"You all right?" Longarm yelled from the doorway.

She nodded. "Is he dead?"

"I'm about to find out!"

Longarm ran back into his room, stomped into his boots and quickly reloaded his Colt. There was no time to dress in anything but his hat and his boots.

He bounded on out of the room and down the hall to the stairs. In the lobby below, the German, who apparently owned the place, was standing behind his desk and shouting loudly in his mother tongue and wielding a small, nickel-plated pistol, waving it at the man just now stumbling past the desk toward the hotel's front door.

"Get down behind the desk, friend!" Longarm shouted as he descended the stairs.

He was halfway down when the ambusher swung around toward the hotelier, a second revolver in his hand. He fired a round toward the hotelier, but he was so wobbly that the slug plowed into the rack of pigeonholes behind his target.

The German screamed louder and triggered his own pistol over the desk, his slug punching into the door just as the bushwhacker opened it.

"Hold it!" Longarm shouted from the bottom of the steps.

But the ambusher pushed on out the door and into the dark night. Longarm didn't want to fire because someone might be in the street beyond him. Instead, he grabbed the hotelier's pistol out of the man's hand, so the man couldn't shoot Longarm in his wild rage, and tossed the pistol across the lobby. He ran out the front door and onto the gallery.

The night was cool and dark though stars glittered in the velvet sky. There were few lights on this end of Broken Jaw, so it took Longarm's eyes a few seconds to adjust. He could hear the would-be killer running away from him, and then he saw his jostling shadow angling across the street and to the left, toward a small, cream-colored adobe cantina.

The man was limping on his left ankle and wheezing shrilly.

There were a half-dozen horses tied to the lone hitch rack fronting the cantina. The gunman seemed to be heading for one of them—likely his own mount.

Longarm ran down the three gallery steps, stopped, and aimed the pistol straight out from his right shoulder. "Turn around and drop the gun or take it between the shoulder blades!"

The man had just reached the hitch rack. He stopped so suddenly that he nearly fell and swung back toward Longarm. Starlight flashed on the revolver in his fist.

Longarm's .44 spoke once, twice, and then a third time. Each shot was followed by a grunt from the man the slugs punched through, until he breathily said, "Fuck!" and triggered his pistol once toward the stars. He fell backward into the stock trough fronting the hitch rack with a loud splash that caused the already jostling horses to whicker and side-step away from the tank.

Longarm lowered his pistol halfway and walked toward the man lolling in the stock trough, the water spilling over the sides glittering in the starlight. Two men walked out of the cantina behind the bushwhacker. Around here, men were accustomed to hearing gunshots any time of the day or night. Hooking their thumbs behind their cartridge belts, they sauntered along the cantina's slim boardwalk and looked down at the man in the trough.

They both lifted their faces in unison, regarding the man dressed only in red balbriggans, a hat, and boots walking toward them. One half turned to the other, dipped his chin toward the trough, and said, "That's Jim Winter."

"No shit?" said the other, poking his hat brim back off his forehead.

Longarm stopped at the stock trough, looked down at Jim Winter staring up at him, legs dangling down the end of it, arms hooked over the sides.

"Who're you?" one of the two others asked Longarm.

The lawman scratched his cheek with his Colt's front

gun sight. "The hombre who just killed Jim Winter, I reckon."

"Jim owed me twenty dollars," said the man who'd identified the bushwhacker.

Longarm shrugged. "You can have whatever's on him as long as you haul him out of here and bury him; same with his two pards in the hotel."

The two men looked at each other, shrugged, and came on down the boardwalk to pull Jim Winter out of the stock tank. Longarm walked back toward the hotel. Footsteps rose on his right and a familiar voice called, "Who's shootin' over here?"

Longarm turned to see a skinny, stoop-shouldered figure tramping toward him. For a few seconds, he couldn't place the bull-legged gent in a long nightshirt dangling to his bony knees, and a night sock, the tail of which hung down over his right shoulder.

"Custis, that you?"

Then Longarm saw the mule-eared boots not unlike his own, though far older, and he lifted his gaze to the drooping salt-and-pepper mustache brushing down past the old ranger's chin. The last time Longarm had passed through Broken Jaw, there'd been no local lawman. It was up to the rangers manning the outpost to keep the town in trim. That must still be the setup. Longarm couldn't help chuckling at Sanders's costume, but then he remembered that his wick had nearly been trimmed.

"What kind of a town you runnin', Roscoe?" he said. "A man can't get a good night's rest without three men tryin' to beef him through his door!"

"Huh? Whuh?" Sanders stopped and looked around, befuddled, indignant. His craggy cheeks darkened, and he spat to one side as he poked an accusing finger at Longarm, who continued walking toward the hotel. "Custis, you're trouble. Always have been, always will be! You pack it like most men pack tobacco!"

Longarm stopped at the bottom of the Arizona House's front steps and stared up at Haven Delacroix standing atop the gallery, dressed in her thin pink wrap, her hair down, her LeMats in her hands.

Longarm shook his head and climbed the steps, growling, "Nah, the trouble's right here."

He glanced at her as he brushed past her. He vaguely noted the smell of booze on her but she looked sober enough now in the wake of the dustup. She arched a peevish brow. "You think I'm to blame for this?"

Longarm walked through the open door and into the hotel, not looking back as he said, "It wasn't me they wanted to fuck."

Chapter 17

Despite having his sleep so rudely interrupted, and not in the way he'd expected after hearing Haven's footsteps in the hall outside his room, Longarm woke at the first flush of dawn. He was sure those first footsteps had been hers. She just hadn't had the courage to knock on his door and ask him to let her in so they could carry on as they'd carried on in Leadville.

Too prideful. Typical of the moneyed class. Cynthia Larimer, of course, was the exception to the rule. Cynthia wouldn't have knocked. She'd have broken the door down and taken him by force.

Longarm snorted at the thought, shaving in the cracked mirror propped atop his dresser. But it was probably a good thing that he and Haven hadn't gotten together last night. They'd likely both have been filled full of buckshot.

He figured the three bushwhackers had learned which rooms they were both in by peeking at the hotel register while the stocky German had snoozed in his rocking chair behind the lobby desk. Their plan had likely been similar to the Jerkwater bushwhackers—get Longarm out of the way so they could have some uninterrupted time with the girl.

Yep, probably lucky that Longarm and Agent Delacroix

hadn't both been in his room. They would have died in each other's arms. He shook his head and then lifted the razor once more to his left cheekbone. But what a way to go!

She was a danger, though, he reminded himself, as he continued scraping his face. He couldn't let his guard down again. Men of nearly every stripe on the frontier would be tempted by such a prize as Agent Delacroix, and that made him, Longarm, a target.

There was nothing he could do about that now. He was stuck with her, so he might as well make the most of it. What had happened last night—at least, last night *before* he'd nearly got sent to Glory in a hail of buckshot—indicated that sooner or later she was going to cave under the wave of her own desires.

He grinned at the prospect as he dressed and set his hat on his head, adjusting it carefully over his left eye. With his rifle on one shoulder, his saddlebags slung over the other shoulder, he strode into the hall and closed the door behind him. She was just then emerging from her own room, her carpetbag and saddlebags slung over her shoulder, her LeMats holstered on her tautly curving hips.

Haven looked at him coolly, but he thought he detected an ever-so-slight bleariness at the edges of her eyes.

The bleariness of drink?

"Sleep well?" he asked her.

"Well enough." She shook her hair back from her eyes. "You?"

"Like a log after your friends died."

"No friends of mine."

Longarm snorted and brushed past her, heading for the stairs. She grabbed his arm suddenly and pulled. She was no match for his strength. Instead of jerking him around, his static weight ended up pulling her up against him. Her cheeks flushed slightly, and she stepped back, glaring up at him, a little breathless.

"I'd just like to know what you're problem is with me,

Marshal Long. Come on. Out with it! Let's clear the air before we continue this investigation!"

He stared down at her. She squinted up at him, fire in her eyes. Her breasts pushed out from behind her shirt, which she wore with one more button open than she'd had open the day before. He was sure of that, because he noticed such things about women.

Her bosom swelled as he gazed at it, not for a second trying to conceal his lust for her. Her lips were full and rich. She looked so damn tempting that he could find no words with which to respond to her demand. And then there was no way he could have said anything even if he'd found the words, because suddenly he'd grabbed her with his free arm, drew her to him brusquely, and closed his mouth over hers.

At first, she squirmed a little, tried to pull away. He held her fast, kept his mouth over hers, mashing his lips against hers, his tongue probing hungrily. She closed against him and started to return the kiss, opening her lips slightly.

But then, as though catching herself, she stepped back.

Glaring up at him, she gritted her teeth and slapped him. It was a resounding slap. But it didn't hurt him. It thrilled him. Her passion was intoxicating in whatever form it came in. Flip sides of the same coin.

He had her, he knew. She knew it, too. Now, it was just a matter of time.

He grinned down at her. She wilted under his gaze, stepping back, lowering her tentative eyes to his broad chest. Her throat moved as she swallowed. The idea was hitting home with her now. She was as certain of it as he was, and it scared her as much as it thrilled her.

Just a matter of time . . .

"Best get our horses and ride out," he said and continued on down the hall, digging a fresh cheroot out of his shirt pocket.

Only fifty miles lay between Jawbone and Defiance Wash as well as the town that had partly taken the wash's name, Holy

Defiance, but the trip would require a good two days. Roscoe Sanders had told Longarm he'd be traveling through rugged country, but the word was sorely inadequate for describing the terrain that Longarm found himself heading into.

It was all broken, rocky desert bristling with cactus and greasewood, scored by arroyos and broad canyons carved by ancient rivers long defunct, though their beds might have seen a little water during the summer storm season, or in the spring when the snows melted in the northern mountains. All around the old Apache trail that Longarm and Agent Delacroix followed were deep, shelving mesas and spinelike sandstone dikes.

To the south and west rose jumbled, craggy outlines of a half-dozen different mountain ranges mounded with chalk- or clay-colored boulders and spiked with saguaros and nearly every other cactus native to the Sonoran Desert.

Ridges of all angles, heights, and pitches rolled up against each other and extended out away from each other in a cosmic mess of ancient, plowed-up dirt, sand, and rock. Even the most veteran of reclusive, crafty desert rats would have a hard time matching all the peaks with their respective ranges.

Somewhere out here, however, was the Black Puma Mountains in which the lawmen had been murdered. Longarm just hoped Big Frank and Ranger Sanders's map wasn't a shovelful of bullshit. As he and Haven rode throughout that first day from Broken Jaw, all the ranges to the southwest appeared to be colored different shades of black or gray.

And none of them as far as he could tell looked anything like a puma.

Or, maybe if you stared at them long enough, they all did . . .

As what had become the norm for them, he and Haven did not speak much as they rode. They were each bound in testy silence.

Only after they stopped for the night, when the sun was a red ball impaled by a high, arrow-shaped western peak, did Longarm say, "Not much grub. You gather firewood, and I'll scout around, see if I can't scare up a jackrabbit, maybe a javelina."

"Hold on."

"Huh?"

She'd just finished tending her horse and hobbling it so it couldn't wander far from the canyon they'd stopped in. Now she swept a flap of her duster back behind the handle of her right LeMat, and strode off through the brush. She walked soundlessly, Longarm noticed. No easy trick if you weren't Apache.

He scowled after her. Finally, deciding she'd merely drifted off to tend nature, he formed rocks into a fire ring and gathered some mesquite branches, piling them all next to the ring. Dry mesquite burned quickly, so he'd wait and build the fire after he had something beside Arbuckles to cook.

He started to slide his Winchester from the saddle sheath he'd leaned against a tree with his other gear, when a bang-bang! sounded, startling the horses. Longarm snapped his head up and his gun from the boot, looking around as the reports bounced off the rocky ridges.

Tossing the empty sheath aside, he racked a shell into the Winchester's breech but off-cocked the hammer when foot-steps sounded. She was moving toward him through the mesquites lining a small, dry spring at the southern edge of their camp. As she came closer, he saw that she held a snake down low by her side, the diamondback's rattles trailing along the ground and making a faint rattling sound that always made his short hairs bristle even when he knew the snake was dead.

She held up the snake, still writhing in death, and said without expression. "Supper."

"Holy shit."

She glanced at him as she walked over to where she'd deposited her saddlebags and her carpetbag. "You don't like snake?"

"I got nothin' against rattler. Tastes like chicken. Just never figured you to like it." Longarm chuckled as he picked up his rifle sheath. "How'd you know that was out there?"

"Slithered across the trail in front of us as we rode into the canyon. You didn't see it?" She'd pulled a sheathed skinning knife out of her saddlebags, and now she knelt by a flat-topped rock and began cutting the snake's head off.

Longarm shook his head in amazement. Would she ever stop surprising him? "Well, why don't I gather that firewood," he said whimsically and strode off into the brush.

He returned a few minutes later and built a fire over which Haven cooked a right tasty rattlesnake stew with a potato and a carrot she'd bought in Broken Jaw and spiced with jerky and dried chili peppers. They washed the meal down with coffee, and then Longarm gathered a little more firewood, in case they needed it later in the night, and took a short stroll around their camp with his Winchester.

It was good dark, stars offering the only light. When he was relatively certain they were alone out here, and that the pretty woman hadn't picked up more admirers since they'd ridden out of Broken Jaw, he spread his bedroll and rolled up in it.

She drifted off to tend nature, then came back to sit by the fire and pour herself one more cup of coffee.

She sat back against a boulder near the fire, and stared pensively off into the darkness beyond the sphere of wan, orange firelight. Longarm stared at her from beneath the brim of his hat, which he'd tipped down to just above his eyes.

"Tell me about yourself, Agent Delacroix," he said as the fire popped and snapped to his left.

She looked at him as though faintly surprised he was still awake.

"Why the interest?"

Longarm sighed and closed his eyes. "Never mind."

He willed himself asleep but before he could get there, she said softly, so that he could just barely hear her above the fire's crackling and the sporadic yammering of a coyote. "I was born in Maryland. My family is wealthy. Civilized and wealthy. We're descendants of the French painter, Delacroix, whom I'm sure you've never heard of."

"He teach you how to shoot rattlesnakes?"

Her voice owned the timber of strained patience. "He's dead. Long dead."

"What's your family's business?"

"They deal in rare art and antiquities, when they deal in anything. For the most part, they entertain and they travel . . . and they enjoy the finer things in life. They educate themselves. They're good people, though. Not spoiled. They give money to the poor."

Longarm poked his hat brim up onto his head and rose onto his elbows, scowling at her skeptically. "If you came from all that, how in hell did you end up out West, workin' for the Pinkertons?"

"None of that was enough for me. I've always had an adventurous edge. When I completed finishing school, I fell in love with a wonderful young man. But . . . I just couldn't marry him. I'm not sure why. My heart fairly boiled with the need to see the world, to experience the world on a grand if often violent scale."

She looked at him, the fire dancing in her hazel eyes. "I know it probably doesn't make sense. I wouldn't expect anyone else to understand. Someday, when I'm ready, I'll return home and take up life where I left it there . . . educating myself and entertaining and appreciating art and ancient relics from the Greeks and Romans. I'll travel to Greece and Turkey, and my beau and I will marry in Paris."

"You stay in communication with him?"

She studied the fire thoughtfully, shook her head. "No."

"How do you know he's waitin'?"

"Oh, I know." Her mouth corners lifted a confident smile.

Longarm studied her for a time, puzzled by her, fascinated. "Where'd you pick up the habit of invitin' strange men to your rooms?"

Her cheeks darkened slightly, and her eyes regarding the wavering flames were slightly abashed. But only slightly. "A girl gets lonely."

"Only strangers?"

She looked at him, vaguely puzzled.

"You only sleep with strangers." He was playing a hunch, but only a slight one. "Anonymously. Never sleep with men you know. Why is that, Agent Delacroix?"

Her voice hardened a little, defensively. "It's simpler."

"Kind of risk-free, too—ain't it? No risk of you tumblin' for the fella. No risk of him tumblin' for you. This way you can sort of stay undercover all the time, even in your real life." Longarm smiled his perplexity. "What're you afraid of, Haven? What're you runnin' from?"

Her brows stitched. "What're you talking about? I don't run from anything! I run *toward* things!"

Longarm nodded thoughtfully as he watched her. "That was you outside my door last night, wasn't it? Before your admirers showed up with their shotguns."

She held his gaze. Her lips opened slightly.

Then she sat back a little, crossed her arms on her belly, and leaned toward the fire as if she'd suddenly become chilled, though the day's heat lingered. Her cheeks had flushed again, and he thought her chest rose and fell more heavily.

"Ain't no doors out here, Haven."

"What's that supposed to mean?" she asked crisply.

"No doors, no walls."

"You believe in mixing business and pleasure?" Now her voice was haughty with reprimand.

"When the sun goes down, I figure I'm off duty."

She sighed and raised her knees. She wrapped her arms around her legs, rested her chin on her knees, and stared into the fire. Since the conversation appeared to be over, Longarm pulled his hat brim down over his eyes and drew a deep breath to try to rid his mind of the image of her naked and writhing beneath him.

But then she said just as softly as before, "I'd like to suck your cock again, damn you."

Chapter 18

Just then one of the horses whinnied.

If at anytime in his life Longarm would have done something as melodramatic as to shake his fist and scream at the cosmos, it would have been then. Haven gasped and turned toward where they'd hobbled the beasts in the near wash, to her right and behind her.

Longarm bit out a curse and gained his feet, his Colt already in his right fist, the hammer cocked. His heart thudded not from fear but from the soft echo in his head of her last words to him, just before she'd started to crawl toward him.

And then the fucking horse had whinnied.

"Stay here," he said softly, stepping wide around the fire, careful not to kick their gear.

Quietly, he stepped through some scraggly mesquite and willows lining the wash and saw the dark shadows of the horses standing before him, head to toe, both switching their tails. Longarm's own horse faced him, but it was craning its neck to look behind, in the direction in which Haven's steeldust was staring, twitching its ears.

"Easy," Longarm whispered, running a hand down along

roan's back as he moved up past it and into the mouth of a smaller feeder wash angling off to the south.

He pricked his ears, listening closely to what the night had to tell him. There was nothing but the yammering of distant coyotes, the hooting of an owl, and the occasional murmur of a vagrant breeze scratching branches together, buffeting slim desert leaves.

He walked several yards into the narrow wash and stopped when he was halfway around a bend. A mewling sounded before him, startling him and causing him to tighten his trigger finger, but he stopped short of firing.

Two coyote-shaped shadows were milling around before him.

One turned its head toward him. Longarm could see the pointed ears and the starlight glistening in one of its eyes. The coyote gave a deep, feral growl and then yipped sharply, frustrated, and wheeled and thrashed some mesquite branches.

Both night hunters were both gone just as suddenly as Longarm had come upon them.

He moved forward and found what had lured them here. A dead fawn. Or what was left of it. They might have dragged it here or found it here, likely carried here by the spring floodwaters.

Longarm walked back the two, still-edgy horses, patting them both to silence, and then returned to the camp. Haven stood at the edge of the firelight, looking toward him, her arms crossed on her chest, her LeMats in her hands, their barrels resting against her shoulders.

"Anything?"

"Coyote." Longarm had holstered his own Colt. He stopped in front of her, looked down at her. "Now, where were we?"

She stared up at him. As far as he could tell in the darkness, with the fire behind her, her face wore no expression whatever.

Slowly, she uncrossed her arms, shoved her LeMats down into their holsters slung low on her curving, slender hips. She unbuckled her cartridge belt and set it down with her gear near the fire, and then turned to him and kicked out of her boots before beginning to unbutton her blouse.

Longarm stood staring at her, his muscles having turned to stone. His heart thudded. And then as she removed her blouse to show a thin, pink chemise beneath, her nipples poking hard against the sheer fabric, he quickly unbuckled his own cartridge belt, swiped his hat off his head, and kicked out of his boots.

He was naked in under a minute. She was a little slower, more methodical, but she soon stood naked before him, beside the fire, which burnished the near side of her body with copper, casting shadow over the other half. Her breasts were dark cones jutting toward him.

Longarm walked toward her, his cock hard and angling nearly straight up.

He stopped before her, until the head of his cock was touching her warm, flat belly. The feel of her flesh against his shaft caused excitement to ripple up the backs of his legs. She wrapped both hands around it lightly.

"Wait," she said in a soft, raspy voice.

She walked over and retrieved his brown frock coat, brought it back, and spread it on the ground in front of him. She knelt on the coat, so that her head was a foot away from his cock, and then she wrapped her arms around his legs, and placed her hands on his buttocks.

He heard a very faint wet crackling when she parted her lips and moved her head forward. It was dark between them so he couldn't see well down past his belly, and he sucked a sharp breath when he felt her tongue touch the head of his cock. He held his breath when she slid her tongue up over the orifice and across the top of the swollen, throbbing head.

Swirling her tongue slowly, she licked every inch of the head of his cock, bathing it in her hot saliva.

After several minutes of this harrowing torture, which he endured with his fists clenched at his sides, heels grinding into the sandy ground under his bare feet, she closed her mouth over the head. Soft warmth engulfed him. He tightened his jaws. Moving her head toward his crotch, she slid her mouth with excruciating slowness down the length of him toward his balls.

When he could feel his cock in the tightness of her throat, she stopped, gagged, jerking her head and shoulders slightly, but held him there taut against her tonsils. He could feel her saliva trickling down from her mouth and warming nearly ever inch of him lodged in her throat.

She squirmed and groaned and then slid her mouth back and off him, drawing a deep, liquid breath, gasping and pumping him with one hand while she gazed up at him.

"So big. You're so fucking big."

Longarm groaned.

She continued to pump him slowly with her soft, gentle hands while she gazed up at him from her knees, her eyes showing blue-green in the starlight. "I've thought about that night in Leadville many times. I'm going to think about it many times more before I die. You're the most man I've ever had."

She kissed his cock, caressed it with her cheek and then cupped his heavy balls in both her hands, staring up at him once more. "It was the most satisfying experience I've ever had with any man. The awful thing about it, though, is that it's all I can think about now. I keep wanting to be so completely filled again. That's why I've been so . . . moody. I haven't meant to be, Custis. Can I call you Custis?"

She seemed to be waiting for an answer to the question.

He said, "Don't see why not," in a pinched voice, grinding his heels back into the sand while she hefted his balls in her hands and sucked the head of his cock with passion, groaning.

She pulled her mouth off him with a slight popping sound and smacked her lips together, drawing a breath between her wet, shiny lips. "It's just that I've never had such complete pleasure, and this need for it again . . . and again . . . and again . . ." She shook her head as though deeply confounded. "I just don't understand it. It frightens me!"

"No need to be afraid."

"I think I want to finish blowing you. I want to feel your hot seed in my throat. And then will you fuck me from behind . . . like last time? Like a couple of back-alley curs?"

"Sure."

"And then, let's please not speak of this, okay?"

He frowned down at her. Every nerve was leaping inside of him, his heart beating slowly, heavily, his pulse throbbing in his temples.

Christ almighty, he'd never known a woman to talk this much!

"I'd just rather not speak of it, no matter what happens again between us in the future." Haven ran her tongue up from the base of his cock to the tip, and then slid her mouth off of him, causing his cock to bob against her cheek. "Will that be all right, Custis?"

"Fine, fine," he said through a moan, fearing he would pass out before she could finish him.

She smiled, slitting her eyes devilishly, and then swallowed him again, gagging on him, and then sliding her mouth back to the head of his cock.

Back down again. Back. Down.

Back.

Down.

Faster.

Longarm's knees turned to putty. He groaned, placed his hand on the girl's head as she rammed it back and forth against his belly. His cock seemed to grow though it couldn't possibly get any larger without exploding.

And then he ground his molars till he thought they'd turn

to dust, arched his back, threw his hips forward, and fired off his load until he thought he could hear the Gatling gun–like reports echoing around the canyon.

She drank every drop.

She gagged on it, but she very dutifully held her mouth down as far as she could, and took every bit of his seed that he let geyser down past her tonsils. When her face turned red and she began convulsing from lack of air, she swallowed one more time. He groaned at the pleasurable feeling of her throat contracting against his nearly spent organ. Falling back on her butt, propped on her arms outstretched behind her, she drew a ragged breath, panting as she smiled up at him.

"Now, that was fun."

Longarm's knees buckled. He dropped in the dirt before her. He, too, panted, feeling his cock droop though there was still some desire there. That's how special this gal was. She could drink him dry and still he was ready to take her again.

Her breasts spilled back against her chest, bulging out across her ribs, her nipples jutting. He leaned down and kissed each in turn and then he rose, picked her up in his arms, and lay her down on his bedroll, resting her head back against his saddle.

"Already?" she said, looking up at his face and then down at his cock.

"No." Longarm shook his head. "Not yet. First . . ." He reached into his saddlebags and pulled out his travel flask. "First, a drink."

He offered her the flask. To his surprise, she took it, took a pull, then another pull. She tipped her head back like a bird, swallowing, and smacked her lips. "Tastes good mixed with your come."

Longarm's ears fairly burned at the change in this girl from earlier in their journey. She'd become the lusty nymphomaniac he'd met back in Leadville. He liked the change in her, couldn't imagine her being any other way now.

Chuckling, he took a long pull from the flask, offered it to her once more. When she shook her head, he hammered the cork back into the mouth with the heel of his hand, set it down against his saddle, and lay down beside her.

She crawled over him to lie between his legs, resting her back against his chest, placing his hands on her breasts.

They lay there together, snuggling against each other, exploring each other's intimate parts gently, slowly, not saying anything. She was more intoxicating than any forty-rod that Longarm had ever drunk—more intoxicating than the explosive *tiswin* the Apaches imbibed in to work themselves up for war.

The fire had gone out.

She reached over and tossed a mesquite branch on the glowing, crackling coals, saying, "I want to see our shadows when you fuck me from behind like a dirty dog, Custis."

"Well, this dirty dog's ready to get to it," he said, drawing her back onto the blankets and gentling her belly down against them. He wrapped his arms around her waist and pulled her up onto her knees.

"Custis?"

"What?"

"Have no mercy."

"Never, Haven."

Longarm shoved his cock into her gaping, waiting pussy. Soon their shadows were jouncing wildly on the ground beside the fire. Both were aware enough of where they were to not make a lot of noise beside the muffled grunts and groans of coupling coyotes, lest someone should hear.

Then they slept entangled in each other's arms.

Chapter 19

Longarm awoke the next morning feeling as though he'd tangled with seven bobcats in the back of a covered wagon.

He slid out from beneath Haven, who slept naked beneath the two wool blankets of his hot roll, and dressed quietly in the predawn darkness. He rummaged around in the brush for more dry wood and laid a new fire.

When he dropped a branch atop the building flames, Haven lifted her head from his saddle with a gasp, clutching her blankets to her breasts, her eyes sharp with fear between tangles of her lustrous brown hair.

"Easy," he said, holding up one hand, palm out. "Just me."

She did not blink but continued to stare at him as though he were a bear that had wandered into her camp. The fear was slow to fade. When it did, her pale cheeks were touched with the pink of embarrassment, and then she rose quickly, holding his blankets around her luscious body, and gathered her clothes.

When she had them all, she tramped off into the mesquites to dress in private.

Longarm got out his pot and made coffee, casting speculative glances at the mysterious creature in the mesquites beyond him. He'd never known a girl quite like her, and he had a feeling there was plenty more to her story than what she'd shared last night.

"Looks like it's going to be another hot day," she said, throwing her hair out from her shirt collar when she returned from the brush, dressed and carrying his blanket roll neatly tied. She looked around and he saw that the earlier, mysterious fear was gone from her eyes, the old Haven Delacroix returned.

At least, the day one.

Very odd how she could be one person during the day, nearly the opposite one at night.

As they ate jerky and biscuits for breakfast and drank coffee, they said little, and what they did say in no way referenced the night before. They discussed the route to the dead lawmen's graves, and they discussed the missing gold and who might have taken it, and where they might find water out here, and that was all. It was almost, Longarm thought, as though they had not coupled like wolves only a few hours ago.

As though theirs were only a cool, impersonal, professional relationship.

Which was fine with him. Odd. But fine.

He did, however, feel compelled to say later, as they finished saddling their horses with the sun nearly up, "Since we're partnered up an' all, Haven . . . I mean, Agent Delacroix . . . you can tell me anything you want, you know. Anything you might want to get off your chest." He draped his saddlebags over the roan's back and looked at her over his saddle. "Just so's you know."

He meant that she could tell him why she'd had such fear in her eyes when she'd first seen him this morning, after their rare, erotic intimacy of the night before.

She took her steeldust's reins and swung into the leather, the saddle squawking beneath her, looking at him with a faint, appreciative smile, the smile of a stranger passing on the street. "Why, thank you, Marshal Long. I do appreciate that, I guess . . ."

She reined away and nudged her horse with her heels.

Longarm chuffed softly, curiously, and swung up onto the roan's back. He followed Agent Delacroix to the old Indian trail they'd been following, and then she held up to allow him to take the lead. He was the one with the map, and as they rode throughout the morning, he consulted the plat frequently, looking around at the changing terrain. It was hard to tell because of the sketchiness of the map and all the various formations sliding around him, but he believed that they were in, or nearly in, the Black Puma Mountains.

They rode between two low, shelving mesas and then dropped into a broad canyon, and suddenly he reined the roan up beside a trail that curved out of the desert on his left and swept off into the desert to his right, disappearing into the humped shapes of what he took to be the Black Pumas. Off the far side of the trail about a hundred yards appeared to be a wash.

When he and Haven had ridden up to the wash, they swung east and rode along the arroyo's sandy bottom for another hundred yards when he heard a low growling up the southern bank on his right. He put the roan up the bank, stopped the horse, cursed, and slid his Winchester out of its scabbard.

Ahead, lay five mounded graves backed with wooden crosses constructed of driftwood branches tied together with rawhide. Two of the crosses were tipped over, resting on their sides. One coyote sat a ways back from the graves, shifting its weight between its front paws and watching another that stood beside one of the rock mounds, tugging and growling at what looked like a piece of red cloth, trying to pull it out from beneath the rocks.

As Haven rode up behind him, Longarm levered a cartridge into the Winchester's breech, and planted a bead on the coyote tugging on the cloth. He dropped the sights and fired, pluming rock dust up from in front the coyote. Both carrion eaters wheeled and ran off through the brush, casting worried, angry looks behind them.

"Good God," Haven said as Longarm swung down from his saddle.

There'd been no point in killing the beasts, for they were only doing what they were naturally inclined to do. As he walked up to the five graves, he saw that what the coyote had been tugging on was a red calico shirtsleeve. What appeared to be a hand protruded from above the sleeve, two of the fingers missing, leaving a thumb and the body's ring finger on which was a gold wedding band ground deep into the swollen flesh around it. The sleeve was badly torn, held together by threads.

Longarm heaved a sigh as he inspected the graves. He wished he had a shovel with which to properly rebury the hand, but he did not. Besides, there was little point. The ground around the graves was a maze of padded footprints, and a foot-deep hole had been dug along one of the graves. There was a hungry pack of brush wolves around here, and they'd probably eventually get to the carrion slouched beneath the rocks.

The men were dead. Now they were food. Just the way it worked.

Longarm looked around at the rocky desert tufted with Spanish bayonet and greasewood, the occasional saguaro and pipestem cactus, as though probing the terrain for the ghosts of the dead men who might be able to suggest who had killed them and why. Haven reined her steeldust around the graves and stopped a few yards away.

"Where were they killed?" she asked.

"A few yards east of where they're buried."

As Haven dismounted, he rode over and joined her, swinging down from the roan's back. She was down on one knee, swinging her head from left to right, scanning the scuffed ground.

There were more coyote tracks here, bird tracks, as well

as several shod hoofprints and men's boot impressions. The
men from Whip Azrael's Double D Ranch had been here,
as well as the dead men themselves . . . when they were still
alive . . . and the killer or killers.

Impossible to separate the tracks of the killers from the
killed and then from those of the men who'd buried the
fallen. There were several brown patches that were likely
blood.

Haven dropped her horse's reins and walked around for
a time, quietly scanning the terrain, the breeze blowing her
duster out away from her hips. Finally, at the southern edge
of the tracks and scuffmarks, she turned to Longarm and
hooked her gloved thumbs behind her cartridge belt. "If only
the rocks could talk."

Longarm was feeling the same frustration, realizing the
long odds of ever finding answers to the questions that had
driven him and her down here.

Five men were dead. He'd known none of them, but Sanders had told him they were all good lawmen. The marshals
had just happened to be visiting the ranger post when Big
Frank Three Wolves had told his story, so they'd ridden
down here on a whim with the rangers.

Apparently, there were no witnesses to the killings. There
was some stolen gold buried around here. Whether it was
still here was anyone's guess. The gold might or might not
be the reason the three rangers and two federal lawmen had
been murdered—gunned down where they'd been riding,
apparently. Ambushed.

Yet another question pecked at Longarm's brain.

Where were Captain Jack Leyton and Ranger Matt Sullivan, who'd ridden down here after the murders to investigate? So far, he'd spied no sign of them.

Had they gotten this far?

"Where did Big Frank say the gold was buried?" Haven
asked, addressing her main concern.

Longarm looked past her to a rise of chalky hills to the

south, on the other side of what appeared another rock-strewn dry wash. "Over there. In one of those creases between the camelbacks. Santana told Big Frank it was between the two biggest humps, near a saguaro and a flat-topped boulder. Atop the boulder, one of Santana's bunch carved a large 'X,' though that 'X' might be worn away by now, since they were here all of a decade ago."

She turned to appraise the bluffs that looked bleached out in the midday light, then turned to Longarm and extended a hand toward the hot, dry-looking formations. "Shall we?"

"Why not?"

He stepped into his saddle and booted the roan across the rocky flat toward the broad wash running along the base of the far buttes. The wash was only slightly lower than the ground he now crossed, and delineated by a few ragged, dusty mesquites and cottonwoods, a few wind-twisted paloverdes. Haven's horse clomped up from behind him, and she rode up beside him on his left.

Birds cheeped in the chaparral around them. There was a streak of red as a roadrunner dashed out from behind a barrel cactus to cross in front of the riders and then disappear in a nest of bone-white boulders piled like a fallen house of cards.

Longarm's attention was drawn to a dark speck atop one of the hills growing larger before him, on the other side of the wash. Squinting, his keen vision revealed what appeared a steeple-crowned sombrero hovering over a rifle barrel extended in Longarm's and Agent Delacroix's general direction.

Longarm threw himself to his left, turning enough that his chest rammed Haven's right shoulder as he kicked free of his stirrups. Sweeping the girl out of her own saddle, they flew down her horse's left stirrup at the same time that what sounded like a distant cannon thundered.

Twisting yet again, Longarm landed on his back, drawing

Haven down on top of him, cushioning the girl's fall, and saw dust blow up about twenty yards straight behind them, the heavy slug screeching as it ricocheted off a rock.

The horses continued walking straight ahead and then, realizing they were without riders, stopped and sort of half turned, reins dangling.

Longarm pushed Haven away from him, yelling, "Take cover!"

She wasted no time scrambling to her feet and then running toward a table-sized rock. Wincing at the ache in his back from his hard tumble to the ground, Longarm scrambled to his own feet as the rocketing blast of the heavy-caliber rifle sounded again, this slug tearing up rocks and sand only a foot in front of him. He jerked to his right and lunged for his horse, which was fiddle-footing nervously now, and shucked his Winchester from his saddle boot.

"Get outta here!" he yelled at the horse, smashing the rifle's butt against its left wither.

He sent the horse running off in similar fashion, both sets of reins bouncing along the ground, and then ran toward where Haven was hunkered down behind the rock.

The big gun thundered again, the slug hammering the ground about two feet from Longarm's pounding boots. Haven triggered one of her LeMats twice over the top of the rock, and Longarm hunkered down beside her, doffing his hat and edging a look over the rock toward the shooter.

"Don't waste your bullets," Longarm told the girl. "He's way out of range of a handgun."

"I know that," she said snidely. "I was just trying to distract him so he wasn't as likely to blow your head off."

"Thanks."

"Don't mention—"

The thunderous *whonk* of another heavy chunk of lead crashing into the ground a few feet in front of their boulder cut her off. It was followed a half second later by the explosion of the rifle.

"A Big Fifty, you think?" she asked.

"I think." Longarm peeked over the top of the rock, saw the silhouetted figure on the bluff eject the spent shell casing from the Sharps' breech.

He nudged her arm with the butt of his Winchester. "You know how to shoot one of these?"

"Of course. I just don't carry one because I like to travel light and I usually have more use for my brains than bullets." As the Big Fifty boomed again, she flinched and pulled her head down lower behind the rock. "In the future, I might reconsider."

He held the long gun out to her. "Cover me. I'm going to try to run on up on him, get around him, find out what in the hell he's so hot about."

Haven holstered her LeMats, took Longarm's Winchester, and smoothly racked a fresh cartridge into the breech.

He paused to wonder vaguely she'd acquired her facility with the weapon, and then handed her five extra cartridges from his belt loops. He slid his Colt from its holster. Looking over the top of the boulder once more, he saw the rifle-wielding, sombrero-clad ambusher hunkered low over his Sharps. Longarm pulled his head down as the big gun hammered another round, this one smashing into the rock behind which Longarm and Haven were hunkered.

Longarm felt the vibration through his shoulder.

Knowing the man had to eject the spent casing and slide a fresh .50-90 cartridge into the breech, he rose quickly and donned his hat.

"Keep him busy, but don't get your head shot off!"

She cast him a faintly worried look through the dark brown hair blowing around her face, and this gave him pause. He'd never seen her worried before—only frustratingly forthright and headstrong.

"Be careful, Custis," she said. "That's a big damn gun."

Chapter 20

Longarm took off running toward the wash and the hills beyond.

Haven began firing the Winchester behind him. She was probably a good two hundred yards away from the man, shooting uphill, so the Winchester would be hard-pressed to hit its target even with an expert squeezing the trigger. But her shots blew up dust along the slope below the man, causing him to jerk his head down behind the rise he was lying against.

Longarm ran hard, tracing a zigzagging pattern in case the man opened up on him again. A Big Fifty could shoot upward of a thousand yards, and the .50-caliber cartridges loaded with ninety grains of black powder, designed for penetrating a thick buffalo hide, would punch a fist-sized hole in a man.

Longarm made it across the wash with the ambusher triggering only two rounds well behind him, while Haven was apparently reloading the Winchester. Longarm ran to the base of one of the hills, hunkered low, and looked up over his left shoulder, holding his Colt straight up in his right hand.

He couldn't see the ambusher from this angle, but the bastard was near. Longarm waited.

The man had stopped shooting. Longarm looked out to where Haven crouched behind the rock. He could see only his rifle barrel poking up from behind the rock, but he knew she was keeping an eye on him.

He waved his gun hand broadly, indicating she should hold fire, and then he slipped into a crease between the hill directly behind him and the next one to the west—the one on which the ambusher lay. The gap was about twenty yards wide, stippled with brush and rocks.

A rattlesnake rattled at him from atop a flat rock, lifting its button tail as well as it flat, diamond-shaped head, sticking out its forked tongue. Longarm swung wide of the rock and turned and began climbing the ambusher's hill, keeping an eye out for more snakes.

All he needed on top of getting ambushed was a load of the excruciatingly painful viper venom. If that happened, in minutes he'd be begging the ambusher to finish him.

He climbed the steep slope, his boot heels slipping in the chalky soil, using his free hand to grab clumps of short grass and shrub branches to steady his progress. When he gained the crest, he doffed his hat, peered down the opposite side, and cursed.

The ambusher was galloping at a slant up the next hill beyond, his black-and-white pinto working hard against the steep climb, lunging off its short rear legs. The rider was too far away for the Colt, but Longarm couldn't help squeezing off a desperate round.

The slug blew up rock dust well below the rider, when the man was about twenty yards below the crest of the next hill. Gravel crunched behind Longarm. In the corner of his left eye, a shadow moved.

He swung around to see a big Mexican moving up on him, holding two Schofields in his hands, the barrels aimed at Longarm's belly.

The man's face was the texture of ancient, black leather. His eyes were washed-out blue, one more than the other, and his two yellow front teeth were chipped. He wore a black sombrero, but his hat was lower crowned than his friend's. He was dressed nearly all in black except for a brown-and-red calico shirt beneath his black vest, and he wore bandoliers crisscrossed on his chest, two empty holsters held up high above his hips and positioned for the cross draw.

"Are you prepared for death, *mi* amigo?" the man said, as he came up level with Longarm and placed his thumbs on his pistol hammers, preparing to rock them back. He squinted his eyes though they didn't seem to focus. Bad eyesight, Longarm thought.

Suddenly, there was a smacking sound, and the man's head tipped sharply to his left. His face crumpled in a deep scowl, and he triggered one of his Schofields into the ground. At the same time, the crack of a rifle reached Longarm's ears, and the would-be assassin staggered sideways, dropping the pistol he'd fired and reaching out with that hand as though to grab something with which to break his fall.

He didn't find it.

He fell hard and rolled onto his back, eyelids fluttering as life left him.

Quickly, his limbs and lids fell still, and he lay staring straight up at Longarm through his washed-out blue eyes, arms thrown out to both sides, legs slightly bent so that the rowels of his spurs touched. Blood leaked out the ragged hole in his right temple and dribbled onto the gravelly ground. The bullet must have exited the back of his head, behind his left ear, because the ground there was quickly growing red, as well.

Longarm turned back toward the west. The other rider had stopped his pinto on the opposite hillcrest, and he was facing Longarm now, clearly outlined in black against the sky. He stared toward the lawman and his dead partner, and then he swung his horse around and dropped down the far side of the hill and galloped out of sight.

Longarm turned toward where the shot had come from.

Agent Delacroix was walking across the broad, pale wash. She held the lawman's Winchester on her shoulder. She kept her head down, likely watching for snakes, as she long-strode toward the hill and the man she'd left dead at Longarm's boots.

"Nice shot," he told her as she climbed the hill.

As she approached the crest of the hill, between strained breaths, she said, "The other one?"

"Gone." Longarm knelt beside the dead man, patted his pockets, finding nothing but a small roll of Mexican greenbacks, a sack of chopped Mexican tobacco that smelled like pepper, stripped corn shucks for rolling, two knives in small sheaths, and ammunition.

Lots of ammunition.

There was nothing that identified him personally.

"A killer," Longarm said. "A hired one, most likely. Wonder if whoever hired him knew his eyes were bad?"

"What would he be doing out here? He couldn't have known we were coming."

"Maybe he works for this Azrael feller who owns the ranch he's on. Nothin' to do but to ask him." Longarm rose and looked around. "His horse must be around here somewhere. When we find it, we'll tie him to it and haul him over to the Double D headquarters."

Haven stood looking around, her hair and her duster billowing in the hot breeze. "While there's still some light left, I'd like to look around here for the gold."

"Might as well, though I doubt we're gonna find it."

"You never know. Big Frank might have it right."

Longarm had just found too many holes in the story about the gold to believe that was true. Not that Big Frank had been lying. Santana was likely the liar. If the Mexican really had hid the gold here, the chance of it still being found here was damn slim.

Longarm found himself scrutinizing his partner admiringly. "That was a damn tough shot from that distance," he said. "How'd you make it, anyways?"

"Why are you so surprised?"

"'Cause you're a girl."

He'd meant it as a joke, because she could obviously shoot her LeMats as well, and as willingly, as most men. She hadn't seen the humor in the remark, however, and brandished a narrow-eyed look as she shoved his rifle at him, barrel-first. He took it, and watched her walk down the hill and into the crease in which Big Frank said that Santana's gang had buried the gold.

Longarm mentally kicked his own ass. "When are you gonna learn to keep your whiskey funnel closed, old son?"

After looking around carefully to make sure the first shooter hadn't circled back around to wreak more havoc with his Sharps Big Fifty, Longarm followed his partner into the crease between the hills. The bottom was a dry watercourse dropping from a high ridge, the top of which he couldn't see from his vantage, for the chasm twisted between high, stony walls.

He could see why Santana had led his men in here when the Apaches had attacked them—there were plenty of strewn boulders offering cover. They'd likely buried the gold in one of the many nooks and crannies amongst the rocks, and then either fought their way out of the chasm or rode on up and over the pass to safety on the eastern side.

"Remember, you're looking for a boulder with a large 'X' scratched into it."

"I remember," the girl said with her customary strained tolerance.

"Just remindin' ya."

"Thank you," she said as she continued walking up the watercourse, swinging her head from right to left and back again, scrutinizing every half-concealed pocket.

"Don't mention it." Longarm looked behind and between

several boulders. "Where did you say the gold was headed when the stage was hit?"

"A bank in Tucson."

"For what?"

"I don't believe it's in the report, was it?" she asked. "You read the same one I did. If my superiors know, they didn't share the information with me."

Longarm kept walking up the draw. "You sound testy. Was it the girl comment?"

She stopped and gave him a sidelong look, her eyes shaded from the blazing sun by her hat brim. "I could have told you that you have mighty poor hearing for a lawman, but I didn't, did I?"

"What's that supposed to mean?"

"You couldn't hear that killer walking up behind you?"

Longarm felt a colicky burn in his gut. "He musta been particularly quiet. Besides, I was hearing the thuds of the horse of that first hombre—the one with the buffalo cannon." He felt injured by her insult mostly because he knew she was right—he should have heard the second man walking up behind him, and he was damn lucky the man hadn't just shot him from a distance. "Remember, Miss Fancy Britches, I've saved your hide a time or two myself."

She stopped and looked back at him again, blinking slowly. "Once."

"Twice. Once in Jerkwater, once in Broken Jaw."

She laughed caustically. "I handled myself well both times!"

"Sure, but only because I culled the herd o' them that was gunnin' for ya. Only they wouldn't have gunned ya till they'd had their fun with you."

She turned to face him straight on from several yards up the rocky wash, between two boulders slanting like tables with missing legs. "Those were not the only two times men have tried to have their ways with me out here, Marshal Long. I'm accustomed to it. I expect it and am always prepared for it."

"Well, I'm glad you're always prepared to take on so many by your lonesome. Next time that many decide to skin your panties off your purty legs, I'll just let 'em!"

"Quit calling my legs 'purty'."

"Pretty, then. What's the difference?"

She raised her voice, and despite her usual restraint, it trembled slightly with barely controlled emotion. "I wasn't mocking your uncultivated mode of speaking just then. What I meant was, I'd rather you stopped speaking about my legs or any other part of my body."

"Your legs are damn purty, and I'll mention 'em any time if I feel I need to in the course of defending myself from your harangues, Agent Delacroix!"

Longarm stared down his arm and extended a finger at her, as though he were aiming a rifle barrel. His face was flushed. He felt it grow even hotter when she just stared at him with mild amusement and then chuckled with even more hilarity.

Shaking her head, she turned away and continued walking up the wash.

Longarm lowered his arm, feeling ridiculous. He'd let himself be lured into her female trap, had been made to look foolish. And, somehow—he wasn't quite sure how—she'd won the argument.

No wonder he had no intention of ever letting himself get hitched.

Well, since he couldn't get any more trapped than he was: "And your tits are mighty nice, too!"

She ignored him and kept walking. He stood in place for a time, let himself cool down despite the stifling heat burning through his hat to seer the top of his head, and then continued looking around at the rocks and boulders and clumps of tough, wiry brown brush.

He'd just inspected the purple shadows between two stacked boulders at the ravine's stony southern ridge, and was about to continue on up the wash, when he stopped suddenly. Haven stood at the far end of the stacked boulders, looking at him with a grim, meaningful cast to her gaze. She held her hands straight down at her sides.

"You come back to thank me for the compliment?" he asked her snidely.

She shook her head, took a step back, and half turned to indicate the wash beyond her. Longarm automatically brought his rifle down from his shoulder as he brushed past her and continued on up the draw, letting his right arm brush the side of the stacked boulders, and looked across their updraw side.

A man lay in the shadows, arms stretched nearly straight above his hatless head. His ankles and boots, worn to the color and texture of older moccasins, were crossed.

Longarm moved closer to the body, saw the thin, dark brown hair combed to the left, the ginger-colored eyes staring through half-closed lids. The man wore a grim smile on his mouth mantled with a brown, dragoon-style mustache. Around his neck was a bloody green neckerchief.

Behind the tightly wound cloth, a long, gaping wound shone. His throat had been cut. There didn't appear any other wounds.

Longarm heard Haven's boots on the gravel behind him, saw her shadow in the corner of his left eye. She came up beside him and stared down at the dead man.

Longarm looked at the Arizona Ranger's badge pinned to the man's cream cotton shirt, partly concealed by a suspender strap. "Matt Sullivan."

"Captain Leyton's likely around here somewhere, too."

Longarm doffed his hat and ran a weary, frustrated hand down his face. "Likely."

Haven dropped to a knee beside the dead man and pressed the back of her hand against his cheek with surprising tenderness. Her voice was matter-of-fact, however, when she said, "He hasn't been dead for more than an hour. Wasn't bushwhacked, though. Disarmed first, then killed. Your dead blind man must have slit his throat with one of those knives of his."

Longarm shook his head. "Damn. If we'd gotten here an hour earlier . . ."

Haven straightened. "Someone doesn't want anyone looking for that gold. Which must mean it's still here."

"Yeah, well, you worry about the gold. Me—I'm gonna worry about findin' out who killed Sullivan and the others. Jack Leyton, most likely, too."

"Since we're on Double D land . . ."

"Yeah, we'd best load up these dead men. I'm gonna go pay a visit to the Double D headquarters."

She scowled. "And *me*?"

"You best hole up out here. Not *right* here, but out here somewhere safe."

"I'm riding to the Double D headquarters with you, Marshal Long."

"No place for a woman. Specially one such as you." Longarm let his eyes flick to her breasts.

She gave him a blandly stubborn look, her eyes faintly smiling.

Longarm blew a long sigh, switching his gaze to the dead Matt Sullivan and then back to his partner.

There was no point in arguing with such a woman. "Then I hope you're ready for another fight, Miss Delacroix. A pitched battle, too, since ole Whip Azrael likely has a dozen or so men on his roll. Well-armed ones, too, judging by those we've met so far."

Chapter 21

Longarm and Agent Delacroix looked up and down the wash for Captain Jack Leyton and/or Ranger Sullivan's horse but saw no sign of either.

They did, however, find the horse of the man whom Haven had sent to heaven . . . or wherever pale-eyed bushwhackers went when they gave up the ghost. It was tethered in the crease between the hill on which the dead ambusher lay and the next rise south—the one over which the dead man's partner with the Big Fifty had fled.

Longarm tied both dead men over the back of the grullo gelding, which to Longarm's eye appeared to have some Spanish barb in it, owing to its deep flank, its short, strong loin and well-shaped head with liquid blue eyes. It wore no brand, but the lawman was still betting that the dead man was a Double D rider.

Maybe the horse had belonged to the dead man and was not part of the rancher's remuda. It didn't have to be.

If so, when Longarm delivered the dead man to the Double D headquarters, he'd likely find the man with the Big Fifty, too. He was looking forward to having a discussion with him as well as his boss, Whip Azrael. They had many things to discuss, Longarm and the rancher and the Big

Fifty–wielding ambusher. Including the gold, which Longarm and Haven had given up looking for after they'd found
the dead ranger.

It had been getting on in the day, and looking for the gold
up that twisting canyon was like looking for the proverbial
needle in a haystack, especially with the dark afternoon
shadows bleeding out from the stony walls.

Longarm and Agent Delacroix followed the stage road
running parallel to Defiance Wash up into higher country
marked by green foliage, including bunchgrass and gama
grass, growing amongst the craggy, sun-bleached bluffs and
mesas that Longarm assumed were part of the Black Puma
Mountains. In the late afternoon, they crested a pass
sheathed in pines and aspens, and the air was fresh and aro-
matic with the tang of pine resin and sage.

As they dropped down the pass, the wash became a shallow stream, the water looking lime green as it rippled over
the pale rocks between stands of trees and leafy shrubs.
After drinking, washing their faces, and refilling their canteens, they continued down the pass, dropping only for a
couple of miles before large, dark, formidable-looking peaks
appeared ahead, seeming to block the riders' westward
passage.

The stage road forked, one tine leading northwest around
a humpbacked jog of low mountains turning spruce green
and copper now in the west-angling light. The fork was
marked with a wooden arrow announcing: BENSON 45 MI.

The other tine meandered southwest toward the high, menacing black peaks. It was marked: AZRAEL DOUBLE D—3 MI.

Longarm and Haven took the southwest fork and they
soon found themselves in rolling, high-desert country, with
two riders dropping down out of the hills to the north. They
were coming fast and yelling, though Longarm couldn't hear
them above the clomping of the galloping mounts.

Stopping the roan as well as the barb that he trailed by
its bridle reins, Longarm slid his Winchester out of its boot,

cocked the weapon one-handed, and rested the barrel across his saddlebows. Haven glanced at him edgily as the two men galloped down out of the hills, their horses' thuds and snorts growing louder, pale dust rising.

They came through a crease between the last knobs and reined up in the trail before Longarm and Haven. They both wore bandanas over their sun-leathered faces and rough trail garb, a couple of pistols each. Sheathed carbines were strapped to their saddles, both of which wore the Double D brand on their left withers.

The lawman didn't say anything as the two men looked him and Haven over. Finally, one rode back behind Longarm and drew rein beside the barb. He looked at the two dead men and then at Longarm, who squeezed the neck of his cocked Winchester.

The Double D rider's eyes flicked to the rifle resting across Longarm's saddle.

"The Azraels don't cotton to company."

"They'll cotton to ours. I'm a deputy U.S. marshal, and she's a Pinkerton. One of the dead men behind me I'm guessin' is one of yours, in which case I got a bone to pick with Whip Azrael, because the stiff's partner tried to drill a fist-sized wad of lead through us both. The other's a dead Arizona Ranger. I'm guessin' he was killed by the same men."

The man behind Longarm rode back up to where his partner waited.

The two men conferred too quietly for Longarm to hear. After a minute, they regarded Longarm and Haven obliquely, jerked their chins toward the trail ahead, and then kicked their horses into dusty lopes.

Longarm glanced at Haven, cocking a brow, silently informing her that now was the time to hang back if she'd had a change of heart about riding into a possible vipers' nest. If she understood, she didn't let on. They both touched heels to their horse's flanks, heading up the trail and eating the dust of their guides.

After a half hour, a ranch portal appeared amongst the chaparral covering the relatively flat canyon bottom they were traversing. The Double D brand was burned into the portal's thick plank crossbar adorned with several sets of deer and elkhorns. Beside the portal stood another sign warning: STRANGERS UNWELCOME.

As he rode beneath the crossbar, trailing the barb and the dead men, Longarm saw the ranch headquarters sprawled along the trail that soon became a broad, dusty yard—the house on the left, bunkhouse and several other outbuildings including a couple of barns and a maze of interconnected corrals on the right. There was a round breaking corral on the near right, constructed of ocotillo branches.

Half a dozen men stood around the corral, leaning on the top poles and watching a hatless cowboy riding a bucking black bronc in hard-pounding circles. The onlookers, a couple of whom sat on the wide wooden gate, whooped and yelled and offered advice.

There were Anglos as well as Mexicans and one black man, who sat on a rock near the gate, a boot hiked on his knee, carefully building a quirley. He wore a red-and-white-checked shirt and sun-bleached sombrero. As the two strangers rode in with their guides, the black man half turned his head toward the others and moved his lips. The others swung their heads around to peer at the newcomers.

A shaggy dog with some German shepherd blood came running out from the direction of the house, barking wickedly and showing its fangs. A small, wizened figure in blue jeans walked out of a stone portal fronting the house and a shaded front patio and garden. A raspy voice of indeterminate sex yelled, "Rascal!" and the dog dropped instantly belly down on the ground but keeping its aggressive gaze on the strangers.

The denim-clad figure in a black shirt despite the heat, wearing a straw sombrero, continued to stride a little gimpily toward Longarm and Haven. The raspy, sexless voice said, "Who in the hell are you, and good Lord—what the hell are you packin', mister?"

One of the two guides canted his head at Longarm and said, "Law, Mrs. Azrael."

Missus, huh? Longarm thought he detected a couple of nubbin' breasts behind the black shirt and knotted red neckerchief, but the rest of the person looked all male. The face beneath the sombrero was like a giant raisin. Black hair was pulled back tight beneath the hat. Longarm thought that her head *might* come up to his cartridge belt, but only because of the high heels of her child-sized stockmen's boots.

"Who's he packin' on the hoss there?" Mrs. Azrael said, scrutinizing the barb with her coal-black eyes.

"Says one's a ranger."

"I'll speak for myself," Longarm said angrily. "One's a dead ranger. The other man I got a nagging suspicion is one of yours, Mrs. Azrael. He tried to kill me. The other tried to kill both myself and my partner, Agent Delacroix, with a buffalo gun."

He looked around the men now facing him from the corral. The bronc rider had dismounted and was watching from over the fence, the bronc standing slouched, reins drooping, its sides moving in and out as it breathed, in the corral's center.

"I'd like to palaver with the son of a bitch out in your wood shed," Longarm added. "Your husband, too, since he hired 'em."

Mrs. Azrael looked at the men standing by the breaking corral and said in her toneless, nasal wheeze: "Stretch!"

One of the men—tall, with a funnel-brimmed hat and pinto-hide vest—stepped away from the corral and walked over to the barb. He pulled the dead men's heads up by their hair, scrutinizing each slack face, then let the heads slap down against the barb's ribs.

Stretch turned to Mrs. Azrael and hooked his thumbs

behind the belt of his batwing chaps. "The ranger was here a few days ago. Him and the other one, Leyton. Askin' about the five we planted over on Defiance Wash. The other one, the Mex, I wouldn't know from Adam's off-ox."

"You never seen him before?" Longarm said skeptically.

Stretch turned his long face toward the lawman, scowling belligerently. "You heard me."

"Who around here carries a Big Fifty?"

"No one," Stretch said after a short, menacing pause, holding his glowering stare on the lawman.

Longarm could hear several of the other men speaking amongst themselves to his right. They were getting worked up. The black man sat on the rock, smoking and glaring toward the newcomers and their grisly cargo.

Longarm turned to Stretch, hooking his thumb over his shoulder. "That bastard and the one with the Big Fifty fired on us when we were on Double D range. Now, why would they do that?"

Stretch stepped toward Longarm, letting his arms hang loose at his sides. "You callin' me a liar?"

"Get your back down, Stretch," Mrs. Azrael said with an amused air, standing a few feet from Longarm with her fists on her hips. "If you're a lawman, how come I don't see a badge?"

"Badges make good targets. I keep mine in my wallet." Longarm reached into the inside pocket of his brown frock coat and pulled out the black wallet of worn cowhide.

He opened it up to reveal the old, tarnished moon-and-star badge he'd been carrying for years. Mrs. Azrael moved in closer to scrutinize the nickeled tin and then looked at Longarm with her black eyes set deep in leathery sockets. She looked past him at Haven.

"She's a Pinkerton?"

"That's right."

"A girl?"

Haven said affably, "Since gaining the age of twenty-three, I'd prefer to be called a woman."

That seemed to win the leathery ranch woman's heart. "Don't blame ya bit, miss. Don't blame ya a bit."

"I'm Long," Longarm said. "This is Agent Delacroix."

"You both look hot and dusty. Miss Delacroix, I bet you'd like to freshen up. Marshal Long, you look like you could use a drink."

Haven might have won the old ranch woman's heart, but Mrs. Azrael hadn't won his yet. "Mr. Azrael around?"

"Oh, he's around. Upstairs napping at the moment. I'll bring him down later, and you can talk to him for all the good you think it'll do." Mrs. Azrael beckoned. "Come on. Light and give them hosses a blow. You're too far out in the high an' rocky to head elsewhere this late in the day. You're welcome to spend the night here at the Double D, and we'll do what we can to answer your questions, though somethin' tells me you're not gonna ride out of here any more satisfied than that dead ranger and Captain Leyton were two days ago."

Longarm swung down from his saddle, and Mrs. Azrael called for a few of the other men to tend the horses and to bury the two cadavers. The lawman had just started to follow Mrs. Azrael and Haven toward the ranch house, when Stretch stepped up to Longarm and said tightly, "Just so's you know, lawman or not, I don't like bein' called a liar."

Longarm half turned in time to see a fist arcing toward his face. He ducked, and Stretch's right fist swiped Longarm's hat from his head.

Stretch grunted, his pugnacious face acquiring a surprised look. It grew even more surprised when Longarm buried his own right fist in Stretch's belly and then smashed an uppercut against the underside of Stretch's chin that was carpeted in a light brown spade beard to match the mustache mantling his long, thin-lipped mouth.

Stretch toppled like a windmill in a midwestern twister, dust billowing.

Mrs. Azrael laughed behind Longarm. She sounded like a whipsaw chewing on a horseshoe. "There you go, Stretch! Now look what you done!"

The ranch woman laughed again, thoroughly satisfied, it appeared, with the state of the man whom Longarm assumed was her foreman. "I told you to get that hump out of your neck, ya damn tinhorn!"

Chapter 22

On his ass in the dirt and ground horse shit of the ranch yard, propped on his elbows, Stretch glowered up at Longarm. Bright diamonds of threat danced in his eyes.

Mrs. Azrael laughed and said, "Come on inside, Marshal. I do apologize for my ramrod's inhospitality. He's a firebrand, that one!"

Longarm picked up his hat and glanced once more at Stretch. The other men had moved up closer to the house, some of them taking fighting stances in case the dustup between Longarm and Stretch wasn't finished. Stretch stayed where he was, however, his glaring gaze filled with both shock and a promise of retribution.

Longarm pinched his hat brim to him and then turned toward the house. Haven stood just outside the entrance portal to the garden, scowling up at Longarm, like a schoolmarm silently chastising an unruly student. He merely hiked a shoulder, and then Haven turned through the portal and followed Mrs. Azrael along a stone walk through the garden.

Longarm followed them both, noting the colorful flowers arranged in flower beds, transplanted shrubs, cacti, and a flowering crabapple tree. The garden appeared to ring the house. As Mrs. Azrael silently walked along the stone path, she stopped and tipped her head back to look up at the tall lawman, who towered over her. She placed a hand on her sombrero's crown to keep it from falling off.

"You're a big man, Marshal. Bigger than Stretch." Her high cheeks covered in wrinkled and dimpled leather, stretched an admiring smile. "Takes one your size to give him his due, which he's never had, as far as I know. If so, he's never told his ma about it."

"Ma?" Longarm said.

"Sure, sure. Stretch is my boy. Favors his father more than his black-Irish ma, don't he?" She called through the portal where Stretch was swiping dust from his leather leggings with his hat. "Stretch, get cleaned up. Supper in an hour!"

The tall ranch foreman threw an indignant look over his shoulder and dragged his boots in frustration toward the corral, where the bronc rider was just now climbing back into the hurricane deck.

As Mrs. Azrael started climbing the steps to the house's front gallery, she stopped again and said, "And this here is Stretch's wife, Vonda."

Longarm hadn't seen anyone standing there before, but he saw her now, hovering near a whitewashed stone piling that supported the gallery's red-tiled roof. He hadn't seen the girl because, being ash-blond and dressed in a white, low-cut cotton dress, her pale shoulders bare, she'd blended in to the piling and the white clapboard house front.

Longarm's heart twisted a little, when he saw the heavy-lidded stare the girl gave him, crooking one corner of her full rich mouth that was just the right size for her delicate, heart-shaped face. Her flawless skin told Longarm she probably wasn't much over sixteen years old, if that, but her body was full-busted, with long legs and ripe hips.

Her eyes behind the heavy lids were the blue of a high-mountain lake at the height of spring. She was barefoot, and now she mashed the toes of one foot down on the other foot—an achingly sexy gesture. Her toes were pink and plump and somehow as alluring as the pale breasts that were half-revealed by the thin, cotton dress. The big lawman's keen male eye told him this woman-child's breasts would not be as large as Haven's, but they'd be full and succulent beneath his tongue.

Had Mrs. Azrael said she belonged to Stretch?

Longarm knew an instant's fleeting jealousy, which he thought he concealed well as he nodded once to the girl, giving a cordial, professional smile. "I'm Deputy United States Marshal Custis P. Long, and I'm pleased to make your acquaintance, Miss Vonda."

Haven stepped up beside him and dipped her chin to the girl. "I am Haven Delacroix of the Pinkerton Agency."

The girl kept her sultry, blue gaze on Longarm, continuing to mash her pink toes into the top of her opposite foot and lean beguilingly against the piling, as though she were imitating a cat pressing its body against a man's ankle.

Mrs. Azrael said in her brusque, raspy tone, tossing her clawlike hand in an urgent wave, "Go on up and tell Angelina to bring ole Whip down. The marshal and Agent Delacroix want to talk to him. We'll be in the parlor. When you've done that, fetch us a jug of fresh water from the well."

The girl smiled at Longarm, who didn't think she'd given Haven so much as a passing glance yet, and then pushed away from the porch post, did a fleet, little, dancer's pirouette, her blond hair flying out from her neck, and then ran through the stout open door and into the house. Longarm heard her bare feet slapping on what he assumed were stone tiles.

"Please, come in," Mrs. Azrael said, entering the house herself and doffing her straw sombrero. "And don't mind Vonda. She's cork-headed and lazy as a rich widow's cat. Why on earth my son chose to marry her of all the girls he's had at his beck and call is beyond my fathoming!"

Walking through the doorway behind Haven, Longarm reflected that it sure as hell wasn't beyond his fathoming.

As he and Haven followed Mrs. Azrael through the cool, dark house, he got the impression that the place had once been much smaller—probably a settler's cabin. Since then, it had been added onto in various fashions until now it was a sprawling maze.

In some parts, the floors were stone; in others, oak. The walls were adobe brick or fieldstone, a few consisting of vertical wood panels. Most were dark with soot from candles, coal oil, and wood smoke from several iron stoves and brick fireplaces.

The little woman led them into a large room with couches and large comfortable chairs, a desk in one corner. There were a few small bookcases, old-model rifles, an oil painting, and hunting trophies on the walls.

There was also a stout liquor cabinet made of oak, Longarm noticed. He was glad to see the rangy woman amble over to it, curling both feet in a little, as though her ankles were sore.

"Drinks all around?" she asked. She'd hung her sombrero on a peg somewhere in the dark house, and Longarm saw that she wore her coal-black hair very short, with a tortoiseshell comb holding it down in back.

"Why not?" Longarm looked at Haven, who stood with her hat in her hands.

She hesitated for a second then, giving Longarm a vaguely defiant look, said, "Sure."

"I got some purty good busthead here," said Mrs. Azrael. "How 'bout some bourbon? Whip used to order it by the case from Kentucky. No doubt played a part in his . . ."

She let her voice trail off as she looked over her shoulder at the study's open doorway, through which a young, plump Mexican woman was pushing a wiry, little gray-haired man in a wheelchair.

"Accident," Mrs. Azrael finished.

The young Mexican woman kept her eyes down as she rolled the little gray-haired man up to the striped rug fronting the cold fireplace and around which most of the chairs and one of the couches were arranged. "Obliged, Angelina," Mrs. Azrael said. "Start supper, will you? There'll be two more this evening."

The Mexican girl did not respond but, keeping her cool, dark eyes lowered, merely turned and strolled back out the study door, leaving the little man in his chair facing the fireplace with all the expression of a blank adobe wall. He was almost as small as Mrs. Azrael, and he wore a black patch over one eye. His skin and his hair was as dry, thin, and as colorless as that of a corpse.

Mrs. Azrael continued pouring drinks at the cabinet. "Marshal Long, Agent Delacroix, meet my husband, Whip Azrael. Don't take it personal if he don't say howdy or shake hands."

Longarm gazed down at the poor old hombre in the wheelchair, both the man's knees together and leaning to one side. In his stockmen's boots, gray suit, and a black string tie, he looked as though he were about ride into town for a night of card playing with his moneyed cronies.

But Longarm doubted Whip Azrael ever left the house much anymore. Or, if he did, he likely didn't know it.

"What happened?" Longarm asked as Mrs. Azrael handed him and Haven their water glasses half-filled with bourbon.

The old woman turned to the door and croaked out, "Where's that water, goddamnit, Vonda!" To her guests, she said, "Have a seat. Anywhere. Please!"

Longarm chose a leather chair near Whip Azrael, facing the unlit hearth. Haven lowered her fine body into the brocade-upholstered sofa on his left, a low wooden table between them. Mrs. Azrael sat on the couch's opposite end, her glass in her clawlike hand.

She sipped the bourbon, made a face, and turned to yell toward the doorway again when Vonda appeared with a stone pitcher and a wooden trivet.

"Hurry, hurry," the girl said in her sultry voice, brushing past Longarm, filling his nostrils with the smell of . . . what? Ripe peaches? There was a tang to it. Maybe peach brandy?

She set the trivet on the table and the pitcher on the trivet and looked at Mrs. Azrael. "Can I have one?"

"You go help Angelina. Skedaddle with ya!"

"You know I'm all thumbs in the kitchen!" the girl responded angrily, fists on her hips.

"Use your fingers, then!"

The girl swung around, showing Longarm her pouting mouth and raking her sultry gaze across his shoulders as she brushed past him again, heading for the door.

Mrs. Azrael added branch water to both hers and Haven's bourbons and offered some to Longarm, who waved her off. When she sat down on the couch once more, she looked at her husband, and said, "Poor Whip. Horse threw him last fall. Landed on a Mojave green rattlesnake. One of the men saw the whole thing. The snake chewed ole Whip's eye out and the poison did somethin' to his brain. I don't know—maybe it gave him a stroke. He ain't said a word since then, and he's never given me a single look that said he recognized me. Brain's plum mush. He's just waitin' to die, now, I reckon."

She sipped her bourbon and shook her head sadly. "I sure never thought it would end like this, but you just never know what's gonna happen to ya, the ones you love."

She favored her invalid husband with a look so sad that it squeezed even Longarm's jaded heart.

Longarm said, "Last fall, you say?"

Mrs. Azrael nodded.

Longarm glanced at Haven, who said, "You're in charge of the ranch operations, then, Mrs. Azrael?"

"Me an' Stretch, that's right. We been runnin' a tight ship. Stretch had his stompin' days same as most young men—that's when he hitched his star to that girl of his he found in a saloon in Benson—but he's grown up now. Pretty much, anyways, if you don't count Friday nights in ole Kimble Dobson's saloon in Holy Defiance."

She cackled her crow-like laugh. "He's headstrong, a good fighter . . . most of the time," she added with a smile at Longarm, "but he's got his pa's good business sense, too. He does all the hirin' and firin'. I just look after the books and keep up my garden. Angelina tends ole Whip. He's in rubber pants now, you know. Can't hardly feed himself. Still takes a snort of bourbon before bed, though. That's how I know he ain't all gone. Not just yet."

"I do apologize for your trouble, ma'am," Longarm said, feeling uncomfortable with the invalided Whip Azrael in the room, the sorry bastard's lamps lit but no one in the house. The old rancher just stared into space, occasionally brushing a thumb across his nose, working his lips, and sighing.

"But getting down to brass tacks, Mrs. Azrael, you've had seven men killed on your land of late."

Chapter 23

"I know," the old ranch woman said. "It's just awful." Her regret appeared genuine. "That ranger you hauled in over that purty barb was here just the other day."

Longarm said, "With another ranger—correct?"

"With Ranger Jack Leyton, that's right. He's been here before. Him and Whip was pards in their day, spent some time in the cavalry together."

"Leyton and Sullivan left here together, I take it?"

Mrs. Azrael nodded. "I sure hope nothin' bad has become of Leyton. He's a nice man. When we was havin' the Apache trouble, all them years, he was a big help. He'd come down here and organize posses with the sheriff over at Holy Defiance. When there was a sheriff there, that is. Not there's nothin' much there but a saloon run by old Dobson and his 'Pache daughter that all the boys go to on the weekends."

Haven sipped her drink, set the glass on the table before her, and crossed her legs with feminine grace, half turning to the old woman sitting on the other end of the sofa from her. "I assume you were here when the stage carrying the gold was robbed, Mrs. Azrael?"

"My, yes. We been here for twenty-five years, Miss Delacroix. Whip built this house himself. It wasn't nothin' but a

stone shack back then, and we spent more time fightin'
Apaches than herdin' cattle, but we proved up on it, sure
enough. Grieves me those men died on the Double D."

She shook her head again. She was so tiny that she looked
like a little brown doll leaning back in the sofa corner, bringing her drink to her lips often with both hands, and taking
large drinks from it. The glass appeared the size of a canteen in her tiny hands scored with bulging, knotted veins.

Longarm sipped his own drink. "So you know it's
rumored that the gold is still on Double D range?"

"That's the story, yes." Mrs. Azrael waved a hand as
though brushing away a fly. "Never seen it, though. I'm not
so sure that Santana's gang didn't take it all and spend it
somewhere. Or maybe there wasn't even any gold to start
with. That ole Santana rapscallion was a crower, he was.
Haunted this border country for years, runnin' stolen horses
back and forth from Mexico, robbin' freight outfits between
Nogales and Tucson, much of it on the outlying areas of the
Double D. This here's a big spread, Marshal Long. Stretches
across more than fifty thousand acres!"

"Oh, the gold was on the stage," Haven said. "I'm quite
sure of that. That's why I'm here. Wells Fargo has a contract
with the Pinkertons to find it and return it to its rightful
owner. The missing gold has left a mark on Wells Fargo's
reputation, and Mr. Pinkerton wants it off his books."

She paused, leaned forward to take another sip from her
drink, and shook her hair back from her face. She turned to
the ranch woman again and said, "Do you know that a gentleman called Big Frank Three Wolves claims to know the
location of the hidden gold? At least, the location of little
canyon it's supposedly hidden in?"

"Oh, sure I do," Mrs. Azrael said, waving her little hand
again with annoyance. "That's why them lawmen came
down here, hopin' to find it. And got themselves killed for
their trouble. And that young one now, too—Sullivan. And
probably Jack Leyton. Dirty shame!"

Longarm leaned forward in his chair, resting his elbows on his knees. "You don't have any idea who might have killed them?"

"Banditos, most like," Mrs. Azrael said. "This country is still peppered with 'em. Maybe Apaches runnin' off their reservation in the White Mountains. We still have problems with them rustlin' our cattle. This is big country, Marshal Long. Still pretty damn wild, even with ole Geronimo in Florida."

"And you've never seen the second dead man I hauled in here today?"

"I never got a good look at him, but I wouldn't recognize half of Stretch's men. They stay away from the house, and I stay away from the bunkhouse and let Stretch run things. He's good at it!"

Longarm said, "Where were Leyton and Sullivan headed when they left the Double D—and when was it they left exactly."

"Day before yesterday. Sullivan wanted to have another look at that draw where Santana hid the gold. Leyton thought it was a waste of time, and so did I, but Jack agreed they'd go out there an have another look-see and then ride around the range for a time, see if they could pick up the killers' sign."

A man's voice had risen from somewhere in the house, faintly echoing. Boots clomped on floorboards. A female voice mingled with the man's—softer, lower, deferring. The voice of Stretch's wife, no doubt.

Mrs. Azrael lifted her chin and crowed, "Stretch! Get in here, Stretch! Let them girls *cook*!"

Stretch kept talking to someone half the house away. His tone was sharp, commanding. Suddenly, his wife's voice rose sharply, as well, giving back as good as she'd been given, and the pair argued loudly and savagely for a few seconds before Mrs. Azrael called for her son once more.

Her grating voice made Longarm's ears ring. Haven winced.

Stretch yelled, "I'm comin', goddamnit, Ma!" His booming voice reverberated around the house, as did the pounding of his boots and the chinging of his spurs.

"Don't you curse with visitors in this house, you peckerwood! And take them spurs off. How many time I gotta tell you?"

"Ah, hell!" Stretch said, his voice louder now as he entered the study. He stopped just inside the door and raised each boot in turn, unbuckling the spurs before dropping them with a raucous clatter near the door.

"Now come in here and meet our guests proper. They got a few questions for you, too."

"I already answered all the damn questions I'm going to," the firebrand said, walking into the room, his glowering stare on Longarm, who'd gained his feet and turned to face the man.

He wouldn't put it past ole Stretch to try to deliver another sucker punch.

"Oh, don't worry," Stretch said, holding up his hands in mock innocence. "I don't roughhouse in Ma's house."

He had a cut beneath his chin. It curled up over the outside edge of the chin, and the blood was smeared in his scraggly spade beard, around the beginnings of a scab. Apparently, he'd washed up, for his sandy, wet hair was slicked straight back from his forehead.

"Good to hear," Longarm said.

"She might take me over her knee," Stretch said, grinning and glancing at Agent Delacroix sitting on the couch opposite his mother. "Who's that?" he asked, jerking his thumb at Haven.

"I can speak for myself," Haven said curtly. "I am Agent Haven Delacroix of the Pinkerton Agency."

Stretch looked at her, his lower jaw hanging slightly, and whistled.

"Oh, quit," his mother cawed. "These folks are gonna think I didn't raise you with a half ounce of manners!"

"You didn't." This from Vonda standing in the doorway behind Stretch, arms crossed beneath her breasts again, shoving them up so that they were half-revealed. They were as creamy as fresh milk.

Stretched whipped his head toward the girl. "Who invited you?"

"No one!" Mrs. Azrael said, jutting her arm. "Git back out to the kitchen and help Angelina so we can eat sometime tonight. I'm so hungry I could eat that bronc out in the breaking corral!"

Vonda slid her eyes from her husband to Longarm, gave her bottom lip a sensuous nibble, and then she turned her mouth corners down, dropped her arms from her breasts, and headed back down the hall, bare feet slapping angrily.

"And get some shoes on!" Stretch yelled at her.

"You go to hell, Stretch!" Vonda screeched.

"That girl," said Mrs. Azrael. "Don't know what this kid ever saw in her."

Stretch looked at Longarm, grinning. "You know, don't ya?"

Longarm dropped back down in his chair.

"She's very pretty," Haven said. "But she's not why we're here. We're here . . ."

"About the dead lawmen," Longarm said.

"And about the gold," Haven added crisply.

"Ah, hell—that gold again. Christ!" Stretch walked over to the liquor cabinet. "I don't think there ever was any gold in the first place. I think that old Santana was full of . . ." Catching himself, he cast a jeering grin over his shoulder at his mother. "Chili peppers."

Mrs. Azrael snorted. "Quit tryin' to charm this woman, Stretch. You're married. Beside, she's got too much class for you. Delacroix, Delacroix. Is that French?"

"Indeed, it is," Haven said proudly.

"I knew it. You got clean lines. I bet you're of noble birth. I am, too—back in Ireland."

"Does that make me a nobleman?" Stretch asked, turning and leaning back against the liquor cabinet.

"You're a cur." Mrs. Azrael snorted, glancing at her husband, who sat staring out his one good eye at the cold fireplace. "You got ole Whip to thank for that. His blood's murkier than a flooded gulch!"

She extended her empty glass to Stretch. "Refill," she said, wagging the glass impatiently, slurring her words slightly. Her black eyes glittered.

Stretch's big, sunburned face darkened with embarrassment, and as he stepped forward, he glanced sheepishly at Haven, who had her back to him. He took his mother's glass and stomped back to the liquor cabinet.

"Who found the dead lawmen, Stretch?" Longarm asked the firebrand.

"A couple of the boys," Stretch said, angrily clanking bottles and glasses.

"I'm going to want to talk to them."

"They ain't big talkers."

"Just the same, we'll palaver," Longarm said, not liking the Double D foreman at all. His suspicions were running off their leash about Stretch. As the lanky foreman splashed more liquor into his mother's water glass, Longarm said, "And you've never seen or heard of anyone having found the stolen gold . . . ?"

"You need to ask that again?" Stretch scoffed.

"Just wanted to hear it plain from your gums. Seein' as how five lawmen got murdered on your land when they came down here to look for it, I'm gonna need a whole lot of other things plain before I leave here."

"I will, too," Haven said.

As Stretch delivered the refilled glass to his mother, he scowled at Agent Delacroix. "Should a woman be in your line of work?"

Haven gave him a blank stare.

"You mind your manners, boy!" Mrs. Azrael said.

"Forgive him, Miss Delacroix. I tried to raise him right, but you can't beat sense into a rock. I do hope you find your gold, though. You're awfully pretty, and I'm pullin' for you. And I'm just so sick of hearin' about that *gold*!"

She looked at Longarm as Stretch resumed his position by the liquor cabinet. He'd already tossed back two shots of busthead and was now sipping his third. "I hope you find whoever killed them lawmen, Marshal. But I don't hold out much hope. Double D Ranch is home to more than a few outlaw trails stretching between the Mogollon Rim and the White Mountains and Mexico. If you stay out there too long, sniffin' around, you best be careful you don't end up the same as them others."

To Haven, she said, "Maybe you'd best stay here with me, Miss Delacroix. It ain't safe out there for a man, much less a pretty girl."

"We'll protect you here," Stretch said with a lascivious leer.

"I'm sure your wife would appreciate that, Mr. Azrael."

Longarm looked at Stretch. "Any of your own men been shot out there?"

Stretch filled his mouth with whiskey, puffed out his cheeks, and swallowed. "Nope. Just lawmen like yourself. Like Ma says, best tread quiet out there." He gave a cold smile, his eyes glittering now like his mother's. "Bullets buzz around like blackflies out there, don't ya know."

Stretch splashed more liquor into his glass and headed for the door. "I best go see if the girls need more wood split for the stove." He grabbed his spurs and clomped off down the hall.

"Don't mind him," Mrs. Azrael said. "All the whippin's in the world couldn't turn him out right, though Lord knows I wore the bark off many a willow sap across that boy's derriere. Stretch's got too much of Whip's blood." She studied the old, one-eyed rancher who sat in a catatonic stare and shook her head. "Oh, but we did have some good times, though, didn't we, Whip? Despite the hardships."

She slapped her hand down on the sofa arm. "My word, you two will want to clean up for supper. Help yourselves to the washtub on the porch. There's a barrel with fresh water there, and I'll have Vonda fetch some clean towels."

"I'd be obliged," Haven said, throwing back the last of her drink and rising.

"On your way out, help yourselves to another drink. Supper will be ready in a few minutes. I'm just gonna sit here a bit with my husband."

From somewhere in the house, Vonda screamed, "Stretch, god*damn* your ugly hide!" She sobbed, and then a plate crashed to the floor.

Mrs. Azrael pressed the front of her wrist to her forehead and crowed, "Lord, give me strength not to shotgun 'em both!"

Chapter 24

They all ate in the dining room off the kitchen, the shutters over a couple of large, arched windows set in the outside brick wall thrown open to the cool of the desert dusk. Birds tittered in Mrs. Azrael's garden, a refreshing breeze rattling the leaves of the pecan trees. Occasionally, a horse whinnied in one of the corrals.

Two more guests arrived as Vonda and the pretty, plump Mexican girl, Angelina, set several cast-iron pots and plates of tortillas on the long, heavy wooden table. One of the guests was the black man whom Longarm had seen earlier building a quirley on the boulder near the breaking corral.

His name was Tallahassee Smith. The other, Jake Wade, was a cadaver-thin Anglo with a bushy black mustache wearing a yellow-and-black-checked shirt beneath a brown leather vest and suspenders.

Wade was the ranch *segundo*, second in command behind Stretch, while Tallahasee was apparently next in line, though Stretch didn't say as much. Stretch didn't say much of anything after he'd introduced the two ranch hands, and he probably wouldn't have introduced them at all if his mother hadn't berated him into doing so, pounding his shoulder with her clawlike little fist.

Longarm got the impression that both these men were regulars at the supper table, and most nights they probably discussed ranch business as they ate and then drank and smoked in the study or out on the front veranda. Longarm's and Haven's presence had thrown a wrench into the social workings here, because no one said much of anything until Mrs. Azrael piped up with, "Jake an' Tallahassee was amongst them who found the dead lawmen, Marshal Long. So if you wanna speak to 'em, you got your opportunity right here. Go on—I don't hold much on meal ceremony. Ask what you want. Jake, you an' Tallahassee cooperate with this man. He's here to pop killers out of the brush here at the Double D, and since you yourselves can't seem to keep my range clear of miscreants, I say it's about damn time someone does!"

Longarm looked over his plate piled high with a chewy but tasty Mexican stew consisting of venison, garden peas, Spanish rice, and chili peppers. He held a fork in one hand, a tortilla scrap in the other, as he regarded Jake and Tallahassee, both of whom kept their heads down over their plates as though the woman had cowed them.

Likely, they were just shy, Longarm thought. Most cowboys were bashful as well as backward and as dull-witted as the cows they tended. Longarm had spied these two as well as Stretch casting furtive glances of unbridled male interest across the table at Haven.

Vonda, sitting beside Stretch, was just now grinning and sliding her own mischievous gaze between the two men and Longarm. She apparently knew how uncomfortable the men were in the presence of strangers including one Pinkerton beauty whom they were all probably imagining with her panties off and her dress shoved up around her waist.

"What'd you find out there, boys?" Longarm prodded the punchers.

"Dead men," said Tallahassee. He was bald on top. He wore long, shaggy sideburns and a mustache. His eyes owned an intelligence and blatant cunning that was missing from the man sitting next to him—Jake—who outranked him. "Five of 'em."

Tallahassee held Longarm's gaze with a defiant one of his own. But lots of men didn't like lawmen; it didn't necessarily mean they were breaking the law or had paper on their heads. In fact, most of the men Longarm had run into distrusted the law outright. Until they needed them, of course.

"Shot?"

"Uh-huh."

"From close up or far away?"

"Medium range," the black man said, then added with a peevish air, "How'm I supposed to know?"

"How many times were they shot?"

The black man had resumed eating. Now he looked up at Longarm with an impatient sigh. "Don't recollect. They was all bad bloody. Some was prob'ly shot once, others twice."

"One got it in the head," the cadaverous Jake said, not looking at Longarm but continuing to shovel food into his mouth, leaving a lot of it on his brushy, dark brown mustache.

Haven cleared her throat. "Would anyone here at the Double D have any idea why someone might want those lawmen dead, including the one that was killed earlier today, possibly yesterday?"

Both men looked at her as though it was the first time they'd seen her. They seemed especially interested in her, and also especially suspicious of her for no other reason than she was a female in authority.

Jake's light brown eyes acquired an amused air as he said, "Why, no man, I don't believe so."

He wasn't taking Haven seriously, and she knew it. She continued looking at Jake while the *segundo* continued eating with an annoyingly mocking smile lifting his mouth corners, and Longarm felt as though he were sitting beside a coiled rattler.

Finally, Haven drew a deep breath, released it, and picked up her fork.

Longarm reached for his coffee cup and saw Vonda staring at him, a smile on her bee-stung lips. She chewed slowly, staring at him, and he held her gaze curiously—was she as horny as she seemed?—until Stretch glanced at her. He turned away, then turned back to her and followed her gaze to Longarm, and then back to his wife again.

He rammed his elbow into her side, hard, and said, "Eat!"

Vonda yelped and jerked back in her chair, dropping her fork and slapping a hand to her ribs. "Goddamn you, Stretch Azrael!"

She climbed to her feet, sobbing, and yelled, "That hurt!" and ran out of the room. No one else said anything. Stretch chuckled as he continued eating. His mother gave him a cold-eyed stare as she chewed her food. "Was that necessary?"

Stretched hiked a shoulder. "She's my wife. I can do what I want to her."

He looked up at Haven as though to see how that last comment had registered. Agent Delacroix kept her eyes on her plate. Stretch looked at Longarm, and his eyes hardened and the tips of his ears turned red.

Oh, boy, Longarm thought. Here we go.

He was beginning to wish he hadn't ridden over to the Double D. About all he'd gotten out of it so far besides a meal was another target drawn on his back. Between the dustup earlier and the incident just now, he'd gained another enemy in Stretch Azrael.

"You have a real talent for making friends," Haven told Longarm later, when they'd slipped out into the rear-walled garden and patio for a private conference away from the rowdy, bickering Azraels.

It was good dark, the dry air silky. All was quiet now that the ranch hands had shut themselves into their bunkhouse for the night.

Mr. and Mrs. Azrael had gone to bed. She'd assigned a room with a door onto the garden for Haven, not far from where Stretch and Vonda slept. Longarm had been allocated the headquarters' first *segundo*'s shack, a one-room stone cabin behind the main house. He'd deposited his gear there a few minutes ago and killed a few of the black widow spiders, though a scorpion crawling on one of the old tomato-crate shelves had been too fast for him and scuttled out a crack in the stone wall.

"You try to make friends with ole Stretch." Longarm winked at Haven as they strolled along the garden's brick paths lit by soft blue starlight. "Without gettin' flat on your back, I mean."

"That's disgusting. The way you were ogling that crazy wife of his was just as disgusting. Don't you men have any pride at all? No sense of civility or moral integrity? Is every potential unwashed thought welcome fodder for your depraved minds?"

"This is obviously somethin' that's been eating you."

"We're out here to investigate murder and stolen gold, and you're making eyes at the wife of one of the suspects."

Longarm stopped and swung toward her. "Hey, just remember how we first met, Miss Santy Maria!"

She wagged her finger at him and narrowed a reproving eye. "I told you not to bring that up ever again."

"How 'bout last night? I shouldn't bring that up, either?"

"We were two mature, unattached adults enjoying each other's company after hours. I saw nothing wrong with what we did, though I see no reason to be so uncouth as to discuss it in the light of day."

Longarm scowled at her, felt himself wagging his head again in utter befuddlement. He'd never understand how her mind worked. It was even more complicated and vexing than most of her sex. She must have been raised pious as hell, her earthly soul riddled with holy guilt yet incapable of keeping her from falling prey to her own female cravings over and over.

"What do you got to be embarrassed about? We threw the blocks to each other, and we'll probably do it again tonight." Longarm grinned. "Got a room key?"

"Don't you think we should discuss what we've learned from our visit so far, and what each of us thinks about these people and their possible involvement in the murders as well as the gold?"

"Shit, I don't know nothin' more than I did before we got here."

Haven glanced back at the house. They were near the garden's stone wall, and the house was about fifty yards away. No windows facing the garden showed light. Longarm thought that Stretch and Vonda had gone to bed, though he wasn't sure about the quiet, plump, long-suffering housekeeper Angelina, who toiled tirelessly and apparently without complaint.

Haven kept her voice low as she said, "I, for one, am very suspicious of Stretch. I think he has the gold. Or he had it."

"If Stretch had the gold," Longarm said, firing a lucifer to life on the wall and touching the flame to a fresh three-for-a-nickel cheroot, "I doubt he'd still be here at the Double D. He'd have left a long time ago and been livin' high on the hog."

"Not necessarily. A fool like that might have spent it already. Frittered it away on cheap women like his wife, and on expensive whiskey and cards."

"Jesus," Longarm said with a dry chuckle, blowing smoke out over the wall toward his little shack hunched in the darkness amongst some still mesquites and Spanish bayonet. "It's frightening how well you know the male way. I have to say, you have a point. But if the gold's been spent, there ain't no way to find it."

"If the gold's been spent, why were those lawmen killed?"

"Maybe ole Stretch and his dear old ma are right, and they were killed by banditos. We could ride out and within a half hour we'd probably flush a half dozen out of the first wash we came to."

Longarm stared into the darkly bristling desert toward the steep peaks forming a black, jagged-topped wall beyond, blocking out the stars.

"What is it?" Haven said, standing just off his right shoulder, looking up at him curiously.

"I don't know." Longarm rolled the cigar around between his lips. "Somethin' tells me you might be right. Somethin' also tells me that them two that ambushed us are part of Stretch's roll."

"That would mean the one with the Big Fifty is here somewhere."

"Possibly, unless Stretch told him to make himself scarce till we left."

Haven groaned in frustration. "What is going on here? Why would his men have ambushed us? Ambushed the other lawmen? Where is Captain Leyton? Could all those killings and attempted killings have happened because Stretch *thinks* the gold is buried up that canyon, and he doesn't want anyone else finding it *first*?"

"You said it yourself," Longarm said. "Stretch ain't all that bright. Why, you can see the rocks rollin' around behind his eyes. And we seen how impulsive he is. You go on in and get some sleep. I'm gonna take a walk around, see if I can flush up some secrets. Sometimes the dark of night is the best time for that."

"What out for Stretch. He might jump you again with a few of his men to back his play."

Longarm chewed his cigar. "Worried about me?"

"I'm worried about ending up alone out here."

"Don't worry." Longarm placed his hands on her shoulders. He was surprised that she let him kiss her forehead.

"This ain't my first rodeo. Give me an hour, and then . . ." He canted his head toward his dark shack. "You'll know where to find me."

"I'm tired," she said dryly. "You need your sleep, too. Big day tomorrow. And probably the next day." Primly, she added, "Good night, Marshal Long."

She turned and strode off in the darkness.

Longarm gave a sardonic snort and whispered loudly, "Knock twice quick so's I know it's you!"

Chapter 25

Longarm left the garden through a wooden gate and strolled over to his shack.

He went inside and lit a lamp, throwing a shutter open so that anyone around and watching would see the light. He took a long drink of water from the jug that the housekeeper, Angelina, had provided, and then swept a hand through his hair beneath his hat. He slipped back outside and stole around the front of the shack to the far side, out of sight from the house.

Stepping carefully in the darkness, he walked back past the rear of the shack and kept striding, threading his way through the sage and greasewood. After a time, he arced back toward the main yard and found himself on the south end of it, gazing back toward the yard proper that was bathed in cool, blue starlight.

The house was on the right and about seventy yards away from him. The corrals, barns, and bunkhouse were on the left side of the yard.

Most drovers tended to keep the hours of the animals they tended, retiring and rising early, and these men appeared no exception. The long, L-shaped bunkhouse between one of the barns and the breaking corral was dark.

He stood beside a cottonwood for several minutes, listening to all the little night sounds of which besides the breeze and the infrequent rattling of leaves, there were few.

Finally deciding he was alone out here, he decided to relight a half-smoked cigar and sit down against the tree to look around and mull over the situation. He'd just dug the cheroot out of his pocket, when he heard a sound off to his left.

It was a scraping sound mixed with . . . what? Panting?

He returned the cigar to his coat pocket and, adjusting his Colt high on his left hip, its butt angled across his belly, he strode into the brush and rocks on the yard's north side. There were a couple of old stone buildings out here—probably a keeper shed for meat and maybe another storage shed of some kind. He walked between them and across a sandy wash.

The sounds he'd heard grew louder. They sounded like an animal digging.

He climbed up the other side of the wash and stopped. Before him, a small shadow jostled. The coyote was kicking up sand around a rock pile. No, not a coyote, he realized now, hearing the ragged breathing and faint, desperate mewling. A dog.

The shepherd-like cur of Mrs. Azrael?

Longarm moved forward, dropped to his haunches, one hand on his pistol butt in case he was wrong and it was really a wolf or a bobcat out here.

"Here, boy," he whispered.

The dog froze, looked toward him. Starlight shone on its wet tongue hanging down over its lower jaw.

"Here, boy," Longarm said. "Come on over here. What you doin', old son?"

The dog whined and dropped to its belly beside the low pile of rocks, staring toward Longarm, panting. The lawman straightened and walked slowly over, keeping his hand on his pistol butt. The dog growled, rose, and backed away several feet, keeping its dark eyes glued to the big man walking toward it.

The rock piles, the lawman saw as he drew within a few feet, were graves. One had a homemade cross flanking it. The other wasn't quite as large as the other, and it was not marked with a cross. The dog had been lying beside the unmarked grave, but now it slowly backed away from Prophet, mewling and groaning deep in its throat, pointed ears pricked.

It had dug a sizeable hole in the side of the unmarked grave, tossing sand over some of the rocks that had been mounded to keep predators away.

"It's okay, boy," Longarm said, dropping to his haunches once more and removing his hand from his Colt's grips. "You're only doin' what dogs do, ain't ya?"

The dog barked once, twice, three times, jerking its head and snapping its jaws. Longarm gritted his teeth as the barks echoed, cutting the quiet night open.

"Shhh!" he said, holding two fingers to his lips. "Enough o' that!" he hissed, knowing the barks were likely heard by every pair of ears around the place. He would have left right then, but he wanted to get a better look at the graves—one marked while the other, curiously, was not.

Why wasn't it?

The shaggy beast appeared ready to bark again, when a man's voice called from the darkness in the direction of the bunkhouse, "Duff? That you, Duff? *Here, boy!*"

The dog yipped eagerly and took off running wide around Longarm and then angling toward the wash and the bunkhouse beyond. Longarm stayed hunkered down beside the graves. The dog's soft foot thuds dwindled into silence. A man's voice, not loud but clear and sharp in the quiet night, said, "What're you doin' over there? Better not be diggin' up them graves. Git home, you mangy critter!"

The dog whined. There was a faint rustling. The animal

had taken off running again. Longarm hoped it was obeying the man and was heading back to the main house.

Longarm stayed hunkered beside the graves, listening. When he heard no one coming over, he looked at the graves. Being fresh, they were most likely the graves of the two men Longarm had hauled onto the ranch headquarters earlier that day. Why was one marked with the traditional cross, the other not?

Which one was the ranger and which the man who'd been about to give Prophet a bellyful of lead?

Men who rode for the same ranch were usually pretty tight. When a man died riding for that brand, he was given a proper burial, which usually included at least a crudely fashioned cross with a properly fortified grave.

Longarm thought he knew who was buried beneath the cross. The answer to that question answered, or at least *started* to answer, a lot more. And it caused his suspicions about Stretch Azrael and the entire role of the Double D to buffet like red flags in the wind.

He turned and walked back toward the dry wash. When he'd crossed it, men's voices sounded off to his left. He froze, turned his head toward the bunkhouse, his hand once more closing over his pistol grips. The voices continued—two men conversing in a low tone. They were roughly thirty to fifty yards away.

Longarm pressed up close to a paloverde and peered through its branches. Nothing but cactus and creosote shrubs between him and the rear of the bunkhouse. He brushed past the paloverde and walked toward the bunkhouse until he saw a privy behind it. Two shadows moved behind the privy. Pinpricks of dull orange light shone against the shadows.

The smell of cigarette smoke touched Longarm's nostrils. The voices were clearer now, from this distance, though the men were speaking in conspiratorial tones.

He stopped behind a mesquite, pressed a shoulder to the trunk, breathing shallowly and pricking his ears, picking out bits of the conversation as the men smoked and talked.

". . . Boss don't like it at all," one man was saying. "All this snoopin' around."

Silence.

A throat was cleared.

". . . Wanna do about it?"

"Same as before."

"Shit."

"Yeah, well, hell—what're we gonna do?"

There were garbled sentences here as the two men turned their backs on Longarm, looking eastward toward the corrals in which the shadows of horses stood stone-still as the animals slept on their feet.

Slightly louder, one of the men said, "U.S. marshal and a Pinkerton? A *woman*?"

"Maybe we don't need to kill the woman."

"Yeah, she'll likely light a shuck out of here if that big lawman gets beefed, eh?"

"That's what I'm thinkin'."

Just then a couple of coyotes started yipping and howling so loudly and closely that Longarm jerked with a start. It must have scared the two men behind the privy, too, because one said, "Shit!"

The other laughed.

After a few seconds, one of the men said, "Tomorrow mornin', early, you ride out and tell . . ."

Just then the coyotes kicked up another racket. A small pack must have been hunting in another wash less than sixty yards behind the bunkhouse.

The men behind the privy tossed their quirleys and stepped out away from the bunkhouse, heading for the wash, speaking too softly now for Longarm to hear. They were probably heading out to scare the coyotes away, in case the predators decided to finish the dog's job of digging up the fresh graves.

As the two men disappeared in the dark desert, Longarm walked straight west from the mesquite and then retraced his footsteps to the yard's west edge. The men's conversation bounced around in his head.

So, their boss wanted him dead. The boss of topic was most likely Stretch Azrael. That Stretch wanted Longarm dead was no big surprise. That alone wasn't enough to clarify any of the mystery of the stolen gold or the dead lawmen. Longarm still didn't have enough hard evidence to bring charges against anyone, including Stretch, for anything.

He needed to know why Stretch wanted him dead.

Trouble was, he needed to stay alive long enough to find out the reason. Confronting Stretch would do him no good. Stretch would merely play dumb—which wouldn't be much of a stretch for ole Stretch . . .

At least it didn't sound like the killers would go after Haven. The lawman was glad that he wouldn't have to worry overmuch about her. He could concentrate on watching his own back and try to find out why it had a target on it.

One thing was sure—he'd watch to see which of the Double D men lit out from the ranch yard tomorrow morning and follow him. If Longarm could find out who that man was, and who he was riding out to pay a visit to, he'd be that much farther ahead of the game.

From them, he might be able to learn the ins and outs of whatever deadly game was being played out here at the Double D. And the location of the gold, if Stretch hadn't spent it all yet . . .

"Stretch," Longarm said under his breath as he wended his way back to his shack behind the main house, "I'm gonna run you to ground, old son. And then you're gonna tell me a few things I wanna know!"

He slipped back into his shack and quickly turned the

wick down on his lantern, so his shadow couldn't be targeted against the light. The killers hadn't sounded as though they'd come gunning for him tonight, but you could never predict when a killer would kill. Trying to do so would get you killed.

He stripped down to his balbriggans, leaned his rifle against the stone wall near his cot, and shoved his Colt under his pillow. He sat on the edge of the cot for a time, staring out the shack's front window at the starlit desert night.

It was as quiet out there as the inside of a dry well on the darkest night of the year.

Just the same, he'd sleep like he usually did when he was on assignment—light as a feather.

He took another drink from the water jug and then rolled up in his blankets, the wooden cot creaking beneath his weight. He'd just drifted into the shallow ditch of a lawman's slumber when something propelled him back to the surface, and he snapped his eyes open, staring at the shack's dark ceiling.

Footsteps were growing louder as someone approached the shack. They sounded like butter in a hot skillet. The person was doing little to conceal his approach. *Her* approach.

Longarm grinned, felt his tense muscles relax.

He'd known she'd come.

Eager, ragged breaths sounded beneath the soft footfalls. A bare foot slapped the wooden floor of the shack's front stoop. A quick double knock on the door.

"Yay-up," Longarm said.

The hinges squealed softly as the door opened and a slender shadow moved toward him, closing the door behind her.

Chapter 26

Longarm looked toward the door.

It was too dark in the shack for him to see much of anything, but he detected an inky movement against the darkness. The floorboards squawked under Haven's tread. There was a sibilant rustle as she removed whatever wrap she'd worn out here and let it drop to the floor.

Then he saw the pale blur of her naked body before him.

He smelled the unmistakable fragrance of woman. His cock throbbed.

"Hold on."

He tossed the covers away, dropped his feet to the floor and quickly shucked out of his underwear.

He lay back on the cot and she was on him like a duck on a june bug, breathing hard and fast. She lowered her head to his, kissed him hungrily, almost painfully, grunting and sighing, and then pulled her head away.

"Christ, if I didn't know better," he said, chuckling, her saliva hot on his lips, "I'd say we hadn't cavorted like two randy Northwoods bears just last night!"

She whipped around on top of him, and suddenly, her hot mouth was closing over his cock while her silky-haired snatch was pasted over his face. Her knees were splayed across his shoulders. He could smell the warm musk of her, and that coupled with the eager way she lapped him, gently kneading his balls with her hands, heightened his desire.

He lifted his hands to her round, tender ass, used his thumbs to spread her pussy wide until he could see the pale pink nubbin of her honeypot just off the end of his nose. He rammed his nose up hard inside it, and she withdrew her mouth from his cock and groaned.

He gave a devilish smile when he felt her knees tighten against his shoulders, and she shivered as though chilled. Sticking his tongue straight out, holding it rigid but curling the tip, he raked his thick mustache and his lips up and down her quivering slit.

She groaned louder, shivering and kneading his balls while sucking his cock wildly, sliding her mouth up and down and lapping the head before sliding it down once more.

The wet sucking sounds engorged him. When she'd brought him with her lips and tongue and hot breath to the edge of his precipice, he withdrew his tongue from her wet pussy and rolled out from under her.

She gave a groan of protest, but when he knelt atop the cot and shoved her down against it, she giggled. It wasn't a raspy giggle but a high squeal. He grinned—she was loosening up more than usual—and brusquely positioned her sideways, her head near the foot of the cot. He lifted one of her long, creamy legs up and wedged her foot against his shoulder.

Reaching down, he found the sopping hair of her love nest, and used his hand to guide his cock through those wide-open, petal-soft doors.

"Oh!" she cried. "Oh! Ahhhh. *Uhnnahhh-gawhhh!*"

He rammed himself deep into her. He'd prepared her for this, so she shouldn't be as tight as she was, but he enjoyed the slow in-and-out work as he slowly pried open her womb once more for the full width and length of him.

A pale blur in the darkness, sprawled in a half twist

before him, she sighed and panted and nodded her head slowly, grinding her hands into the cot, bunching his blankets in her fists. When she'd become more malleable, he worked faster, and soon her head was bobbing wildly on her shoulders while he fucked her long and hard, feeling the cot leap around on the floor beneath him.

Her foot beat against his shoulder, increasing his desire. Her toes flexed and curled.

"Fu-uck!" she said through a long, ululating sob. "Oh . . . oh . . . oh, fuck *meeee!*"

When his blood started to boil, his cock seemed to grow even larger inside her. He rose up high on his knees and thrust against her harder, harder, his hips slapping her ass loudly.

Her cunt was like a warm, wet, furry creature gently nibbling his rock-hard manhood. She grunted loudly, until he was afraid she'd awaken Mrs. Azrael and Stretch and Vonda. But when he began to explode inside her, she grew suddenly, almost eerily silent.

She tensed every muscle in her body and bowed her head as though in prayer.

Her pussy expanded and contracted as his cock fired its seed deep into her boiling womb. She ground her little foot into his shoulder.

Slowly, his spasming abated. He held her foot against him, and stopped thrusting, leaving his cock halfway inside her. Her threw his head and shoulders back, gulping deep draughts of the fresh air pushing through the open windows.

He lifted her foot to his lips, kissed the little toe.

He held the foot in front of his face, feeling a scowl carve deep lines across his forehead. The foot he held before him was smaller and plumper than the one he'd kissed last night. He looked down the length of creamy leg angling up from the cot in front of him.

Too creamy, and not long enough to belong to Haven Delacroix . . .

Then he saw the blond head atop the pale shoulders. Vaguely, he'd noticed the paleness of her before and thought it a trick of the moonlight. But there was no moon tonight.

The girl pulled her foot out of his hand and rose up on the cot before him. She pressed her bee-stung mouth to his and then pulled her face away, sandwiching his jaws between her hands. Vonda Azrael's heart-shaped face smiled at him, her blue eyes narrowed to jeering slits.

"You just fucked a married woman, Marshal Long," she said with mock castigation. "You just fucked *Stretch's* woman, and she's been needin' it *bad*!"

She laughed like an evil child as she clambered up off the cot, stooped to grab the shift she'd worn into the shack, opened the door, and ran skipping into the night.

"Holy shit," Longarm growled when he woke the next morning after a bad night's sleep, "did I really fuck Stretch's wife?"

He sat up on his elbows in the predawn, pearlescent darkness, and looked around the small stone shack. Last night all came back to him. Her mouth on his cock. Her pussy in his face. He smacked his lips. Her tang, like a freshly minted penny, was still on his tongue.

"Yep, that's just what I done, all right."

He'd been so sure that the woman who'd walked into his shack had been Haven, had been so intoxicated with the prospect, that it hadn't occurred to him to make *sure* it was her.

Who would have thought he'd need to?

As he dropped his feet to the hard-packed floor and reached for his socks, he couldn't help chuckling. There was only a little humor in it, however. Fucking the wife of the prime suspect in his current investigation could only complicate things further, and the details of this case were so complicated as they stood, and so damn befuddling, he might never get them all nailed down.

The very real prospect that he might have to head back to Denver with his tail between his legs and his hat in his hands to detail his failure at finding neither the killers nor the gold to Billy Vail sobered him right quick.

He couldn't let that happen. He was the best lawdog in Billy's stable, by God, and he wasn't about to let the chief marshal down.

Remembering why he'd wanted to rise well before the sun—to follow whoever rode out of the ranch yard before first light, ostensibly to rendevous with someone else in the Double D's conspiracy of killers—he quickly pulled on his socks and then gathered the rest of his clothes from where they hung from wall spikes.

He rinsed out his mouth with a mouthful of rye, which he swallowed because it was a sin to waste good Tom Moore. He donned his hat, adjusted the angle, and headed on out of the shack with his saddlebags draped over one shoulder, loaded Winchester resting on the other. He paused, adjusted his crotch with a wince. Vonda had chafed him good.

As he strode up past the main house toward the yard, he brushed his thumb across his right vest pocket. His double-barreled derringer was there, opposite the old, dented railroad watch to which it was attached with a gold-washed chain.

Out here, not knowing for certain sure that he had a target on his back, he'd needed every weapon close and ready.

The house was dark though a fire rose from a stone hearth over the kitchen. Longarm knew that the Mexican housekeeper was probably stoking the stove in preparation for breakfast and that she probably had coffee boiling. The thought made his stomach growl, but he ignored it. He didn't have time for breakfast or even a cup of much-needed coffee.

He needed to find out who was riding out of the ranch yard this morning and follow him. The gent might just lead him to the man or men who'd killed the lawmen and even, possibly, to some answers concerning the fate of the stolen gold. It might just be that Stretch's entire payroll was in on the killings, but Longarm needed some hard evidence before he started trying to arrest up to twenty curly wolves.

That Stretch was the "boss" mentioned by the two men he'd eavesdropped on last night, Longarm had little doubt. Mrs. Azrael might be in on it, too—she seemed rougher than a dry-wash floor bristling with coiled rattlers—but there was little doubt in Longarm's mind that her son was the one in charge.

At the moment, whoever was due to ride out of the ranch yard was his first real lead to substantiation of his suspicions. He couldn't let the man leave without shadowing him to see where he went and whom he visited. To make sure he didn't miss him, he'd ride out first and keep an eye on the trail to the east, since east was where most of the mischief had been taking place.

"Sleep well?"

The female voice rose out of the shadows near the house's west front corner. It stopped Longarm in his tracks, and he was about to drop his saddlebags and raise his Winchester, heart thudding, when he saw Haven's slender, duster-clad figure walking gracefully toward him from his left. Her duster flaps were drawn back behind the handles of her matched LeMats, as though she was preparing to wield the savage blasters.

"Where'n the hell did you come from?" he asked through a growl. He didn't like being spooked.

"Got up early, took a walk around. Never know what you'll turn up if you keep your nose to the ground." She stopped and stood with her boots spread wide, hands in her duster pockets. "I asked you if you slept well."

"The cot was a little hard," he said, wobbling his head around. "Got a stiff neck."

"Maybe that's from wrestling with the little catamount known as Vonda Azrael. You know—Stretch's wife?"

Longarm glowered at her.

Haven said, "I saw her heading back to the house after midnight. Skipping."

Longarm gave a sidelong look. "You were keeping an eye on me."

"Not a chance. Couldn't sleep. Needed a little air."

Longarm felt genuinely chagrined. His shoulders slumped beneath the weight of his saddlebags, his rifle, and his guilt. "I thought she was you."

She wrinkled her brows skeptically, as though he'd just told her that he and Stretch's wife had spent their time together reading Bible verses.

"That's a steel-tight, copper-riveted fact," he insisted, keeping his voice down. "Only, when we was done—"

"Look, it doesn't matter. Congratulations. Another conquest. I'd just hoped you were smarter than to get yourself involved with the woman of the man we're most likely . . ." She stopped and looked around at the dark house and shadowy yard, as though to make sure they were alone. "Most likely *after*," she finished.

Her tone burned him. Who the hell did she think she was? His *boss*?

"It was after hours. She threw herself at me." Longarm continued around the house's garden wall, heading for the main yard and the barn. "You stay here today. I'm headin' out alone."

"Do you think that's wise?"

Longarm turned to her. "Lady, I always work alone. I shoulda come down here alone. Women are trouble. Always have been, always will be."

"Only because you have a tendency to *make* us trouble."

"I'd love to palaver, but . . ."

He started to turn away again, but she stopped him with: "What am I supposed to do?"

"What you do best, Agent Delacroix. Investigate. Watch your back, 'cause someone's done etched a bull's-eye on mine." He continued striding toward the barn in which his horse was stabled. "Don't wait up, hear?"

He continued on into the barn, where he found the hostler, a middle-aged man in suspenders, denim jacket, and floppy-brimmed black hat, forking hay to the stabled horses.

"You're up early," he muttered, giving Longarm the suspicious eye as he forked another bunch of hay from a pile beneath a door to the upper loft.

"Figured I'd give the roan a little run."

"You think you're gonna find that stolen gold," the hostler said.

"Don't you?"

The roan was enjoying breakfast, so Longarm decided to smoke a stogie and wait. The man wasn't that old, but he had gnarled, arthritic fingers, which was why he'd likely been relegated to barn chores. "Nope. That gold ain't there. If it ever was there, it's gone by now."

Longarm bit the end off his cigar. "How're you so sure?"

"'Cause I ain't an idjit. Santana didn't have time to hide it that well. Them draws where the Apaches pinned him down done been scoured by every ranch hand who ever worked for the Double D. I for one have been out there . . . oh . . . a good fifty times or more. Every free day over the first couple of years after the holdup."

The hostler chuckled as he scraped hay off his fork with a stall partition behind which two matched sorrels—likely buggy horses—ground their breakfast and snorted eagerly for more. Longarm's roan was still munching oats from a trough and nudging the tin water vessel hanging from a nail, making tinny scraping sounds. The barn, in fact, was filled with the sounds of horses eating and switching their tails contentedly.

"If it was there, I'd have found it. Or one of the old desert rats who also scoured them draws."

"I suppose you were going to turn it in for the reward money," Longarm said, standing in the barn's open doorway and looking out at the yard as he smoked. He smiled foxily over his shoulder at the hostler.

"Somethin' like that," the man said with another wry chuckle.

Longarm drew deep on his cigar and watched a couple of men stirring out front of the bunkhouse on his right. They were yawning and stretching. One was strapping his spurs on while another wrapped two holstered six-shooters around his waist.

Without looking at the hostler but keeping his gaze on the bunkhouse, Longarm said, "Who do you think killed the lawmen?"

"Mescins," the man said matter-of-factly. "Banditos up from Mexico to haunt the stage trail. The stage line through there has suffered holdups for nigh on twenty years. Same for the freighting outfits. I don't really see what keeps 'em in business. I guess just enough coaches get through between Las Cruces and Nogales or Tucson to make it worthwhile."

"Well, I reckon I'll just go out an have a sniff around, anyway, if you don't mind."

"Hell, I don't give a shit. You ride out alone, though, you'll likely end up as dead as them others."

"Well, riding together didn't do them a whole lot of good, did it?"

The hostler chuckled. "You got a point there, lawdog."

Chapter 27

While the hostler continued talking, Longarm watched one of the men from the bunkhouse walk toward him. The man was smoking a quirley, and he wore a long, gray duster. He wore two big Colts over his belly, butts facing each other. The spurs on his high-topped boots rang as he walked, glowering beneath his high-crowned Stetson at Longarm.

"Well, look—that lawman's up with the birds," he said snidely to no one in particular. Thick wavy hair curled over his collar as he approached the barn.

"Mornin' to ya, friend." Longarm smiled and pinched his hat brim.

The man stopped in front of him, gave him a hard, belligerent stare, and then brushed past Longarm, sliding his elbow very lightly but with brash menace across Longarm's belly, and headed into the barn. There was his quarry, the lawman thought as he remained outside, smoking, hearing the hostler and the newcomer talking desultorily inside the barn as the newcomer saddled a horse.

He was the one Longarm would follow. There was a chance the man was heading out on ranch business, but doubtful. The sun wasn't even peeking above the eastern horizon yet. Besides, this man was better armed than most ranch hands, who didn't weigh themselves or their horses down with excess iron.

Longarm was just finishing up his cigar when the man led his horse—a big Appaloosa—out of the barn and into the yard. He gave Longarm another cold look as he swung into the saddle to which a rifle scabbard was attached and cast yet another hostile look over his shoulder as he rode away. At the east end of the yard, he touched spurs to the Appy's flanks, and the horse bounced into a trot and then lunged into a gallop.

Horse and rider disappeared around a bend in the trail twisting through the desert.

Longarm took the final drag from his cigar, wanting to appear in no hurry though he was genuinely eager to get after the man. Not wanting to tip his hand, he dropped the cheroot into the dust and ground it out with his boot. He went into the barn and saddled the fed and watered roan with painstaking casualness, humming under his breath while the hostler went about his chores.

Finally, he shoved his Winchester down into its saddle boot, and bid the hostler good day. The man only grunted as he climbed wall rungs into the hayloft.

Longarm led the roan outside, stepped into the saddle, and booted the horse westward across the yard at a fast but unhurried walk. He figured eyes were on him, so he'd ride west, the opposite direction from the other man, so as not to evoke too much suspicion. Later, when he was a couple of hundred yards west of the ranch yard, he turned off the trail that appeared to rise higher into the craggy, menacing Black Pumas, and made a broad circle around the headquarters.

An hour later, he rode to the top of a low mesa and swung down from his saddle, scanning the desert terrain stretching out to the east. The sun was above the horizon now, and Longarm was looking right into it, so he shaded his eyes.

He was starting to think he'd lost the man and that he'd

have to go back to the main trail to pick up the rider's tracks when he spied movement. No larger from this distance than Longarm's thumb, the rider was galloping at an angle across the desert, heading south.

"There we go," Longarm said, his heart lightening, and swung up onto the roan's back.

He followed a deer trail down the sloping side of the mesa. When he reached the flat bottomland bristling with Sonoran chaparral, he put the horse into a hard gallop, keeping his quarry's bobbing and weaving silhouette in front of him.

Occasionally the Double D rider would gallop up and over a rise, and Longarm would naturally lose sight of him. When this happened, Longarm slowed his pace, resting his horse as his quarry was probably also doing as he rode down the incline. When the man had left his field of vision, Longarm would look keenly around him, listening to every sound, wary for another ambush.

Over the course of the morning, the rider might have spied him and decided to shed the lawman from his trail.

Longarm rode for over an hour. The sun blasted down like liquid coals from the brassy sky unobscured by the smallest cloud. Nothing moved in the bright, shadowless land around him. All the animals were tucked away in their burrows.

Longarm shed his frock coat and wrapped it around his bedroll. He rolled the sleeves of his cotton shirt up his forearms and tipped his hat down low over his eyes.

Still, sweat ran down from his forehead and burned in his eyes. He dragged a handkerchief out of his back pocket, dampened it from his canteen, and dabbed at his eye corners to relieve the sting.

He rode between broad, rounded hills—low mountains, really, tufted with cactus. Beyond the mountain on his right lay another, lower hill on the far side of a crease between the two formations.

Nothing appeared out of sorts. The tracks of the man he

was shadowing continued scoring the red dust before him, leading off in the same direction the man had been heading all morning. Longarm had not seen the man for nearly a half hour.

This fact laid a dry, cool hand of unease between Longarm's shoulder blades. He'd almost been dry-gulched once on this assignment. He'd be damned if he'd let it *almost* happen again.

Ahead, the side of the second hill was about thirty feet high and steep. Almost straight up and down. The crest of the hill was a jumble of adobe-colored boulders of all shapes and sizes. There wasn't a living thing around. Just rock.

Plenty of rocks to hide behind and effect an ambush.

Longarm shucked his Winchester from his saddle boot, swung his right boot over his saddle horn, and dropped straight down to the ground, landing quietly flatfooted. He wrapped his reins around the apple. Slowly, gritting his teeth, he levered a cartridge into the rifle's breech and then tapped the butt plate against the roan's hindquarters.

The horse gave an indignant whicker as it lurched ahead with a start, trotting on down the trail, obscuring the preceding horse's tracks with its own.

Dust lifted like tan feathers behind it. Squinting against the dust, Longarm ran behind the horse, letting it slowly outdistance him. He ran crouching, holding the cocked Winchester across his chest with both hands, keeping within a few feet of the steep slope on his right, so he couldn't be seen from its crest.

Ahead the horse clomped around a slight bend in the trail, following the curving face of the steep slope on its right. Longarm quickened his pace to keep the horse in sight. Just as he rounded the curve in the slope's face, a rifle belched shrilly.

Dust plumed to the left of the horse and ahead a bit. Longarm knew that if he'd been in the saddle, however, the slug likely would have gone in one of his ears and out the other.

The horse buck-kicked fiercely and lunged into a hard gallop, empty stirrups flapping, bedroll bouncing. One of its reins came free of the saddle horn and bounced along the ground beside it.

Longarm stepped out away from the slope, saw a ribbon of smoke rising above a gently shelving, flat-topped boulder. Beneath the boulder, his quarry stood aiming a rifle and staring down the slope before him, a deep, angry scowl on his face.

Longarm raised his Winchester at the same time that his would-be assassin spotted him. Longarm fired as the man turned.

The man fired his own carbine and stumbled back against the boulder. Longarm fired again as the man twisted around and ran up the hill. The lawman's bullet tore up rock dust at his quarry's heels. The Double D rider turned toward him again and fired his carbine twice from the hip, levering quickly, spent shell casings arcing back behind him.

Longarm fired again, and the man screamed and jerked back. He continued climbing until he was up and over the hillcrest.

Cursing, Longarm ran up the steep slope, grinding his heels in the sand and gravel and using his Winchester's stock to help hoist him. It was hard going, for the gravel was loose between the boulders, and he had a hard time getting a firm purchase.

Halfway up, he saw his quarry peer around a boulder at the top of the ridge. Longarm jerked back behind a boulder to his right as the man's rifle thundered twice loudly, both slugs screeching off the side of the boulder near Longarm's right shoulder.

Longarm leaned out from behind the boulder and pumped four quick shots up the slope. At least two punched into the dry-gulcher's chest, jerking him back.

His knees buckled, and he leaned forward and dropped his rifle to the gravel before him. He fell to his head and his knees simultaneously, and rolled over and over down the slope. He rolled straight past Longarm and piled up at the base of another boulder about ten feet away.

He lay on his back, blood pumping from three holes in his chest, another from his arm just up from the elbow, and yet another just above his left knee.

Longarm shook his head and immediately, automatically began to reload his Winchester from his cartridge belt. "You're in the wrong line of work, old son."

He was not reveling in the kill. In fact, it burned him. He'd wanted to follow the man, find out whom he was riding off to rendezvous with and maybe learn from both men why Stretch wanted him dead.

Now, because the man had spied him on his back trail, Longarm's plan had been foiled.

Longarm raked an angry sigh.

He slipped and slid down the hill to the trail, walked up the trail hoping to see his horse not far ahead. That wasn't the case. He walked a hundred yards, then another hundred. No sign of the beast.

He came to where the horse's tracks angled off to the south, but looking that way he saw nothing but piñon pines, cactus, greasewood, bunchgrass, and occasional cedars cowering beneath the merciless sun. He had to find the horse; his canteen was looped over the saddle horn. If he had to, he'd go back and look for the dead man's horse, which was likely carrying the dead man's water, but he'd backtrack only if he couldn't find his own mount in a half hour.

He swung right from the trail and began following the horse's tracks through the chaparral. When he'd walked only twenty yards, a rumbling rose.

He squinted against the sun, saw riders galloping toward him from nearly straight ahead. Apprehension poked at him. He looked around for cover. There was nothing but the dry, gray-brown shrubs and modest-sized rocks.

The riders appeared to have seen him, because they were

heading for him—five or six men coming fast. The lead rider appeared to be trailing a spare horse. A roan.

Longarm's horse.

A vague, cautious optimism gave the lawman's overall anxiety a little nudge. Just a little one. He didn't like the setup. He wondered if this was what the dead lawmen had seen in the minutes before they had died—a blur of riders growing steadily against the brown of distant mountains and trailing a rising cloud of tan desert dust.

He stood his ground, holding his Winchester in both hands straight across his belly. Neither a defensive nor a threatening stance, but a cautious one. As the group approached to within seventy yards, he saw the gaudy sombreros and neckerchiefs, the bearded, dusky-skinned faces.

Several wore charro jackets and flared slacks. Cartridge bandoliers flashed in the sunlight.

Mexicans.

Banditos.

Shit.

The group slowed and then stopped around the lead rider, who was leading Longarm's roan by its bridle reins.

The man was short and stocky. He wore a black leather jacket stitched with white thread, and a billowy red neckerchief. His face was round and pockmarked, and it was trimmed with brushy black muttonchop whiskers that formed arrow points near his mouth corners. Mantling his mouth was a brushy, black mustache.

He and the others sat their horses staring blandly at Longarm. Their mounts snorted and blew, stomping their hooves. Dust wafted around the group. Longarm could smell the hot horses and the man sweat and the leather mixing with the tang of pine and creosote.

The group was well armed. The lead rider held his right hand down near a six-shooter jutting from a tooled leather holster.

Longarm waited, saying nothing. There were five of

them. Three were holding carbines. He might be able to take one or two before the others cut him down and left him as the other lawmen had been left to swell and rot.

Finally, the lead rider's truculent face brightened with an unexpected grin. His black eyes flashed in the sunlight. "Vonda sent you, no?"

The question rocked Longarm back on his proverbial heels. Vonda?

He knew he must have frowned dubiously but covered it by spitting to one side and then nodding, keeping his face a stone mask.

The lead rider raised his fist with the reins in it. "Yours?"

"That's right."

Longarm started forward but stopped when the lead rider lowered his hand clutching the reins and drew it slightly back behind him. He frowned suspiciously. "Why she send you?"

Longarm kept his expression plain as he shuffled quickly through several options. When he chose one, he'd have to ride it out to wherever it led him. That place might be a shallow grave scratched out right here in the thin desert dirt beneath his boots.

"Another lawman snoopin' around," he said. "Back at the ranch."

A man behind the leader said, "Probably the one who Fuentes saw yesterday, Mercado. The one who killed Maximillian."

"*Si*," said the leader called Mercado, keeping his eyes on Longarm but turning his head slightly back and to one side. "Why does she not kill him? Why tell us? It's not like we don't have our hands full looking for that new Bolivar route as it is!"

"I reckon she figures there's gettin' to be an awful lot of lawmen to kill, wonders if this one might be one too many." Longarm kept his index finger curled through his Winchester's trigger guard, knowing that, improvising as he was, he might very well say something that could get him blasted to hell in a heartbeat.

He said, "She thinks maybe Fuentes should try him one more time, take him down out here, away from the headquarters."

In Spanish, Mercado asked one of the other men where Fuentes was. The man replied that Fuentes was off scouting the Javelina Buttes—for what, he didn't say. More lawmen? Or the Bolivar route? Whatever in hell the Bolivar route was . . .

Mercado pondered this and then slid his dark eyes back to Longarm. "How did you lose your horse, amigo?"

"Bastard saw a rattlesnake and threw me." Longarm gave his best tough-nut glare to the roan, half meaning it.

Mercado tossed him the roan's reins. He caught them and asked, "What're you fellas doin' out here? You think the Bolivar route is this far east?"

"Who knows where it is?" the leader said, more frustrated than angry. "All we know is that one payroll shipment was due to pull through here last month, but we saw no sign of it. It passed through somewhere out here—it had to, it's the only way across the border—but Leyton thinks that after the other lawmen were killed, the company got spooked and switched the route through the buttes southwest of Holy Defiance."

The name "Leyton" rocked Longarm back on his heels a second time. *Ranger Jack Leyton?* How in hell was he tied to this—whatever *this* was?

"You look like you could use some tequila," the gang leader said, winking at Longarm.

"You know it," the lawman responded, swinging into the roan's hurricane deck.

"We were just heading back to Holy Defiance when we spotted your horse. You can join us. Jack will want to hear about this new lawman. He will need to be dealt with, also." The Mexican leader held out his gloved hand, suddenly most gracious. "I am Mercado. No doubt you heard of me from Vonda."

"Oh, yeah," Longarm said, manufacturing his best wolf-ish grin.

Mercado chuckled proudly. "What is your handle, amigo?"

"Me?" Longarm hesitated for only an eye blink of time though to him it felt like seven long years. "I'm Longabaugh. Clyde Longabaugh." He thought he'd seen the surname on a wanted circular offering a reward for a gang of mostly nonviolent, small-time bank robbers from up Wyoming way.

Longarm shook Mercado's hand and then followed the gang east through the chaparral toward Holy Defiance and a meeting with Ranger Jack Leyton.

Uneasiness rode like a heavy second passenger behind him. Things were either about to become really clear really fast, or Longarm was about to become really dead for a long, long time.

Chapter 28

"You like girls, Senor Longabaugh?" asked Mercado, the leader of the small pack of Mexicans who'd rescued Longarm.

They were riding over a bench and into the little town of Holy Defiance—a handful of dilapidated buildings hunkered down in the sunburned desert between two piles of black boulders that some volcano must have vomited from the earth's bowels several hundred eons ago.

Defiance Wash ran through the heart of the town. A rough plank bridge stretched across its twenty-foot width.

Clouds had moved in, blocking out much of the sun now and painting the town nearly hidden amongst the rocks in dark, gothic hues. Thunder rumbled. A summer storm was in the works.

"Sure, I like girls all right," Longarm said, wincing slightly as he became conscious of his still-chafed dick.

"Senora Concepcion has turned her old hotel into a brothel and brought in three pretty girls from Tucson." Mercado raised a hand to his chest and pantomimed the hefting of a succulent female breast. "All with big tits, too!"

"Is that right?" Longarm liked tits as well as the next man, but between his chafed dick and the prospect of soon meeting up with Ranger Jack Leyton, who had apparently wandered over to the wrong side of the law, he was having trouble working up much enthusiasm.

Mercado laughed as they trotted on into the town, obviously a ghost town—probably one that had boomed due to gold or silver and promptly went bust when the minerals had played out. The brothel was a humble, two-story mud-brick affair with a wooden front veranda as well as wooden second-floor balcony. The wood was old and gray. Originally, the building had probably been a hotel.

A couple of scantily clad girls were on the balcony, leaning forward against the splintering rail, one smoking as Mercado and Longarm approached. A couple of Mercado's men called out lustily to the girls, who smiled and fluttered their lashes. One—a plump, pretty, green-eyed blond—caressed her breast, pushing it up out of the thin, cotton nightgown she wore, one strap hanging off her near shoulder.

She flicked her tongue across her nipple and laughed enticingly.

The men riding behind Longarm and Mercado whooped and hollered and galloped on past their leader and the man calling himself Clyde Longabaugh. They swung down from their saddles in front of one of the brothel's two hitch racks. The five men ran up onto the porch, yelling and calling to the whores, and filed quickly through the brothel's open front door.

When the last man had gone in, and their boots and spurs could be heard thudding and chinging from inside, a severe-looking woman in a flowered blue dress stepped out. She had brown hair pulled back in a tight bun, and while she was pale-skinned, her almond-shaped eyes were large and brown. A brown mole sat just off the corner of the right one.

Mercado leaned forward on his saddle horn and spoke in Spanish, grinning. "Senora Concepcion, as you can see, my men and I are back."

"So soon?" the woman answered in Spanish, arching one severe brow and ignoring the buoyant din rising from the brothel behind her. The two whores had gone into the building to welcome their eager clients. "I expected you to be gone for longer than a couple of days, Senor Mercado. Your business seemed so important!"

"It was, it was," said Mercado. "But enough about my business, senora." The Mexican gang leader's smile hardened, and he pitched his voice with mild but unmistakable menace. "My business is not something for old ladies to concern themselves with. Your only concern is to please my men with your women. And for that we pay you very well, do we not?"

The old woman just stared at Mercado, her brown eyes betraying little motion though there was a hesitancy in the rigid set of her shoulders.

Mercado glanced across the street and the deep, gravelly wash running down its center, toward another building whose sign over its porch roof announced: BLACK PUMA HOTEL, SALOON, AND DANCE HALL. On the saloon's front porch, to the right of the open plank door, sat a solitary, dark-skinned female dressed in a long, flowered purple skirt and a red blouse with a matching red neckerchief knotted at her throat.

Longarm had spied the saloon and the young woman a minute ago, and he'd been keeping a curious eye on the girl, who sat unmoving on a long bench against the saloon's front wall.

Her Indian-featured face was stoic as she stared toward the brothel on the other side of the wash from her. She had one moccasin-clad foot propped on the bench, and one arm draped casually over her upraised knee. The cinnamon-skinned girl, obviously an Apache, though possibly Pima, wore a thin bandana around her forehead. Coarse, black hair fell straight down her back.

Mercado looked back at Senora Concepcion. "It is too

bad the silent one does not work over here, on this side of the wash. I find Dobson's girl somewhat intriguing."

"If that mute was working over here, Mercado, you know as well I do that you would probably get a night's fun out of her but then wake up with a knife in your balls the next morning."

Mercado laughed at what the woman had told him so matter-of-factly, in uninflected Spanish. Longarm was slow to translate it, but when he did, a few seconds after Mercado started laughing, the lawman looked across the wash again. The girl sat as before, one foot on the bench, before her.

She sat as still as if she'd been carved out of wood.

Mercado glanced at Longarm and slitted his eyes like a wily coyote. "A witch, they say. A mute Chiricahua. Her father was a shaman. If a man looks too long at her, his cock shrivels up like dried leather and falls off!" He shook his head sadly as he glanced once more at the girl. "It is too bad. What I wouldn't give, just once, to . . ."

Senora Concepcion shook her head darkly and turned her mouth corners up knowingly. "That is all it would take."

"Enough about Dobson's little witch," Mercado said, swinging down from his saddle. "Where is Leyton? I have someone he will want to speak with. Upstairs, huh?"

"No," Senora Concepcion said. "He and Fuentes rode out together this morning. Fuentes came for him, eager to show him something he found. Looking, you men. Always looking for something out in the desert . . ." The severe-looking old *puta* smiled cunningly.

"You forget about what we are looking for, *puta*," Mercado warned through a snarl. "When will he back?"

The whorehouse madam shrugged. "How should I know? Tonight, maybe. Everything is a secret around here.

Mercado turned to Longarm and threw his hands up. "Oh, well, I guess we have to wait until tonight to see Leyton."

Just then thunder rumbled louder, and rain began to fall

as though someone had pulled a plug in the sky. White water streaked straight down. "I, for one, am going to go in and warm myself with your girls, Senora! Come on in, Long-abaugh. There aren't enough *putas* to go around, but my men don't take long!"

Laughing, Mercado followed the madam into the brothel, leaving Longarm still mounted on his roan and hunched against the rain. The lawman wasn't worried about getting wet. The cool rain felt good against his hot, sweaty skin caked with several layers of desert grit.

He was relieved to still be alive, which he might not have been if Leyton had been here. He'd have gone down shooting, of course, taking as many killers with him as he could. But he'd have died just the same.

Now, he'd been given a reprieve. A chance to plan another course of action.

He looked across the street at the Black Puma Saloon, being hammered by the white javelins of rain. The bench was now vacant, the Apache girl nowhere in sight.

Two Mexican boys had run out of the brothel in front of Longarm, and were quickly gathering up the reins of Mer-cado's men's horses. The boys had apparently been ordered to stable the beasts.

Longarm swung down from the roan's back. He slid his Winchester from the saddle boot, slung his saddlebags over his shoulder, and tossed his reins to one of the Mexican boys, who caught them deftly as he gathered up the other sets of reins. As the boys ran around the side of the brothel, leading the trotting horses that arched their tails at the weather, Longarm strode across the bridge spanning the wash.

Back in Denver, Billy Vail had mentioned an old desert rat and his Apache daughter who now ran a saloon in Holy Defiance. Dobson must be him.

From Dobson maybe Longarm could gain some idea about what in hell was going on out here—something apparently so lucrative that a man he'd once known to be as good as they came—Ranger Jack Leyton—had gone over to the other side for it.

As Longarm took the saloon's porch steps two at a time, he could hear beneath the drumming of the rain on the roof the strumming of a guitar—soft, melodic strains of what sounded like an old, sad song. He stopped at the open door and peered into the dingy place.

The brightly dressed Apache girl sat in a chair near what appeared an ancient player piano and a roulette wheel—both probably relics from the town's as well as the saloon's more prosperous and rollicking days. She sat in a Windsor chair at a scarred round table—one of about a half dozen in the entire place.

She had one leg crossed over the other one, and now she looked up at the tall man in the doorway and continued to strum the guitar. Her face showed no interest whatever.

She lowered her face again to watch her fingers slowly raking the guitar strings.

An old Anglo man in Mexican peasant garb and with long gray hair sat straight back in the room's deep shadows, about halfway down the long, low-ceilinged room. There appeared a dance floor at the far end. A balcony, probably where gambling tables had once been set up, hovered above it. Game trophies limned the front of the balcony over the main drinking hall—a black puma, a cougar, a mountain lion, a couple of wolves, and a grizzly.

The old man was hunched forward over a fat, open book on the table before him. There was a bottle there, a shot glass, and a cigarette sending smoke curling up from an ashtray into the shadows above the table. He looked up at Longarm, squinted his startlingly blue eyes that contrasted the pastiness of his pockmarked face, and then placed round-rimmed spectacles on his nose, and looked again.

"I'll be damned," he said in a throaty voice. "I do believe we got us some business, Cocheta."

The girl kept her eyes on the guitar and continued strumming the instrument that the rain now threatened to drown out entirely.

"Come on in," the man said, gaining his feet a little awkwardly, a little drunk. He stuck the quirley in the corner of his mouth. His peasant's pajamas hung on his long, rangy frame as he walked around the far end of the bar and came up behind it.

"Whiskey? Tequila? Come on, name your poison."

Longarm walked into the room and set his saddlebags and his rifle on the bar. "Tequila." He removed his hat, tilted it to drain water from the brim, set it on the bar, and ran a hand through his damp hair.

"Tell me, amigo," the barman said as he splashed liquor into a shot glass, "are you amongst Leyton's men or are you a lone desert wanderer seekin' shelter from this welcome desert rain?"

"How 'bout if we say I'm both and neither?" Longarm threw the shot back and held up two fingers to indicate a refill.

The barman chuckled and looked up after he'd refilled the shot glass. "The secretive sort. I don't blame you. This is the country for it. Loose lips get men killed."

He chuckled again, swiped the back of his hand across his mouth.

"I'm just glad to have some company over here, not to mention the business. Ever since that Mex bitch, Concepcion, rolled in here with her wagonload of whores and tequila, and set up shot in the old hotel yonder, my income has taken a deep dive. Oh, I get a few freighters and desert rats now and then, but most of the business, like Leyton's and Mercado's boys, stay holed up over at Concepcion's."

"How long they been holed up over there?"

Leaning forward against the bar, the pasty-faced old man considered Longarm over the tops of his spectacles. "Didn't I see you ride in with 'em a few minutes ago?"

"So what if I did?"

The man smiled conspiratorially and then splashed more tequila into Longarm's empty shot glass. "On the house. To answer your question, they been comin' an' goin' for about two months now."

"Why?"

"I don't ask that question. No one does unless they want their heart carved out with a dull stiletto."

"Concepcion seems mighty curious."

"Yeah, well, that old *puta*'s too curious for her own good. Her old ticker's likely gonna be dried and hangin' from Mercado's neck when him and Leyton finally get what they're here for and ride on south across the border."

The old man leaned on his arm, shifting his head a little closer to Longarm and lowering his voice though no one was here except the Apache girl strumming the guitar.

"You law?"

Longarm knew he was treading in very shallow water, but he had a feeling he wasn't going to learn what the outlaws were here for, and why they'd killed the rangers and the U.S marshals, unless he tipped his hand to this man.

"For the sake of argument," he said, "let's say so."

The man nodded once. "Don't tell no one I said this, because I'll deny it an' call you a raving lunatic, but I got it in on fairly good word from an old desert rat who knows this desert as well as most Apaches do that—"

Outside, a horse whinnied above the pounding rain. Men's voices rose. One was speaking Spanish with a heavy American accent.

Presently, boots pounded the porch floor. A man's medium-tall, compact frame appeared in the saloon's open doorway, clad in a dripping, yellow, India-rubber rain slicker. Rainwater sluiced off his gray, high-crowned Stetson.

The man's voice resonated above the frequent thunder and driving rain. "Well, if it ain't my ole friend Custis Parker

Long his own mean an' nasty self!" The man laughed, showing white teeth under a salt-and-pepper mustache and a long, pitted, hawk-like nose. The whiteness of his teeth and his eyes stood out against the old-leather color of his weathered skin.

Longarm turned toward the door, stiffening, sliding his right hand very slowly across his belly toward his gun. "Well, well," Longarm said, managing a grin despite the cold hand of fear splaying its fingers across his back. "If it ain't my old pal Captain Jack Leyton."

Chapter 29

Captain Jack Leyton walked into the saloon. Mercado followed him, glowering angrily at Longarm.

Obviously the Mexican now knew he'd been duped. The big man with the Big Fifty—a tall, beefy man with dark skin but green eyes and dressed much like a vaquero—walked in behind Mercado. He had his Sharps on one shoulder.

The rest of Mercado's men filed in behind the big man. They were all holding pistols in their hands, and they walked into the room, spreading out in a ragged semicircle to Longarm's right.

"Custis, get your hand away from that .44, now, damnit!" Leyton said with disgust. "You ain't gonna shoot your way out of here, and you *know* it!"

Longarm looked at the men holding pistols aimed at his belly and glowering at him. The Apache girl had stopped playing her guitar now, and she was watching the events unfolding before her with only vague interest, the way one might watch a couple of coyotes fighting in the street.

Longarm lowered his hand to his side. Rage burned in him as he glared at the pompous, self-assured Leyton, who now removed his hat and tossed it atop the bar beside

Longarm's rifle and ran both hands back through his thick, wavy, salt-and-pepper hair.

"Why'd they have to send you, of all people, Custis? Now, I'm most likely gonna have to kill you, and that genuinely grieves me. We was *pals*!"

"Why'd you do it, Jack? Why'd you kill those men— lawmen, just like you and me?"

Leyton sighed. The rain had let up some but it was still slashing against the sides of the building in the blowing wind, making the ceiling and the walls creak. Thunder pealed occasionally, causing the puncheon floor to vibrate and the bracketed oil lamps to ring.

The ranger said, "Let's have a drink, and I'll spell it all out for you. Might as well. You're here now, and I reckon I'm gonna have to kill you here pretty soon, anyway." He shook his head again grimly and looked at the barman, Kimble Dobson, who stood tensely behind the counter.

"Bottle of your best whiskey, Dobson. Three glasses. Tequila for my men."

Leyton glanced at Mercado, who was still glowering indignantly at Longarm, and canted his head toward a near table. The Mexican walked over and both him and Leyton sat down. The others watched Longarm, guns aimed at the lawman's belly.

When Longarm finally sat down across from Leyton and Mercado, facing the front door, the others, including the man with the Big Fifty—Fuentes—lowered their weapons and sank into chairs around two tables near the front.

No one said anything except Dobson, who said sharply, "Cocheta!" as he looked nervously through the dusty bottles lining the shelves on his back bar.

The girl rose from her chair with a bored, tired expression, set the guitar down against a ceiling support post, and started toward the bar. One of Mercado's men reached out and pinched her ass. She gave a sharp grunt and turned her fiery eyes on the man who'd pinched her.

The men laughed, but the man who'd pinched the girl soon cowered slightly under her menacing glare. Mercado snickered. Jack Leyton smiled, and then watched as the girl walked around the far end of the bar and came up behind it to help Dobson.

"Pretty, ain't she?" said Leyton. "A pretty savage. Mercado thinks she's a witch."

"She is a witch," Mercado said, watching her now as she set a couple of trays atop the bar while Dobson filled shot glasses. "Her mother was a sorceress, her father a shaman. Her family is well-known amongst my people south of the border."

Longarm only hazily wondered how the girl had come to be with Dobson, living here in this virtual ghost town. All eyes, including his own, were on the strangely silent girl as she came out from behind the bar, picked up a tray with a bottle and three filled shot glasses on it, and set it on Longarm, Leyton, and Mercado's table.

Indeed, she was an Apache beauty, with a smooth, oval face the color of dark honey. There was a wild, unbridled aspect to her that was hard to pin down and a coppery sheen in her otherwise chocolate eyes.

Apparently, she wore no underclothes beneath her red calico blouse, which was unbuttoned to reveal an enticing view of her cleavage. Longarm could see her large breasts swaying behind the fabric, her nipples pushing out the cloth as she bent to distribute the shot glasses. Her blue-black hair, coarse as a horse's tail, hung down to just above her round ass. A faintly feral musk emanated from her. It smelled like the cooling desert in late fall.

"Mute, they tell me," Leyton said, looking up at the girl admiringly.

"Oh, but she wasn't born that way," Mercado said. He looked up from the girl's swaying breasts to her face and said commandingly, "Show them, senorita!"

She glowered down at the man. She did not look at

Longarm or the others but kept her blandly malevolent gaze
on Mercado as she reached up and pulled her neckerchief
down to reveal a thick, nasty-looking scar across her throat.

Longarm felt himself inwardly recoil at the grisly wound.

"Christ!" Leyton said.

As the girl swung haughtily away from the table and
retreated behind the bar, Mercado said, "Soldiers cut her
throat when she was a little girl. Raided her camp, killed
her family and all the others in her band. Cut her throat and
left her to die. Only, being the demon she is, she didn't die.
Dobson found her and adopted her."

The Mexican gang leader favored the tense barman with
a sly look. "It's my guess he's sold his soul to the devil and
partakes of his adopted daughter's lovely wares nightly. Eh,
Dobson, you old rapist? But who could blame him—living
under the same roof as that?"

The other Mexicans laughed uncertainly, their limited
understanding of English preventing them from getting the
full gist of their leader's tomfoolery.

"Enough of that," Longarm said, casting his wrathful
gaze on Leyton once again. "What's your game, Jack?
Why'd you murder those men?"

"Ah, shit, Custis," Leyton said, looking down at the filled
shot glass in front of him. "I didn't kill those men. That was
Vonda's doin'. Or the doin' of them stupid killers she has
runnin' with her."

Longarm still couldn't wrap his mind around the idea of
Vonda being an outlaw much less having had anything to
do with the lawmen's killings. She'd seemed so lazy and
sexy and benignly stupid. He'd let it go for now. Eventually,
he hoped, everything would become clear.

He waited, holding his acrimonious gaze on Leyton and
suppressing his urge to drill six bullets into the man from
beneath the table.

Leyton was reading Longarm's mind. "Yes, Vonda.
Smarter than she looks. A saloon girl. A devilish one. Hell,

a leader of men albeit a tad on the emotional side. She married that cork-headed Stretch a year ago, but he doesn't know what she's up to. Eight of Stretch's men are hers . . . and mine, includin' his *segundo*, Wade, and Tallahassee Smith. She was in on this thing from the beginning—a whore from Texas with money on her mind. Big money, and a small gang of Texas bank robbers to go along with her aspirations. But to make a long story short, a couple of her men were out looking for the new route for the gold shipment last month when they came upon the rangers and the marshals down from Broken Jaw and drilled all five because our boys thought the lawmen had gotten savvy to our game down here."

Longarm said woodenly, "Stretch's *segundo* and Tallahassee Smith."

Leyton chuckled and threw back half his shot. "I was in Tucson at the time and didn't even know about Big Frank tellin' the others about the gold from that old stage shipment. Shit, that one-armed bastard is so full of shit he'd float in shallow water. If Santana really did bury that gold where he told Big Frank he did, it's long gone. Some old desert rat got it, or maybe one of Whip Azrael's boys, back before Vonda came on board and convinced Stretch he needed more men, and a new *segundo* an' such, and suddenly our cutthroats were in Stretch's bunkhouse and that fool didn't even know it!"

Leyton threw back the last of his shot and refilled his glass from the bottle on the table between him and Mercado, who sat listening with a sly smile on his mustached face, hands laced on his small paunch.

Longarm said, "So, what's game, Jack? Might as well tell me, since we was pards once and you're gonna kill me an' all." He gave his ex-friend a cold grin.

Leyton told him between peals of thunder and sips of a second whiskey shot that the Bolivar Company out of St. Louis had a secret gold mine in the hills south of Nogales.

The company had been hauling the gold up from Nogales in nondescript freight wagons—two wagons loaded with a quarter-million dollars in gold bars every three months—to the Atchison, Topeka and Santa Fe railroad in Las Cruces. From Las Cruces, the gold was shipped to the government mint in New Orleans.

Leyton had learned about the Bolivar Company mine and about the gold from a former colleague of his who'd gone to work as a freight guard. The former colleague had convinced him to throw in with Javiar Mercado and the Texas outlaw saloon girl known as Vonda, to rob one of the gold shipments and be set up moneywise for the rest of their lives.

Only problem was they'd just finalized plans for their first robbery on information relayed to them by Leyton's former colleague when the Bolivar Company had unexpectedly changed the route and hadn't informed the gold guards until they'd been well on their way across the Mexican border and heading north into Arizona Territory. The outlaws had figured it had been too risky for their inside man to get the information out to them. Or that his ploy had been found out.

Possibly, he'd been unofficially done away with. The punishment wasn't unheard of.

"The former route was across Azrael's Double D range," Leyton said. "Unbeknownst, we reckon, to Azrael himself. I reckon when a gold company's in cahoots with the U.S. government and Mexico, they figure they can do what they want. Anyway, I knew the new route had to be somewhere around here, too, because Azrael's land is about the only place the route *could* go because of the mountains on both sides of it. Since they must have taken several bullion shipments along that route recently, we figured we'd cut their sign. Hard to hide the tracks of one heavy wagon and a four-mule hitch as well as a good half dozen or so horseback riders."

"Since you look so pleased with yourself," Longarm said, "I take it you did cut it."

Leyton glanced behind him at the big man with the Big Fifty, who sat sipping a beer and a tequila shot and staring owlishly at Longarm. "Fuentes and the man you killed, Maximillian, stumbled onto it a couple days ago.

"Not only did he discover the new route, my friend, but Fuentes and I spied the wagons crossing the border. Early today. Moving at a snail's pace. Tomorrow, we ride out, wait for them, and hit them!"

Leyton slapped his hands together sharply, causing several of the Mexicans in the room to jump.

He laughed, pleased with himself, and Longarm thought he must be an imposter. The Jack Leyton he'd known was nothing like this gold-hungry monster before him who saw the killing of five good lawmen as merely a sad misstep. Then, again, a fortune in gold will bring out the worst in just about everyone. Longarm had seen it many times in the past.

Leyton added, "I just sent a rider back to the Double D with the information, including the place where we're all going to meet and wait. As slow as the gold wagon's moving, there's no hurry. The rain might slow them further. Whenever they arrive, we will be there, waiting."

Longarm hardened his jaws. He looked at Leyton and then at Mercado grinning like the cat that ate the canary beside the ranger. He looked over at the six other men parked at two tables on the room's right side. Longarm's trigger finger itched.

The muscles in in his back and legs were bunched, coiled, ready to spring.

He had to fight hard to keep himself from bounding up, blasting away with his .44. Leyton and Mercado's pistols were holstered. He might be able to shoot both of them. *Might.* The others were watching him closely, reading his mind, a few quirking their lips as though daring him to attempt what he was on the verge of attempting.

If he did manage to take out both gang leaders sitting

across from him, he'd be dead a half second later. On the other hand, he was likely on the verge of death right now.

What did he have to lose?

Leyton and Mercado stared at him, both with similar expressions on their faces, their eyes bright with the whiskey they'd been swilling. Longarm's heart thudded heavily. His trigger finger kept itching.

"Custis, let it go," Leyton said. "There's not a damn thing you can do to stop us. We got us a brand-new Gatling gun we stole from the *rurales*—the locals—just across the border. We've been planning this takedown for over a year. Shit, Vonda even got herself hitched to that stupid Stretch Azrael so she could keep a closer eye on his range and add his money to our takedown. Them Azraels are loaded, don't ya know, and Vonda'd never let even a single three-cent piece slip between her greedy fingers. Besides, she liked ole Stretch's company, I reckon. She likes big men, Vonda does. Likes to use 'em and break 'em like a branch over her knee."

The ranger grinned lustily. "That's a girl that can't get enough of it. I wouldn't doubt it if you found that out for yourself." He winked.

Longarm's ears couldn't burn anymore than they already did. He was trapped. He knew the whole story, and like Leyton said, there wasn't a damn thing he could do about it.

"What happened to Sullivan?" he asked.

Leyton grimaced, glanced over his shoulder at the big man with the Big Fifty lying across his table. Fuentes said, "Maximillian," and then slid his right index finger across his throat and grinned.

"I gave him the chance to throw in with us, Custis. He wouldn't take it. Young and brimmin' with honor, that kid."

"Too yellow to do it yourself?" Longarm said, wrinkling a nostril at the ex-ranger whom he now wanted to kill as much or more than he'd ever wanted to kill anyone.

"It grieves me; it really does, but he would have thrown a wrench into everything we had going down here."

"You bastard."

Leyton shrugged that off. "I got a proposition for you, Custis. Don't make Matt's mistake. Throw in with us."

Longarm laughed, flabbergasted. "You think I'd switch sides now, after all these years. What kind of a man do you think I am, Jack?" He slitted his eyes, felt the fire of fury searing his cheeks. "A man like *you*? A gutless turncoat *coward*?"

He said to hell with it and started to come out of his chair, sliding his hand toward the walnut grips of his Colt. The Apache girl, replacing a new bottle with an empty one on the table of Mexican cutthroats to Longarm's right, gasped amidst a shrill tearing sound.

Longarm whipped his head around to see one of the men at that table holding her torn shirt in his hands and grinning lasciviously. She swung around, dropping the empty bottle and cupping her heavy, brown breasts in her hands, her brown eyes firing copper spears of hatred at her aggressor.

Longarm's boiling rage suddenly targeted the man who'd ripped the girl's shirt off. But as he bounded up from his chair, he heard the ratcheting clicks of two gun hammers—one right after the other. He looked down to see both Leyton and Mercado aiming pistols at his belly.

He had his own Colt only half out of its holster.

Leyton said in the heavy silence that followed the tearing of the girl's shirt, "Custis, you set that hogleg on the table. The derringer in your vest pocket, too. Or I'll kill you right here, right now, and let Mercado's brutes do what they want to that savage."

He spread his lips away from his teeth and wrinkled his leathery hawk nose. "And I think you know what that is."

Chapter 30

Longarm knew that Mercado's men would have the girl naked and on a table with her legs spread if he didn't do what the ex-ranger had ordered. They were a superstitious lot, but drink trumped superstition, and over the course of the past half hour, they'd each had a snootful of busthead.

They'd probably do it, anyway, but as he looked around the room at the men switching their hungry gazes between Longarm and the girl standing before them with her hands on her breasts, he decided he had little choice but to comply.

Longarm turned to the short, stocky man holding Cocheta's torn shirt and barked, "Give her the shirt back!" His voice pealed like the thunder that was now starting to roll off to the east.

The man looked at Mercado, who nodded once, his own lusty eyes on the girl, whose shoulders looked so bare and vulnerable there to Longarm's right, her shirt in the stocky Mexican's hand. The man tossed her the shirt. She clamped the shirt to her chest and glanced sidelong at Longarm. He canted his head toward the bar, and she strode past him, flaring her nostrils, her jaws tight, and then climbed the stairs at the back of the room.

Knowing the men could still do what they wanted to the

girl, Longarm tossed his Colt onto Leyton and Mercado's table. He followed it up with his derringer along with the watch to which it was attached.

"We could use you, Custis."

"Kindly fuck yourself, amigo."

"That's no way to talk to a friend tryin' to help a friend. How long you been in the service? Too damn long. You ain't as young as you used to be, Longarm. And I bet you're making little more money than a thirty-and-found cowpuncher. Shit, I sometimes wasn't even making that much. Didn't even always get paid. And I put in seventeen years!"

"We don't do it for the money," Longarm said, balling his fists at his sides. "At least I don't. And I know there was a time when you didn't, either, Jack."

Leyton paused. The others drank and glowered owlishly at the tall U.S. marshal standing before them, glaring hard at Leyton and Mercado, who still had that sneering, self-satisfied grin on his face, his pistol on the table before him.

The ex-ranger said, "I'd hate to kill you, Custis. You'd be hell on hooves, ridin' with us. Tell you what, I'm gonna give you tonight to let you think about it. In the meantime, you might think better if we take that hump out of your neck."

Leyton glanced at Mercado, who laughed and snapped an order in Spanish to his men.

Almost instantly, they were all on their feet and unbuckling their shell belts. Longarm looked at his gun just as Mercado, grinning so broadly that he showed the gaps where his eyeteeth had once been, swept it along with his own from the table.

Longarm stepped back and into a broad space between the room's few tables. The Mexicans moved toward him quickly from around both sides of Leyton and Mercado's table.

Eagerness was bright in their eyes. These were men who loved using their fists almost as much as using their pistols, especially on a man who had made fools of them. The big man, Fuentes, came harder and faster than the others, stopping just a few feet away and regarding Longarm blandly but with a dark flush in his broad cheeks, his green eyes crossing with malevolence.

The others moved up on both sides of him.

Longarm saw no reason to wait around for these men to make the first move. He was badly outnumbered. Fuentes was just bunching his thin lips and starting to bring up his right fist when Longarm delivered a savage, flashing right jab to the man's face. The slug surprised Fuentes, who howled angrily as he stumbled back and into one of the others behind him.

The other man righted Fuentes, who gave another howl and, his face swollen with fury, bulled toward Longarm.

The lawman stepped sideways, grabbed Fuentes by the collar of his leather charro jacket, and rammed his head so hard against a ceiling support post that the unlit lantern hanging from a nail fell from the post to smash on the floor, instantly filling Longarm's nostrils with the sooty smell of coal oil.

Fuentes dropped to his knees without a sound other than the thud his head had made against the post, clamping both hands over his ears and bowing as though in prayer.

Longarm had just swung back toward the room when one of the others buried his fist in Longarm's belly. It was a powerful punch, doubling the lawman up with a great *whuff* of expelled air. He couldn't draw any air back in—not with his lungs feeling as though they'd been hammered flat against his spine—but he couldn't go down. If he did, he was finished.

He lunged forward off his heels, burying his head in the belly of the man in front of him, bulling the man straight over on his back and smashing the back of the man's head into a chair with a wicked crack!

Longarm tried to suck air into his mouth but it was a

stillborn gasp—his battered lungs weren't having it. They felt shriveled to the size of prunes, filling the lawman with a natural panic at not getting oxygen. He didn't have to dread long what was coming next, because then a boot toe was rammed into his ribs on one side.

As he fell to the opposite side, another boot toe was buried in his ribs on that side.

And then they were all on him at once, someone lifting him from behind so the others could punch his face. After several nasty blows that lifted a steady screech in his ears and filled his head with a hammering pain, he fell to the floor and rolled onto his back.

Boots kicked him several times and then he was on his feet again, someone holding him upright from behind this time while the others worked him over, taking turns. They hammered with lefts and rights and haymakers until he could no longer feel his jaws or his cheekbones and he vaguely detected the heavy pressure of one eye swelling shut.

After a time, he found himself being flung in a circle, being propelled from man to man by fists to his face, head, and body. Just when he'd start to fall, another fist would lift him and turn him until he rammed into another.

During one such pirouette, he saw through the one eye that was not swollen shut as badly as the other one the Apache girl standing halfway down the stairs. She wore a striped poncho now. At least, Longarm's dull, battered brain thought it was a poncho.

All he could really tell in the second or so he had to peer at her was that she had a look of silent, wide-eyed horror on her pretty, coffee-colored face with those strange copper eyes of hers.

Her face was the last thing he registered before he felt the floor slam against his knees, and then a warm, soupy, pain-filled blackness washed over him and dragged him into an unconsciousness filled with misery.

It was her whom he again saw when he managed to open one eye—the one that didn't feel as though an elephant were standing on it. Her face hovered over him, and those strange eyes had a strange, otherwordly glassy cast.

He lowered his gaze slightly, and he saw that she was no longer wearing the poncho. Her breasts were bare and slightly slanting down toward him, heavy and brown-nippled, as she leaned toward his chest on her knees.

Her legs were bare. In fact, she wore nothing at all. He could see the long, pink gash across her throat, but all it did was complement the fire in her eyes, add an erotically savage aspect to her elemental beauty. Her legs were tucked under her, and he could see the black tuft of her groin hair up high between her thighs.

He groaned. It was a groan of pain as well as pleasure, he suddenly realized. Looking down, he saw where the pleasure was coming from.

His cock rose straight up out of his balbriggan fly, red and fully engorged. Her right hand was wrapped around it, pumping it slowly, gently, bringing the foreskin up over the head and then back down again. There was a crackling sound of whatever grease she had lubed her warm hand with.

Lard, his nose told him.

It felt delightful.

Her hand rose, pushing the skin up with it, and fell again, making the grease crackle softly. The fat glistened in the candlelight beween her hand and the hard flesh it was wrapped around.

He groaned again, sighed.

He was dressed only in his longhandles and socks. He lay on a bed in a dimly lit room somewhere, he assumed, in Dobson's saloon. He lay on the bed, dreaming the girl was here, naked on the bed beside him, stroking his cock and gazing at him with those peculiar, copper-irised, erotically charged eyes.

At least, he thought he was dreaming. He would have to be dreaming, wouldn't he?

In fact, going a step farther, maybe he was dead and these images and sensations were merely the last vestiges of his consciousness firing like miniature rockets in his dwindling soul as said soul was being hurled off to wherever souls went when the body dies.

She tilted her head slightly to one side, brown-copper eyes crossing slightly. A fine sheen of sweat glistened above her lip. Her oiled breasts sparkled in the candlelight, as well. She followed his gaze to one of the orbs and then with her free hand she lifted one of his and placed it on the tip of the breast he was staring at it.

And then, feeling the firm, rounded flesh beneath his palm, he realized that he was not dreaming. He wasn't dead, either.

He'd been hauled up here to this cozy little room lit by a dozen candles on a near dresser, and this Apache witch had undressed him and was now massaging his cock with excruciating slowness and gentleness, so that he was only vaguely aware of the sundry other miseries squealing in the rest of his body.

She swallowed and parted her lips, her breasts rising and falling heavily as she breathed and massaged him. His aches and pains were dulled by the wild, warm pulsing in his loins. Even the ringing in his ears and the steady pounding in his brain dulled when, keeping her hand on his engorged member, she straddled him, rose up over his belly on her knees, and positioned her black-furred pussy directly over the head of his shaft.

Slowly, she lowered her crotch over the head of his swollen organ. He stared down his belly at his cock and her snatch and groaned when he saw the pink folds of her pussy opening as the bulging head of his purple mushroom head slid into her.

He sighed as the pink petals closed around him, warm and slick with her own warm honey.

She gritted her teeth and stared at the ceiling as she slowly lowered her pussy over his cock until her ass was on his hips. She pivoted at the waist, twisting and turning, corkscrewing around on him and tipping her head back, making animallike sounds deep in her chest.

She got her heels under her, squatting, and then began bouncing up and down on him, making the bed's leather springs complain like rusty door hinges. She growled and snarled as she bounced up and down on him, increasing her pace until she was a dark-skinned blur before him, her long hair sliding across her face and hiding it.

Longarm's blood churned. His ears were so hot that he thought smoke must be curling out of them. His balls throbbed deliciously, tingled as though little firecrackers of sheer ecstasy were exploding in them. He felt like he was being fucked by some rabid beast of the Arizona wild.

The lard crackled as she rode him.

Her hair danced wildly, the ends brushing his chest.

His blood sang in his veins.

Finally, after he thought he couldn't take another moment of the sexual pummeling she was giving him, she leaned back toward his feet, placing her hands on his knees. Her brown breasts flatted slightly against her chest, bouncing, hard nipples lengthening to the size and shape of .45-caliber slugs.

Just that slight repositioning, the shifting of the angle of her rising and falling pussy, was too much for him. He couldn't hold back the dam of his desire for another second.

He spasmed hard and violently, rising up on his elbows and bucking into her. The girl flung herself straight up and forward, grinding against him so that he could feel the coarse hair of her snatch scratching his belly.

She mashed her nose against his left cheekbone and he could smell the sweet musk of her hot breath as she grunted and panted and snarled, pummeling him harder and harder and more violently with her hips, shuddering wildly as she succumbed to her own craving.

He must have passed out after that.

When he woke, she lay twisted beside him, half-covered by a twisted sheet. She was snoring softly. Her round ass shone in the starlight slanting through an open window over the bed. The candles were out but their scent as well as that of the lard she'd lubricated him with lingered.

He stared at the ceiling. Aside from her quietly raking snores, silence. He took inventory of his aches and pains. The eye that had been swollen shut was now open a slit. The other was sore, but he could open it fairly wide. His ribs and jaws ached, and he could feel the jelled blood on his cut lips with his tongue.

He rose up on his elbows, slid his legs over the side of the bed, and dropped his feet to the floor. His ribs barked at him, but he couldn't feel any splintering or grinding around inside him. They were badly bruised but he didn't think that any were cracked or broken.

Leyton's cutthroats had given him a good pummeling, taken the "hump" out of his neck. But they'd left him alive because Jack Leyton was genuinely mad enough to think that Longarm would actually join him.

Longarm had to find his horse and ride the hell out of here. He was in no condition to even attempt to do anything more about Leyton and Mercado's plans beyond locating the wagons hauling the gold and alerting the drivers and outriders to the imminent ambush. Then he'd have to get help from the army in running Leyton and Mercado to ground.

He doubted he'd be able to accomplish even half of that, but he had to try. As he heaved himself to his feet and managed not to pass out though it was close there for a minute, he thought he was well enough to ride . . . if he could stand the agony of it, that was . . .

The girl really must be some kind of witch. Taking a tumble with her was like soaking in a mineral spring.

He could sure do with a gun, though.

As if in response to his thought, the girl grunted. He turned to her. She was kneeling on the bed—a vague, brown form in the darkness, black hair hanging over her shoulders.

Something glistened in her hand. Longarm frowned. He reached out and wrapped his hand around the cold steel of a pistol.

He held it up to his good eye. "I'll be damned."

The girl grunted.

Chapter 31

Longarm took about ten minutes to dress, stumbling around as though drunk.

He couldn't see well in the darkness through only one good eye; the other was still swollen and a little blurry, likely from caked blood. Finally, he wrapped his cartridge belt and holster around his waist, and donned his hat. He plucked the girl's gun off the dresser and spun the wheel.

Loaded. A .44, which meant he had extra loads for it in his cartridge belt.

Things were looking up even higher than right after the beating, when he'd awakened to find the girl with her larded-up hand around his cock. He walked over to the bed. He'd intended to kiss Cocheta good-bye and thank her for the help, but she was lying on her side, her back to him, snoring again.

Longarm gave a wry snort. Apaches weren't the most sentimental of folks.

He limped over to the room's door, opened it quietly, and stepped into the dark, quiet hall. He drew the door closed softly behind him and looked around in the darkness.

A wall appeared at the end of the hall on his left. He moved to his right, the rotting floor puncheons creaking loudly beneath his weight.

A door latch clicked to his left. He stopped, closed his right hand over the Remington's grips. The door on his left opened a foot. Dobson appeared, a lantern burning behind him. He wore a frayed plaid bathrobe over a dirty gray undershirt. He held an open book and his steel-rimmed glasses low against his leg. The front of the book was tipped slightly forward so that Longarm could make out the title: *The Monk* by Matthew Lewis.

Dobson kept his gravelly voice down as he said, "Cochilo Gulch."

"Say again?"

"That's where they're comin' through."

"The gold train?"

"I'm not talking about the Cinco de Mayo parade, Marshal."

Longarm beetled the brow over his widest eye. "How do you know?" His voice sounded a little funny due to the swelling of one side of his tongue, which he must have bit, and the puffiness of his lips.

"Hell, I know everything that goes on within a hundred square miles of here."

"Where will I find Cochilo Gulch?"

"Just this side of the pass from the Double D headquarters. Intersects with Defiance Wash."

"Near the graves?"

"Damn near straight west—couple miles."

"Shit," Longarm said, rubbing his chin.

Dobson's mouth slanted in a wolfish grin and he slid his eyes toward Cocheta's door. "She give you a good workout?"

He didn't wait for a response. "Good. She's been needin' her ashes hauled. Them Apache wimmen, you know. Big appetite. I wouldn't know personally, you understand. I consider myself the girl's father as well as a gentleman. Since I spread the rumor about her bein' a witch to keep her from bein' overly pestered when she was younger, she don't get many gentlemen callers."

"I understand."

"Go with God, Marshal. You're gonna need him if you're goin' up against them killers. A good bit of luck, too."

"I'll take both."

Dobson retreated into his room and closed the door. Longarm continued on down the hall and down the stairs. He left the saloon through a back door and hunched in the darkness for a time, getting his bearings and listening and watching for Leyton and Mercado's men.

The night was misty, and lightning flashed in the distance, but it appeared the main storm had rolled away to the east. The only sounds were the trickle of water from the eaves of the saloon and from the roofs of the empty buildings around him. The air was fresh and desert fragrant. Coyotes yapped in the distant mountains.

Longarm touched the grips of the Remington, grateful for the gun. He had a chance now. Not much of one, maybe, but a better chance than he had a few hours ago. And the girl's touch had soothed his aches and pains.

He wasn't so sure about Dobson's being right about her not being a witch or a sorceress of some kind.

Hearing or seeing nothing threatening around the saloon, he traced a broad semicircle around it to the south. He moved slowly because of all his sundry miseries and the steady ache in his head, and because he didn't want to trip over something left behind by the town's now-vanished inhabitants and kick up a racket that might get him killed.

A hundred yards south of both the saloon and the whorehouse in which Leyton and Mercado's bunch was holed up, he swung back west, wincing with the grating ache that each step evoked in his battered ribs.

He came to the wash. It was flooded. Murky water slid driftwood, leaves, and other bits of flotsam quickly past

Longarm in the darkness. He found another bridge farther
west and crossed it, noting that the water had nearly
swamped it.

He stumbled around in the darkness behind the whorehouse before, following the smell of horses, he found the adobe
stable hunched in the wet brush and dripping mesquites.

Water slithered from the stable's eaves as Longarm
looked around carefully, and then very slowly, pressing a
tongue to one corner of his mouth, opened one of the heavy
wooden doors. He turned toward the whorehouse, which
was dark and silent. Leyton and Mercado's bunch appeared
to be asleep—tired after a rainy night of beating hell out of
a deputy U.S. marshal and then probably fucking themselves
into mild comas.

He could have done without the first part of that, but the
last part was just fine with him. He'd get his horse and follow the flooded wash out of town and then ride as fast as he
could in the darkness toward Cochilo Gulch to warn the
gold train.

The more lives he could save, the better. Later, if Leyton
and Mercado got away from the trap Longarm hoped to
spring on them, he'd get help in tracking them down. Thinking of Leyton caused him to clench his battered jaws. He'd
run the turncoat killer down if he had to follow him into
Mexico to do it.

With one more careful glance at the back wall of the
whorehouse, he stepped into the stable. The smell of horses,
dung, and moist hay wafted over him. There was another
smell, and he'd just identified the stench of a sweaty man
when a gun hammer clicked a few inches away from his
right ear.

Longarm froze, his strained muscles tensing.

The barrel of the gun was pressed to the side of his head,
just above his right ear. The man holding the gun said in
Spanish, "You think the boss wouldn't post a guard in the
stable, stupid gringo?"

Another man to Longarm's left chuckled delightedly. Longarm saw a big shadow with a steeple-brimmed sombrero, the whiteness of a bandage around the big Mex's forehead.

Fuentes.

Dread didn't have time to wash over Longarm. Both the guards laughed. And then the gun smashed down against the side of Longarm's head, and before the searing pain had time to blossom throughout his body, everything went black once more.

He woke to aching, miserable darkness just as black.

He tried to move, but he could only lift his thundering head a couple of inches before his forehead pressed against solid wood rife with the smell of pine resin and gun oil. He wobbled from side to side, and suddenly realized as a fist of panic clenched his heart that he was in a pine box.

The box was being carried. He could hear the snickers of the men carrying it, could hear their ragged breaths and the wet sucking sounds of their boots in the mud.

There was another wet sound—the tinkling lapping of the wavelets he'd heard when he'd crossed the bridge over the flooded arroyo. He was near the wash.

The thought had no sooner flicked across his mind than the bottom of the box slammed down on something yielding. The concussion caused Longarm's forehead to smash against the top of his makeshift coffin—probably a rifle box, or maybe the box in which a Gatling gun had been housed— and set the bells in his ears to tolling louder.

He drew a breath through gritted teeth as the box wobbled from side to side. His back was instantly cool. And then it was damp. Water was oozing through the box's seams.

That fist of panic squeezed the lawman's heart more violently. The sons of bitches who'd been guarding the stable had dropped the box in the arroyo . . .

The box lurched and pivoted and scraped against the sides of the wash. Locked in the small, dark, humid enclosure, Longarm felt the sensation of movement above all of the other myriad things he was feeling—most of them pounding pain. The panic of being drowned in a small box in which he had barely enough room to waggle his shoulders was growing quickly.

In his mind's eye, he saw the box hurling down the flooded wash, down the steep incline of the mountain on which the ghost town sat, bouncing off the sides of the cutbank. Steadily, he felt the water seeping through the slight gaps between the boards.

It must have been a good two inches deep in his makeshift coffin by now, slowly crawling up his arms and legs, soaking his clothes. It would soon be over his face.

He rammed his already battered head against the wooden lid but he couldn't build up enough momentum in the tight confines. The lid didn't budge. The two guards must have nailed it tight to the box; that must have been the pounding he'd heard when he'd been unconscious, though it had blended with the invisible little muscular man in his head smashing a ball-peen hammer against his brain.

He was jerked sharply to one side, then to the other, and the coffin must have bounced off the bank or a rock as the floodwater continued hurling him ever down the steep incline. The water was now covering his shoulders. Longarm had never been a fan of water in the first place, and he cared even less for it now as it threatened to drown him in a sealed pine box!

Panic was growing and growing, making his heart pound.

The adrenaline coursing through his veins had dulled the pain in his head and body, and he continued to try to hammer his forehead against the coffin lid to no avail.

He ground his molars as the box rose sharply on his right. It turned over completely, and suddenly he was facedown in the box as it continued to jerk and sway and bounce violently off both sides of the arroyo.

He drew a sharp, involuntary breath, and sucked a pint

of grit-laden water into his lungs for his effort. He lifted his head as far as he could, arching his back slightly, trying to keep his face above water, but he couldn't do it. He heard himself blowing bubbles as he grunted and twisted his shoulders, sort of bucking as though he were making hard love to a woman, and then, as suddenly as it had gone over, the box righted itself once more and the water dropped down to around Longarm's jaws.

The trouble was he still had two lungs half full of water, and the more he gasped for air, the more he choked and coughed and felt unconsciousness closing over him like a slowly tightening, giant fist.

The coffin swerved more sharply than it had so far and slammed violently, loudly against either a boulder or the side of the ravine. The coffin lid rose about three inches from the top of the box, showing the murky blueness of early morning.

Desperately, Longarm crossed his arms on his chest and pushed his arms and head against the lid until it rose farther. With a giant, coughing grunt of panicked desperation, he sat up higher and finally blasted the lid off the coffin. It sailed off to the side as the box continued sliding on down the ravine.

Instantly, the coffin overturned and sent the lawman tumbling headlong into the water. The coffin rolled to one side and then straight out away from him.

He dropped his legs straight down in the stream, twisted around, and his chest slammed into a rock protruding from the side of the cutbank. His head about a foot above the water, he pressed a cheek against the cold, rough surface, and hugged the rock like a long-lost relative.

The murky water streamed around his waist and on down the ravine. He held on to the rock for a long time as he coughed up the dirty water from his lungs, until he was finally able to suck a breath without choking on it.

Feeling as though he might actually live to see the dawn

of a new day, albeit painfully, he looked above the rock with his one good eye. The bank rose on his right. A root protruded from it. He grabbed the root and pulled, his weak arms feeling as though they'd tear out of their sockets.

He kicked and clawed his way up the muddy side of the bank. When he finally lifted his head above the lip, breathing hard and rasping from the remaining water in his lungs and throat, he froze.

His old friend, dread, seized him once more as he heard the ratcheting click of a gun hammer being drawn back.

He looked up. The round, dark maw of a pistol glared back at him.

Chapter 32

The maw of the pistol tilted upward. The gun hammer clicked again as it was eased down against the firing pin, and Agent Haven Delacroix scowled at Longarm from beneath the wide brim of her light brown Stetson. "Custis?"

Longarm heaved a sigh of relief, felt his cracked upper lip curl a grin. "What happened to Marshal Long?"

"What in the hell are you doing?"

"Making mud pies. Wanna help?"

Behind her, her horse cropped weeds between a couple of boulders still damp from the previous night's rain. It was dawn, the sun not yet up, the rolling, rocky, creosote-stippled desert relieved in misty blue shadows.

Longarm extended a hand to the woman squatting before him. "Help me up?"

She half straightened, extending a gloved hand to him. "You look *awful*!"

When he stood before her, his soaked, muddy clothes sagging on him, he spat mud from his lips and said, "Ah, hell"—he gulped a breath—"I been hurt worse shaving."

"What happened?"

"Long story." Longarm felt weak, like he might pass out. His head pounded from all he'd been through. His heart was still hammering. He leaned forward, pressed hands to his knees, and took a deep breath.

"You'd better sit down for a while."

He spat more grit, drew another breath, and shook his head. "No time. We gotta get to Cochilo Gulch, warn the gold train."

"The *what*?"

"I'll explain on the way. Where in the hell are we, anyway?"

Longarm straightened, looked around at the purple hills and bluffs spilling rocks down their sides. Morning birds were chirping in the brush. The flooded wash gurgled and chugged against the sides of the wash behind him. The surrounding terrain looked vaguely familiar, but because of the near darkness and his scrambled brains, he couldn't quite make it out.

"We're a half mile away from the canyon where Big Frank said Santana buried the gold. I rode out here yesterday from the Double D."

Longarm frowned at her. "Why?"

"*Why?*" she said, grimacing as though she were dealing with a half-wit. "That's my *assignment*, remember? To find the stolen *Wells Fargo* gold!"

"Ah, Christ." The exhausted, battered, and bloody lawman laughed without mirth. "There ain't no fucking gold, Haven."

"Clean up your language, please," she said, reverting to her prim daytime self and planting one fist on her comely, duster-clad hip. "And whatever are you talking about? Big Frank said it was there, and I believe him. I have to believe him. I'm finding that gold!"

Longarm walked over to a flat-topped boulder and sagged onto it. He needed to get to Cochilo Gulch as fast as he could and be there when the gold train arrived, to warn the guards and drivers about the coming ambush by Leyton and Mercado. If he tried to ride out at just this moment, however, he was likely to pass out and tumble out of the saddle.

He needed a breather, time to unscramble his brains and gather his wits.

"Like I said, there ain't no gold. Them rangers died for nothin'. No one was worried about them finding Santana's gold. Vonda's men saw 'em snoopin' around out here, and the Double D riders shot 'em because they thought they was onto Leyton, Mercado, and Vonda's plan to rob the gold being hauled out of Mexico from the secret American mine."

"Vonda Azrael?" Haven walked over to him and sandwiched his face in her hands. "Poor man. I'm afraid your ride down the arroyo has turned you into a blubbering fool. I mean, even more so than before."

"It's true, damnit!"

Haven shook her head, walked to her horse, removed the canteen from her saddle, popped the cork, and handed the flask to Longarm. "Maybe this will help."

"The only thing's gonna help is a couple pulls from a whiskey bottle." He took the canteen, anyway, and drank greedily, unable to stop himself. He hadn't realized how thirsty he was in spite of all the mud he'd drunk in the wash.

When he'd had his fill, he lowered the flask, sloshed around what water was left in it. "I hope you have more."

"Fortunately, I brought both of my canteens," she said ironically, taking back the one he held out to her. "Now, suppose you tell me how you ended up in that flooded wash? Where's your horse?"

"My horse," Longarm said. "Yeah, damn!" He looked at her steeldust idly chomping galleta grass. "I suppose that's the only one you have?"

"Two canteens," she said in her patient way, dead certain she was dealing with a man who'd gone soft in his thinker box. "Only one horse. We're gonna have to ride double back to the Double D."

"Not to the Double D," he said, rising with effort from the boulder and unwrapping the steeldust's reins from a creosote shrub. "Cochilo Gulch."

He groaned as he hauled himself into the saddle and then extended his hand to Agent Delacroix. "Come on," he said. "I'll explain the whole thing on the way. We have to get there ahead of Leyton and Mercado, not to mention Vonda."

"Vonda?" Haven said again, her voice pitched with the same disbelief as before as she took his hand, thrust a boot into the stirrup he freed for her, and hoisted herself onto the steeldust's back behind him. "How in the world could that silly wife of Stretch's have anything to do with *robbing a gold shipment*?"

As he rode on along the flooded arroyo and then crossed it where it leveled out and became only a few feet deep, he told Haven about ex-ranger Jack Leyton, Mercado, and Vonda's alliance. He outlined how Vonda, Mercado's woman, married Stretch to get closer to the mine company's secret gold-shipping route as well as to get her hands on the Azraels' small fortune.

He told her about how Leyton had by then already thrown in with Mercado because if you couldn't beat the border bandits, why not join them and make some *real* money?

But then Leyton had learned of the covert gold shipments from the secret mine in Mexico. He shared the information with Mercado and their female partner and former Texas saloon girl, Vonda.

Now, likely knowing there was a whole lot more money to be had on Double D range than what was in Whip Azrael's office safe and in Stretch's remuda, Vonda arranged for Stretch to hire several men from her and Mercado's gang, so they could all keep a sharp eye out for the gold train route without attracting suspicion from the rangers.

"Incredible," Haven said, riding behind Longarm as they made their way southwest, across the gradually lightening desert.

"Yep."

Quickly, the sky turned from pink to salmon to yellow. Rocks and desert flora stood out in relief against the rolling buttes and mesas. As the sun climbed, steam snaked along the damp ground.

Longarm followed a flooded wash toward Cochilo Gulch, rising and falling over the broken land, threading his way between rocky slopes and shelving mesa walls.

He kept his eyes and ears open for Leyton's men, who would be riding in from Holy Defiance in the east though he didn't know by which route. He cursed to himself, knowing he wasn't making good time. But he couldn't push the steeldust overly hard on the wet desert terrain in the intensifying steamy heat, for fear of maiming or killing the beast.

He wished he had a second horse. He'd have left Haven in a shaded arroyo and ridden on ahead himself astraddle her horse and come back for her later, but with Leyton out here, Longarm could very well have been throwing the Pinkerton agent to the wolves.

He couldn't leave her alone out here on foot.

Mid-morning, he reined up suddenly, turned his head and cocked an ear, listening. Crackling sounded in the distance, straight ahead along the wash they'd started following when the floodwater had gone down. Few guns made a cacophony like the one he was hearing.

It was the Gatling gun opening up on the gold train.

"Oh, shit!" Haven said.

Longarm yelled, *"Hi-yahh!"* and ground his heels against the steeldust's loins, putting the horse into a gallop. The horse was already tired, and Longarm couldn't get much speed out of it. His heart hammered and twisted in his chest as he continued to hear the staccato, seemingly endless belching of the Gatling gun.

When the machine gun fell silent, there were a few cracks and booms of pistol and rifle fire. Men shouted and screamed, horses whinnied. Hooves thudded.

As he put the steeldust up the long, gravel-floored wash that sloped up to a pass dead ahead, Longarm thought he recognized Leyton's jubilant voice rising above the din.

The steeldust was slowing and shambling uncertainly, blowing hard. Longarm could feel the pounding of the horse's heart between his knees. It couldn't go much farther. No point in killing the poor beast in trying to get at the most a dozen more yards out of it.

Longarm stopped the weak-kneed horse, and as he hiked his stiff right leg up over the horn and leaped to the ground, Haven frogged back over the horse's tail, landing on her boot heels.

Longarm turned to her. "I'm gonna need one of your LeMats."

She unholstered the pistol in her left-side holster, tossed it to him butt first. He snatched it out of the air, rolled the cylinder across his forearm, and turned to stare up the rocky slope. All of his senses were alive, ushering into the background all of his physical aches and miseries.

On the other side of the pass there was only silence now.

The guns had stopped clattering. The battle was over. After having heard Leyton's voice, it wasn't hard for Longarm to decide who the victor was.

He glanced at Haven. "Stay here."

"Like hell!"

They jogged together up the wash. Only a little water remained, the rest having run down to the flat land or soaked into the wash's gravelly bottom. There wasn't much water around here, which meant there probably hadn't been as much rain in this neck of the mountains as up at Holy Defiance, and the gold train had kept to its schedule.

And Leyton and Mercado and probably Vonda, as well, had been waiting for it.

The slope wasn't steep but it was long, and the fatigued and badly bruised lawman was breathing hard when he and Haven reached the crest of the pass a half hour later. Bending forward, hands on his knees as he gulped air, he stared down the long slope of the wash before him. Horror clamped down hard on his belly, and he felt his knees weaken.

"We were about an hour too late to warn them," Haven said, staring down the slope, her face grim beneath the brim of her hat.

Longarm took another deep breath and ran forward down the wash, staring ahead at the dozen or so bodies strewn across the wash's floor a hundred yards away.

Leyton's men had hit the gold wagon about halfway up the pass and where the rocky walls rose steeply around it. Here, the driver had no escape. He hadn't been able to whip his mule team into a run ahead because of the steepness of the grade, and because the canyon wasn't wide enough to turn what was likely a four- or six-mule hitch, he hadn't been able to retreat, either.

Leyton's men had likely scouted the canyon well and had known exactly where to set up the Gatling gun where it could cut down the gold guards most efficiently.

They'd done their job well, judging by the carnage before Longarm now, who ran heavy-footed, wincing, Haven jogging beside him. They'd also worked quickly. They were gone, leaving blood and bullet-torn bodies to mark their passing.

The gold wagon sat, its tongue drooping, in the middle of the wash and at the center of the carnage. It was a non-descript Murphy freighter that would draw little attention. No one would suspect it was being used to haul a fortune in gold.

A dirty cream canvas cover had been stretched over the box; the canvas now hung in bullet-torn tatters from the wagon's ash bows. The mules that had pulled it were gone, likely used to pull the wagon that Leyton and Mercado had brought for transporting the gold back down the wash and, probably, south to Mexico, where the outlaws intended to live as rich men.

Only dead men were left here. Dead men and several dead horses.

A ways down the sloping wash beyond the wagon, three live horses stood cropping grass along the base of the wash's east wall, reins dangling. The saddle of one of the horses hung down the mount's side.

The riders were bleeding out on the floor of the wash—twisted and slack, some grimacing up at the sky, teeth bared beneath mustaches—likely the same expressions they'd worn when they'd started hearing the savage hiccupping of the Gatling just before the bullets had shredded them.

The freight team had relied too heavily on the secrecy of their route. The mine administrators hadn't hired enough guards and the guards they had hired—likely ex-cowpunchers or lawmen—hadn't scouted the trail ahead of them thoroughly enough. Most of these men—three appeared Mexican, were older, judging by the liberal gray in their hair. They'd gone soft and careless, and they'd paid for it with their lives.

Longarm stared off down the wash, his own fateful grimace creasing his muddy, blood-crusted, swollen-eyed face.

No sign of the outlaws. As he stepped around the dead men and the wagon, he saw where the gang had pulled their own wagon up behind the gold wagon. He saw the boot prints they'd made when they'd switched the gold bars from the gold wagon to their own, probably smaller wagon, which they'd likely turned around before they'd hitched the team to it.

A couple of the outlaws must be good with mules. They'd switched the team quickly to the first wagon, while the other men had switched the gold, and then fogged off down the wash at a fast clip, heading for the border.

Longarm kicked a rock in frustration, cursed loudly, hearing the reverberation of the epithet dwindle gradually between the canyon's stony walls.

"Custis," Haven said sympathetically, "don't blame

yourself. You didn't even know this was going to happen before last night. There's really not much either of us—both of us together—could have done to stop it. We'll have to alert the nearest ranger outpost, the army . . ."

"I'm going after 'em, goddamnit." Longarm continued to stare down the wash. The gang was probably not yet a mile away though he couldn't see them because of the bending floor of Cuchilo Gulch.

He looked at the three horses standing thirty yards away. They still had their saddles. Carbines even jutted from their scabbards. Leyton had struck so quickly that some of the guards hadn't even had time to unsheath their weapons.

Longarm turned to Haven, tossed her LeMat to her. She grabbed it with one hand, keeping her eyes on Longarm, shaking her head fatefully. "No."

"They'll be in Mexico soon, and then I'll never find 'em again."

"Custis, there must be twenty of them altogether."

"I've faced long odds before. I don't expect you to. You're a detective. This is law work."

Longarm slitted his good eye at her, knowing that he probably didn't look very threatening, as beat up as he was. "You go on back to Denver, report to Billy Vail for me. Tell him to send an army, if he has one lyin' around somewhere."

Longarm walked over to one of the dead men. The man had three pistols holstered on his body. Longarm took two Colts chambered for the .44 rounds he carried in his shell belt. He also took a bandolier wrapped around the man's waist, and slung it over his head and shoulder so that it slanted across his chest.

He twirled the Colts on his fingers, liking the weight of the guns, both of them being the older-model Colt Navy with seven-and-a-half-inch barrels and ivory grips. They'd do.

He holstered one, wedged the other behind his cartridge

belts, and took the man's hat. It was a black slouch hat, not all that different from his own Stetson, which he'd left back in the stable at Holy Defiance. Habitually adjusting the angle of the hat, he walked on down the wash toward the three horses.

The mounts eyed him apprehensively, sidled away as he approached. He cooed to one—a coyote dun with one white front leg—and managed to grab its reins while the others trotted a ways off. Longarm swung up into the saddle, slid the Winchester carbine from its saddle boot, and held it up to inspect it.

An 1869 model. The mine company hadn't outfitted its guards with the newest model weapons—that much was obvious. Leave it to large, greedy companies to cut corners even at the detriment of the folks on whose shoulders the company stood. But the gun would do.

Longarm levered a round into the chamber, off cocked the hammer, and rested the barrel against his saddlebows.

As far as he was concerned, a war had just broken out in southern Arizona. He'd go down fighting it.

Chapter 33

Longarm did not say good-bye to Haven. He didn't see the point. He knew he'd be seeing the beautiful detective again in just a few minutes.

One, she wasn't accustomed to taking orders from anyone but Allan Pinkerton himself, much less from Custis P. Long. Two, she wouldn't leave him out here to go up against twenty cold-blooded killers alone.

It wasn't in her to do that.

All that Longarm felt when he heard her clomping up behind him on one of the other two horses—a rangy cremello that she, not surprisingly, looked sexily regal on—was a poignant but fleeting sadness that he'd likely gotten her killed now, too. But if he was going to go down fighting beside a woman, he'd just as soon it be Haven Delacroix, who had as much grit or more than most men he knew, including seasoned lawmen.

They rode down the winding wash, following the deep, narrow furrows of the wagon heavily loaded with gold. The tracks of many shod horses shone in the damp sand and gravel along both sides of the furrows. A good twenty riders. It didn't look as though Leyton and Mercado had lost even one man in the ambush, which didn't surprise Long-arm, having seen where the bushwhack had occurred.

When he and Haven had ridden hard for a quarter hour, the sides of the canyon dropped abruptly. The main wash disappeared into the greater desert stretching washboard flat toward Mexico, while another, shallower arroyo twisted off to the southeast.

Near where Longarm and Haven reached the shallow gully angling between sparse mesquites, the wagon tracks as well as the accompanying horse tracks swerved from the gold thieves' nearly due-south course and headed west.

"West?" Longarm said. "What the hell? I thought they'd be headed for Mexico."

Stopping the coyote dun, he swung down from the saddle and walked around to give the tracks a closer scrutiny. As he did, a horse whinnied nearby, and Longarm wheeled, bringing up the carbine he held in his right hand, thumbing the hammer back.

Two riders were moving toward him and Haven from the east, trotting their horses, dust rising behind them. One was dark skinned but brightly dressed, and with the sensual curves of a female.

She was riding a black-and-white pinto pony. The other rider, a man, had long, gray hair and was riding a mule. Round-rimmed spectacles sagged on Kimble Dobson's pale, hawklike nose beneath the narrow brim of a tall, black opera hat.

Haven slid, with lightning speed, both LeMats from their holsters.

Longarm said, "Hold on."

Dobson and Cocheta stopped their horses, and Cocheta slid down from her Apache-style blanket saddle. She strode fluidly toward Longarm, her face expressionless, and placed her hands on his face. Gently, she caressed his torn, scabbed lips with her thumbs, frowning up at him questioningly. The neckerchief concealing the scar at her throat fluttered in the hot breeze.

Dobson spoke the girl's question. "What the hell happened?"

Self-consciously glancing at Haven, Longarm removed one of Cocheta's hands from his face, his other hand holding the carbine. To Dobson, he said, "Took a little swim."

"We seen your horse in the stable this mornin', after they left. Figured somethin' was up. Cocheta wanted to ride out here, see if you got tangled up in the ambush on the gold train."

Haven arched a brow at Longarm, planted a fist on her hip as she sat her fidgeting horse, and slid her eyes to the mute Apache girl staring obliquely up at the tall lawman. "You've been even busier than you let on, Marshal Long."

To Dobson, Longarm said, "I was too late. They got the gold. I figured they were headed to Mexico, but . . ." He stepped away from Cocheta and walked over to where the two wagon furrows and shod hoof prints drifted off across the desert to the west. "There's nothing that way, but . . ."

"The Double D," Dobson finished for him.

Longarm stared toward the west, across the vast, rolling desert hemmed in on all sides by dun-colored mountains. In the far west rose the black peaks of the Black Puma Mountains, near the base of which sat the Double D headquarters.

"Why go there?" Haven said, echoing Longarm's own confusion. "Why not just head on across the border?"

"There's something they want at the Double D, apparently." Longarm walked over to his coyote dun, picked up the reins, and switched his gaze from Cocheta, who stood near him, to Dobson. "You two go on back to Holy Defiance. There's gonna be one hell of a dustup out here."

Dobson shook his head and looked at Cocheta, who stared at Longarm and hardened her jaws, also shaking her head slowly. "You're only two against twenty," Dobson said. "We'll lend a hand. I'm right good with a rifle, as I fought the Sioux up on the Plains. And Cocheta . . . she's been waitin' to get a chunk of Ranger Leyton."

"Leyton?"

"He was the cavalry officer who led the soldiers into her family's camp, killed her folks, and cut her throat. He left her to die. Only, she didn't die. But she harbors one powerful hate. Been bidin' her time. That's the way of the Apache. They can wait a long time for just the *right* time to cut a man's throat." Dobson's thin lips stretched a dark smile. "She thinks that time is up."

Longarm looked at Cocheta, who stared back at him. "Does Leyton know?"

Dobson shook his head. "Don't have the faintest idea. Don't recognize her, I reckon. Him and his men were likely too drunk at the time . . . on *tiswin*. He was known for that—gettin' drunk on the Apaches' own brew and killin' 'em. Cocheta was only twelve. Now, of course, she's grown up, filled out."

Longarm moved to her. He saw that she wore a green sash, and behind the sash was a long-barreled Remington revolver and a horn-handled bowie knife.

The lawman placed a hand on her arm and squeezed it. "This is law business. You and Dobson go on back to Holy Defiance. I aim to take down Jack Leyton if I have to die doin' it." He shook his head slowly. "It'll get done. You can rest assured he won't see another sunrise."

She shook her head and grinned savagely. She walked back to her pony, swung up into the saddle, and batted her moccasin-clad heels again the horse's flanks. She and the pony trotted past Longarm, crossing the wash and following the wagon tracks to the west.

"Shit," Longarm said with a sigh, stepping into the saddle. "Looks to me like a lot of folks are eager to die today."

He reined his horse around and booted the coyote dun into a gallop, heading after Cocheta, Dobson and Haven putting their own mounts into gallops behind him.

They rode hard, chewing up the ground behind the wagon that Longarm was sure wasn't far ahead. Haven rode beside him, Dobson and Cocheta falling in behind but staying close. Longarm kept his gaze on the bristling desert around him, wary of Leyton sending rear scouts and possibly ambushing him.

The wagon couldn't be moving very fast. He should be able to catch up to it well before the gang reached the Double D headquarters, if that was in fact what they were aiming for.

He slowed his pace, raising his right hand. The others slowed their mounts, as well, scowling at him curiously. He didn't say as much, because he was going over strategies for taking out Leyton and Mercado in his head, but he knew that with all the brush and rock out here, making it impossible to see more than a few yards ahead, there was a good possibility they could ride right up on the gang before they saw them. That would get them killed for certain sure.

Longarm didn't want to encounter them before he was ready. Even then he was likely to get himself, Haven, Dobson, and Cocheta killed deader than hell . . .

Longarm reined in the dun as he studied the terrain ahead of him. The others stopped around him. He dismounted, rummaged in a saddlebag pouch until he found a spyglass. He carried the spyglass to a knoll capped in rock and gingerly climbed to the top of the rock pile, moving slowly and stiffly.

At the top of the formation, he stood tall and extended the glass. A couple of miles ahead, several rocky bluffs stood like a jumble of adobe-colored dominoes. He looked around and then returned his attention to the rocky bluffs. He couldn't be sure from this vantage, but they appeared to be the same bluffs in which Vonda's man had tried to ambush him yesterday morning—sent out by the woman after she'd enjoyed his bed.

Lusty bitch.

If so, maybe Longarm could use them in a similar fashion. If he and his small band could reach them before the gold wagon did, that was.

"I know what you're thinking."

Longarm looked over to see Haven atop a hill on the other side of Dobson and Cocheta from him. She stood staring in the same direction he was, holding one hand up near her hat brim, shading her eyes. Longarm said, "What am I thinking, if you're so smart."

She turned to him, cocked her mouth in a lopsided smile, and nodded slowly. "I know what you're thinking."

Dobson shuttled his incredulous gaze between them. "What's he thinking?"

"He's much cleverer than he looks," Haven said.

Longarm climbed slowly, carefully down from the ancient pile of boulders that had been dropped there by some long-defunct volcano. "Come on," he said, returning his spyglass to his saddlebags and the stepping up into the leather. "I'll show you."

Galloping hard despite the thunderclaps that the rough ride evoked in his tender head, Longarm led his riders in a broad semicircle around the gold train and its escort of armed killers.

Of course, he didn't know where the wagon was exactly, because he couldn't see it for all the brush and low buttes, but he rode far enough south of where he thought it was that his chance of running into it was minimal—and then only if the outlaws made a radical course change.

He and the others came up on the rocky bluffs from the south, heading straight for the rugged formation. A narrow arroyo led into them, and he followed it until the arroyo became little more than a rock- and cactus-strewn gulch, impassable by horseback.

The small party left its mounts in the shade of a couple of paloverde trees, then grabbed their canteens and arms and walked up into the bluffs. When he came to the north side of the formation, he stopped on a flat-topped boulder about halfway up the bluff from the ground and stared down at the gap through which he'd been riding when Vonda's man had ambushed him.

Below and to his left was where his .44 rounds had deposited the dead man. The man himself was gone, though his hat remained hung up on a tuft of Spanish bayonet, and the rocks around were splattered with his blood. The man himself had likely been dragged off by a mountain lion.

Longarm inspected the crease below and the rocky bluff face rising on the other side of it. The gap was about seventy yards wide, and it was the only way through this rocky neck of the desert. Leyton and the other outlaws had to be headed for it.

"Ambush, eh?" said Dobson.

Longarm nodded. He studied the desert to the west, saw what appeared a murky mirage, but there was enough color in it to tell him it was most likely the wagon and its escorts heading toward him.

He regarded Dobson and Cocheta standing to his far left. They looked at him with grim expectance. Haven stood just off his left shoulder. "You all spread out along the side of this bluff. Hide good in the rocks. Don't let them see you until the wagon's straight below you."

"We just gonna start shootin'?" Dobson asked. "Shoot 'em like ducks on a millpond?"

"Just like they did the mine company guards, that's right."

Dobson racked a round in his Henry rifle. "I like that."

Cocheta's copper irises glinted hungrily.

Longarm said, "I'm gonna go on over to the other side. We'll catch them in a cross fire. No one shoot before I do. But after that, cut loose—tear down as many of those sons o' bitches as you can."

"You stay here, Custis," Haven told him. "No point in you moving around any more than you have to. No offense, but you look half dead."

She started down the slope with the rifle she'd taken off

one of the dead gold guards. She stopped and turned back to Cocheta. "We'll *both* go over there, we women," she said with a cold, snide smile.

Cocheta looked at her. The Apache girl glanced at Longarm, turned back to Haven, hiked a shoulder, and canted her toward it, as if to say, "Why not?"

She followed Haven down the slope, both women moving gracefully, skipping from one boulder to the other. Sometimes Longarm wondered if Agent Delacroix didn't have a little Indian blood in her herself.

At the bottom of the slope, they ducked low, scouted the desert to the west, and then ran crouching across the canyon. When they got to the other side, they began climbing quickly, spreading out until they'd both holed up in separate niches in the rocks about halfway up the bluff.

Longarm glanced at Dobson. "Shoot true."

"Don't you worry about that," the saloon owner said, thumbing his glasses up his nose and moving off to Longarm's right, weaving amongst the boulders, some of which were as large as small cabins.

Longarm settled into a near cleft in the rocks. The bottom of one boulder slanted over him. The side of one slanted on his right. A straight, low wall of rock abutted him on the left. He poked his head out of his pigeonhole to cast his gaze to the west.

He could see two lead riders now, both men holding rifles barrel up on their thighs. The wagon was behind them, being led by mules. The other riders flanked the wagon, spread out across the horse trail they were following.

They were within a hundred yards now, closing quickly. Longarm could hear the hoof thuds and the banging and rattling of the buckboard wagon that appeared to have a cream tarpaulin stretched over its box, concealing the gold and, most likely, the Gatling gun.

The men were talking loudly and laughing, apparently confident they weren't being followed.

Or that they were riding into a trap.

At least, Longarm hoped it was a trap for the outlaws and not for himself, Haven, Cocheta, and Dobson.

He turned to the opposite slope and saw the two women crouched amongst the rocks with their rifles. He waved his own rifle slowly above his head, giving the "get ready" signal.

Chapter 34

Longarm doffed his hat and edged a peek around the slanting rock to his right.

The gang was close enough now that Longarm could see the distinguishing features of each rider. One of the lead riders was the black man, Tallahassee Smith, in the red-and-black-checked shirt, red neckerchief, and funnel-brimmed Stetson that Longarm had seen near the breaking corral when he and Haven had first ridden into the Double D headquarters.

The big, burly man riding to the black man's right was Fuentes in his black, steeple-crowned sombrero, holding his Sharps Big Fifty across his saddlebows. The two were talking as they rode into the crease between the bluffs, about twenty feet ahead of the mules pulling the wagon. Longarm couldn't hear what they were saying because of the wagon's clattering and the team's clomping hooves.

Ex-ranger Jack Leyton and Vonda rode in the wagon, Vonda driving, shaking the reins over the team's backs.

Leyton leaned back with his elbows on the top of the seat back, boots propped on the dashboard, smoking a fat cigar and grinning. Longarm could see a glimpse of the man's large, white teeth beneath his salt-and-pepper mustache and long-angling hawk's nose, the glint of his self-satisfied eyes beneath the brim of his high-crowned Stetson.

Longarm pulled his head back into his niche, waiting for the outlaws to draw near enough for him to pick out a target and to take that first shot. Leyton would go first. Then . . . who? Vonda?

Why not? Her being a woman didn't make her any less than a conniving, cold-blooded killer.

He'd pick Mercado out of the gang, and, if one of Longarm's cohorts hadn't taken him down by then, he'd make sure the Mexican bandito would be the next to snuggle with diamondbacks. Then the snake's three heads will have been sliced off, removing the gang's teeth.

Longarm just hoped that his partners would wait for his signaling shot before they cut loose with their own rifles. One misstep here, when they were so badly outgunned, would cost them their lives.

The clomping of horse and mule hooves grew louder. The wagon's rattling grew more raucous, echoing off both rocky butte faces. The outlaws were talking in laughing, jubilant tones.

No, they thought they'd gotten off scot-free. And they were headed for the Double D. Why?

Maybe they thought it would be safer to hole up there for a while than to head across the border with a slow-traveling wagon loaded with gold, where they'd likely draw the attention of some wandering band of *rurales*. When word about the theft of the gold got out, they'd also likely be hunted by every bandito gang in northern Sonora and Chihuahua.

Longarm supposed that with the Gatling gun, the outlaws would have a fairly easy tome of dispatching Stretch's loyal segment of ranch hands.

Or . . . was there something at the Double D that Vonda had discovered and wanted?

In the crease below Longarm's niche, the rattling and thudding grew louder. Tallahassee Smith came into view, straight down the slope from Longarm. Fuentes rode on the other side of the black man.

Smith carried a Winchester Yellow Boy rifle with a buffalo head carved into the rear stock. And then the mules slid from right to left in the lawman's vision field, and a second later he could see Vonda and Jack Leyton sitting the wagon's wooden seat that jerked on metal springs.

Longarm's heart beat slowly, calmly, his hands steady. This wasn't his first rodeo. He knew exactly how to play it.

He'd just raised his rifle and started to plant his Winchester's sights on the left cheek of Jack Leyton, just beneath the upcurved brim of his hat, when a rifle barked below him and to his right. A rider who'd been trotting his horse up on Longarm's side of the wagon—it was Mercado—flew down the far side of his horse with a shrill yell. His head slammed against the top of the wagon's side panel with a cracking, smacking noise, and then he sagged down beneath his horse, his foot apparently hung up in his right stirrup.

Jack Leyton's voice bellowed, *"Amm-buuush!"*

But by then all the riders were sitting straight in the saddles and raising their rifles. At the same time Vonda shook the reins over the mules' backs, screaming, "Giddyup, you sons o' bitches!"

Deciding his next target had to be the wagon driver, so she couldn't get away with the gold, Longarm planted a bead on Vonda and fired. He watched her buck sideways with a shrill yelp as his slug punched through her upper left arm.

Longarm rose to his feet and continued firing, levering his Winchester as fast as he could, spraying the wagon box with .44-caliber lead. He couldn't see Leyton now because the wagon had passed Longarm's position, rattling off down the crease, but he thought he heard the turncoat ranger bellow as the other member of Longarm's party opened up with their rifles.

"Goddamnit, Dobson!" Longarm couldn't help taking the time to shout. "I told you to wait for my signal!"

"Mercado seen me!" Dobson bellowed in reply as smoke from his Yellow Boy wafted up from his niche in the rocks.

He was a good shot, because three riders trying to check down their prancing horses were thrown out of their saddles. Longarm resumed firing, as well, drilling one rider through his knee and hammering a round through the ear of another man taking aim at Haven on the other side of the canyon.

Return fire barked and screeched off the rocks around Longarm and Dobson.

As Longarm paused and dropped to a knee to punch fresh shells through his rifle's loading gate, he saw three of the gold thieves wheel their frightened horses and gallop back the way they'd come. At the same time, Vonda was whipping the mule team off to the west, the wagon bouncing and fishtailing and kicking up a thick, billowing dust cloud.

Longarm pumped a fresh shell into the Winchester's breech and cast a quick glance toward the opposite slope. Haven and Cocheta were both hunkered atop boulders and firing at the handful of remaining riders in the crease, a few still on horseback, a few hunkered behind rocks and returning fire at their ambushers.

The killers were bellowing at each other as they returned fire, thoroughly shocked to find themselves in such a predicament, the tables turned, their brethren dying bloody around them.

Longarm's sundry physical grievances had died down considerably under the hot coursing of his blood through his veins. He couldn't help grinning wickedly now as he descended the bluff, leaping from rock to rock and firing his Winchester from his hip.

Another killer—this one the cadaverous Jake Wade, Stretch Azrael's so-called *segundo*—went down hard, turning and triggering his own rifle into the air above his head.

Haven and Cocheta each accounted for two more outlaws, the murderous bandits blown out, screaming or cursing, from behind their covering boulders, blood splashing their shirt and leather vests.

By the time Longarm had leaped to the bottom of the canyon, automatically punching fresh shells through his loading gate, all the outlaws were down and either lying still in death or writhing as they died. One man was crawling back in the direction from which the caravan had come.

It was Mercado.

Cocheta was just then leaping from a boulder to the canyon bottom. She walked coolly over to Mercado, stepped around in front of him, blocking his progress. The Mexican bandito leader looked up at her, his shaggy hair hanging down over his blood-streaked face.

He screamed in Spanish for the girl to spare him.

She punctuated the plea with a bullet from her Spencer carbine.

Longarm looked around, saw that the other outlaws were no longer a threat, the last living one expiring quickly, quivering in a pool of his own blood near his dead horse. Haven leaped to the floor of the canyon, looking around as she reloaded one of her LeMats.

"The gold," she said.

Longarm was staring to the west. The wagon was dwindling into the distance.

"She won't get far."

He'd wounded Vonda and probably Jack Leyton, as well. Leyton must have stayed on the wagon, because Longarm didn't see the turncoat ranger anywhere around the canyon. The lawman took long strides westward and reached for the reins of one of the riderless horses standing around, wide-eyed and jittery from the fusillade.

Haven ran up behind him, ran down a horse of her own, and swung into the saddle. Together, they galloped up the trail, following the twin wagon furrows, both hunched low in their saddles.

Longarm could feel the malicious little man with the

hammer in his head again, but only dimly, beneath the more violently pounding desire to run Jack Leyton down and either kill him or throw him into a federal prison where he'd have a good, long time to reflect on his transgressions. There was nothing more cowardly than a lawman gone bad . . .

His adopted horse tore up the trail, head down. He and Haven ripped through the chaparral, following the wagon furrows as they rose and fell over the low, sandy swells, creosote shrubs and mesquites occasionally scraping against Longarm's legs. They came around a jutting thumb of rock, and the wagon was just ahead, thundering westward.

"Look out!" Longarm yelled as Jack Leyton, lying atop the canvas stretched over the top of the wagon box, triggered a Winchester.

Amidst the wagon's banging and clattering, the rifle's crack sounded little louder than a branch snapping. Dust puffed from the maw once, twice, three, four times. Haven yelped and jerked sideways in her saddle. Longarm turned to her just as she twisted around and fell down her saddle's far side, hit the ground, and rolled.

Longarm raised his Winchester as Leyton fired at him once more, and cut loose with his own rifle, taking his reins in his teeth and triggering and levering as he rode. When he'd fired his ninth round and the rifle's hammer had pinged on an empty chamber, he tossed the gun away and watched Leyton's slack body bounce over the side of the wagon.

The ex-ranger struck the ground and rolled.

Longarm could hear the man groaning as he continued to roll madly, limbs akimbo, out away from the hammering wagon before piling up against a rock and a spindly desert shrub. At the same time, the mules pulling the wagon turned sharply to avoid a jumble of boulders ahead.

The wagon fishtailed abruptly, slammed nearly sideways into the mound of rock. Vonda gave a high-pitched, agonized scream as she flew up and over the rock mound while the wagon disintegrated behind her.

She rolled as the mules tore loose of the hitch and continued galloping, still strapped together, to the south.

Longarm jerked back on his horse's reins, leaped out of the saddle, and ran back along the trail toward where he'd seen Haven fall. He came upon her just as she was climbing to her knees, clamping one hand over her arm. Her hat was gone and her hair was a mess, but her eyes were all business.

"Don't worry about me, Custis. What about Vonda and the gold?"

Longarm shook his head as he reached her. "I don't take orders from you, Agent Delacroix. How bad you hit?"

"Ah, hell," she said, mimicking him with a smile. "I've cut myself worse shaving."

Longarm inspected her arm, then removed her neckerchief, wrapped it around her arm, pulled her to him, and kissed her. It was a wild, lingering kiss. He was damn glad she was alive. Losing such a sand rattler of a female as her would have grieved him no end.

When he pulled away from her, he braced himself for a slap. But she merely stared up at him with a smoky cast to her hazel eyes. "That's a little unprofessional—don't you think, Marshal Long?" She drew a breath, causing her breasts to rise sharply beneath her shirt, and swallowed, lifting her mouth corners.

"Yes, ma'am, I sure as hell do." He winked at her and gained his feet. "I'm gonna see about the wagon."

He walked to the west and swerved over to where Jack Leyton lay against the rock and the desert shrub. The man was still alive, chest rising and falling sharply as he breathed. Longarm looked down at him, saw the several holes his Winchester had punched through the killer's body. He was alive, but he didn't have long.

Leyton's eyes stared up at Longarm with an odd blandness. "They . . . Mercado's men . . . said they done kilt you, Custis. What are you, anyway—a damn *cat*?"

Longarm saw that one of the two pistols the man was

carrying was his own double-action .44. He ripped it out of the ex-ranger's holster and hefted it in his hand, glad to have it back. "Trophy, Jack?"

"Yeah," Leyton said with a faint, sly grin. "Somethin' like that." He coughed up blood, gasped, said, "Good Lord, Custis—I think I'm dyin' here!"

"Couldn't happen to a more deserving son of a bitch, Jack."

He turned away from the dying ex-ranger and walked over to the gold wagon. Gold bars, strewn amongst the wagon's broken boards, steel chassis, and iron-shod wheels, glittered in the harsh sunlight. Beyond the rocks and wagon debris, a blond-haired figure was staggering away from Longarm. Vonda, holding her wounded arm, was heading west.

A pack of riders was galloping toward her from the same direction.

Chapter 35

Longarm paused as the riders thundered toward him.

He raised his carbine. Vonda stopped, looked forward, and then dropped to her knees, bowing her head as though in prayer.

Stretch Azrael was leading the pack of riders, which, Longarm was surprised to see, included his little, wiry, wizened-up mother on a smart-stepping palomino, in the saddle of which she appeared doll-sized. Mrs. Azrael was dressed for the trail in a cream shirt, denims, and an ornately stitched leather vest, with a flat-crowned, broad-brimmed hat on her black head, chin thong dangling down her spindly chest.

"Vonda, what in Christ?" Stretch yelled, hauling back on his grulla's reins and leaping out of the saddle. He looked at his wounded, sobbing wife kneeling before him, and then at Longarm and the broke-up wagon behind the lawman.

Longarm doubted that Stretch had ever been at a loss for words before. Well, he certainly was now. He cuffed his hat brim back off his forehead and regarded Longarm incredulously.

"What's goin' on? She disappears in the middle of the night. I wake and eight of my riders are gone, including my first two lieutenants—slipped out around the same time as Vonda, not a word to anyone . . ."

"I told you she was about as good as rattlesnake ahead of a wildfire," said Mrs. Azrael, looking down her nose at the blond girl sobbing before her and her son. The old ranch woman looked beyond Longarm at the gold. "What in God's name did she get herself involved in?"

Longarm walked up behind Vonda. She had a pistol in the holster strapped to her right hip. He pulled the gun out, tossed it away, and she jerked her dirty, tear-streaked face at him, scowling savagely. "I should have killed you when I had the chance! Know why I didn't?"

She laughed devilishly, glanced at Stretch, and then turned back to Longarm. "'Cause you satisfied me like I ain't been satisfied since I moved out to the Double D—that's why!"

Mrs. Azrael gave a disapproving chuff and clucked while she shook her head.

Stretch glared at Longarm, his face as red as an Arizona sunset.

Longarm turned to Vonda. "Why were you heading back to the Double D?"

"To get the gold!" she fairly screamed, laughing again and casting her hate-filled gaze at both Stretch and his still-mounted mother.

"What gold?" grunted Mrs. Azrael.

"The gold under your bed, you old hag!" This she screamed at the tops of her lungs, shaking her head wildly and clamping her hand over her bloody arm. "The gold your husband found where Santana buried it and was saving for when he decided to run off with your housekeeper—*Senorita Angelina*! Only, he got thrown by his horse before he could make his escape!"

Mrs. Azrael and Stretch just stared down at Vonda as though she were speaking some foreign tongue.

"How do you know he was going to run off with the housekeeper?" Longarm asked.

"Oh, I just guessed it . . . after I saw Angelina giving the old boy a blow job in his office, a few nights before he fell and turned his brains to mush. I seen 'em together before that. Many times! And I heard 'em talking about the gold many times, too, snickering to themselves while ole Whip had Angelina bent over his desk in his office! That's when I started scheming to add the Wells Fargo gold to the plunder I got today—and could have damn near *doubled in size* if it weren't for you, *you son of a bitch of a crafty ole lawdog!*"

Longarm stared down at the girl with an expression similar to the one on her husband's and her mother-in-law's faces.

"Old Whip saw the holdup," the girl told Longarm, enjoying every minute of telling her story. Wounding the Azraels was at least some compensation for the bitter end of the trail she found herself facing. "He told as much to Angelina. I overheard him. He was hidden in the buttes near the stage.

"After the Indians attacked Santana, Whip went out and dug up the box, brought it back to the ranch, and hid it under his bed. Mrs. Azrael, you been sleepin' on a hundred thousand dollars in gold coins for the past three years, you silly old bitch! Hah! And you and Stretch both thought you was so much smarter than me! *Ha-ha-hahh!*"

Vonda laughed like a witch ready to fly off on her broom, pointing a jeering finger at Stretch. "He didn't tell his own son because he didn't trust him! He was afraid Stretch would tell his mother, and old Whip just wanted to be rid of 'em both! I don't know why he didn't just take off right away. Maybe he was waiting for the right woman to come along . . . a *puta* like *Angelina*! I reckon you couldn't satisfy Whip any better than Stretch could satisfy me, Mrs. Azrael!"

Vonda laughed even harder.

Then she fainted and fell face-first to the ground.

Stretch, Mrs. Azrael, and the seven riders behind them just stared down at Vonda as though at some creature that had winged in and landed here from outer space. Longarm swung around and walked back through the brush, looking over the wagon wreckage and the strewn gold.

He spied movement ahead. Haven was walking toward him, her wounded arm in a makeshift sling. The flaps of her tan duster were tucked behind the butts of her twin LeMats.

The Pinkerton agent was looking off to Longarm's left, where Kimble Dobson sat his horse looking down at Cocheta. The Apache girl was standing over Jack Leyton, who was flopping around like a landed fish, blood spurting from the long, deep gash across his neck.

Cocheta leaned forward to wipe the blade of her bowie knife on the man's trouser leg. When the blade was clean, she slid the knife back into its sheath on her hip and glanced at Longarm.

It was the first time he'd seen her smile.

Epilogue

Two weeks later, all the stolen gold was heading back to its rightful owners. All the bodies, including that of Jack Leyton, were buried.

Cocheta and Dobson returned to their saloon at Holy Defiance.

Vonda was on the mend at the ranger post in Broken Jaw, where she was also preparing to stand trial for thievery and murder. Longarm didn't think that Roscoe Sanders had chained her to an iron ball and put her to work, slinging drinks at Slim's while she awaited trial, but he wouldn't put it past the old ranger.

Whip Azrael remained out at the Double D. Longarm and Haven both agreed that the elderly ranch owner had gotten and, under the care of his angry wife, was continuing to get his just desserts for making off with the stolen Wells Fargo gold.

Longarm and Agent Haven Delacroix were heading back to Denver on the Atchison, Topeka and Santa Fe flyer, enjoying the Pullman sleeper car they shared.

"Custis, I should really be very angry at you," she said late one desert night, four hours north of Santa Fe, while sucking his cock in the Pullman berth they were sharing.

"Because of Cocheta and Vonda?" Longarm said through a groan. "Haven, you ain't gonna believe this, but I didn't start any of it with them two gals."

"You were an innocent bystander?"

"You could say that, yes."

"Not that you mean anything at all to me, you understand," she said, sliding her mouth off the swollen mushroom head of his cock and looking up past his bare belly and chest, her intoxicating hazel gaze melding with his. "It's just that I prefer gentlemen to callous rogues."

"Well, with you comin' from such aristocratic French blood, with some highfalutin painter for a long-lost cousin or such, you would."

He looked down at her. Haven lay belly down and naked between his bare legs, holding his cock in both her hands, her wet lips glistening in the flickering light of a bracket lamp.

Beside them was her own reflection in the dark window, holding his cock before her as though praying to it. She appeared there in the misty darkness, limned with wan lamplight, a lovely girl shrouded in mystery.

A mystery he hadn't yet even begun to plumb or to solve.

She touched her tongue to the head. He shuddered at the keen pleasure the sensation gave him.

"Well, this works out just right, then, Agent Delacroix. There's nothing callous about me."

He smiled. He threw his head back and sucked a breath when she lowered her warm, wet mouth down over his jutting cock once more.

She sucked him very slowly for a time before she lifted her mouth back off of him again with a slight wet, popping sound and licked her lips. "Do you think we'll ever work together again, Longarm?"

"I hope so, Agent Delacroix. I sure as hell do certainly hope so." He wanted . . . needed . . . to solve her mystery.

"Mhmmmm." She smiled. "It's nice to work with a fellow . . . uh . . . professional. Even if he is a lusty cur."

She rose to her knees and straddled him, her full breasts jostling just inches in front of his face. She wrapped her arms around his head and drew his face against those beautiful, heaving orbs, waggling her shoulders to rake his longhorn mustache across her nipples, which hardened instantly beneath his lips.

He took her breasts in his hands and squeezed them as he nuzzled them. Reaching down behind her, Haven closed her hand over his cock and lowered her warm and welcoming love nest down on top of it.

"Oh, Jesus," he said. "Yeah, this lusty ole dog does certainly hope to be workin' with you again real soon, Agent Delacroix!"

GIANT-SIZED ADVENTURE FROM AVENGING ANGEL LONGARM.

BY TABOR EVANS

penguin.com/actionwesterns

M456AS0812

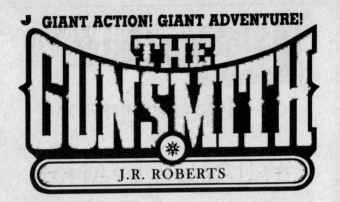

GIANT ACTION! GIANT ADVENTURE!

THE GUNSMITH

J.R. ROBERTS

penguin.com/actionwesterns

M455AS0812

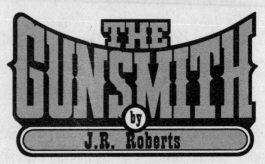